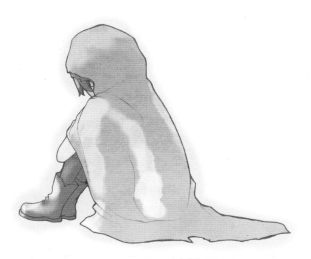

D1501610

**FUJINO
OMORI**

ILLUSTRATION BY
**SUZUHITO
YASUDA**

© Suzuhito Yasuda

IS It WRONG to TRY to PiCK UP GiRLS iN A DUNGEON?

VOLUME 6

FUJINO OMORI

ILLUSTRATION BY SUZUHITO YASUDA

YEN ON

NEW YORK

IS IT WRONG TO TRY TO PICK UP GIRLS IN A DUNGEON?, Volume 6
FUJINO OMORI

Translation by Andrew Gaippe
Cover art by Suzuhito Yasuda

DUNGEON NI DEAI WO MOTOMERU NO WA MACHIGATTEIRUDAROUKA vol. 6
Copyright © 2014 Fujino Omori
Illustrations copyright © 2014 Suzuhito Yasuda
All rights reserved.
Original Japanese edition published in 2014
by SB Creative Corp.
This English edition is published by arrangement with SB Creative Corp.,
Tokyo, in care of Tuttle-Mori Agency, Inc., Tokyo.

English translation © 2016 by Yen Press, LLC

Yen On
1290 Avenue of the Americas
New York, NY 10104

Visit us at yenpress.com
facebook.com/yenpress
twitter.com/yenpress
yenpress.tumblr.com

First Yen On Edition: August 2016

Yen On is an imprint of Yen Press, LLC.
The Yen On name and logo are trademarks of Yen Press, LLC.

The publisher is not responsible for websites
(or their content) that are not owned by the publisher.

Library of Congress Cataloging-in-Publication Data

Names: Ōmori, Fujino, author. | Yasuda, Suzuhito, illustrator.
Title: Is it wrong to try to pick up girls in a dungeon? / Fujino Omori ; illustrated by Suzuhito Yasuda.
Other titles: Danjon ni deai o motomeru nowa machigatte iru daröka. English.
Description: New York : Yen ON, 2015– | Series: Is it wrong to pick up girls in a dungeon? ; 6
Identifiers: LCCN 2015029144 | ISBN 9780316339155 (v. 1 : pbk.) |
    ISBN 9780316340144 (v. 2 : pbk.) | ISBN 9780316340151 (v. 3 : pbk.) |
    ISBN 9780316340168 (v. 4 : pbk.) | ISBN 9780316314794 (v. 5 : pbk.) |
    ISBN 9780316394161 (v. 6 : pbk.)
Subjects: | CYAC: Fantasy. | BISAC: FICTION / Fantasy / General. |
    FICTION / Science Fiction / Adventure.
Classification: LCC PZ7.1.O54 Du 2015 | DDC [Fic]—dc23 LC record available at
    http://lccn.loc.gov/2015029144

ISBNs: 978-0-316-39416-1 (paperback)
    978-0-316-39420-8 (ebook)

10 9 8 7 6 5 4 3 2 1

RRD-C

Printed in the United States of America

VOLUME 6

FUJINO OMORI

ILLUSTRATION BY SUZUHITO YASUDA

BELL CRANELL

The hero of the story, who came to Orario (dreaming of meeting a beautiful heroine in the Dungeon) on the advice of his grandfather. He belongs to *Hestia Familia* and is still getting used to his job as an adventurer.

HESTIA

A being from the heavenly world of Tenkai, she is far beyond all mortals living on the lower world of Gekai. The head of Bell's *Hestia Familia*, she is absolutely head over heels in love with him!

AIZ WALLENSTEIN

Known as the Sword Princess Kenki, her combination of feminine beauty and incredible strength makes her Orario's best-known female adventurer. Bell idolizes her. Currently Level 6, she belongs to *Loki Familia*.

LILLILUKA ERDE

A girl belonging to a race of pygmy humanoids known as prums, she plays the role of supporter in Bell's battle party. A member of *Soma Familia*, she's much more powerful than she looks.

WELF CROZZO

A smith who fights alongside Bell as a member of his battle party. He forged Bell's light armor (Pyonkichi Rabbit Armor MK-II). Belongs to *Hephaistos Familia*.

LYU LEON

An elf and former adventurer of extraordinary skill, she currently works as a bartender and waitress at The Benevolent Mistress.

CHARACTER & STORY

EINA TULLE

A Dungeon adviser and a receptionist for the organization in charge of regulating the Dungeon, the Guild. She has bought armor for Bell in the past, and she looks after him even now.

The Labyrinth City Orario——A large city that sits over an expansive network of underground tunnels and caverns known as the Dungeon. Bell Cranell came to this city in hopes of meeting the girl of his dreams, and he joined *Hestia Familia* in the process. Lilly, the supporter, and Welf, the smith, have teamed up with Bell many times during his adventures in the Dungeon, but he has had only a handful of chance encounters with his idol, Aiz Wallenstein. Now, it appears that the god Apollo has taken an unusually strong interest in the boy...

LOKI

She leads Orario's most powerful *Familia* and has a mysterious western accent. Loki is particularly fond of Aiz.

RIVERIA LJOS ALF

High elf and vice commander of the most prominent *Familia* in Orario, *Loki Familia*.

TIONA HYRUTE

An Amazonian adventurer and Aiz's best friend. She and her older twin sister Tione belong to *Loki Familia*.

FREYA

Goddess at the head of *Freya Familia*. Her stunning allure is strong enough to enchant the gods themselves. She is a true "Goddess of Beauty."

SYR FLOVER

A waitress at The Benevolent Mistress. She established a friendly relationship with Bell after an unexpected meeting.

NAHZA ERSUISU

The sole member of *Miach Familia*. She gets extremely jealous of other women who approach her god.

ASFI AL ANDROMEDA

A very gifted creator of magical items. She belongs to *Hermes Familia*.

MIKOTO YAMATO

A girl from the Far East. She feels it is her duty to make amends to Bell and his battle party for using them as a decoy. She is a member of *Takemikazuchi Familia*.

CHIGUSA

Another member of *Takemikazuchi Familia*.

HEPHAISTOS

Welf's goddess and the head of *Hephaistos Familia*. She has loose ties with Hestia dating back to their time in Tenkai.

BETE LOGA

A member of a race of animal people known as werewolves. He laughed at Bell's inexperience one night at The Benevolent Mistress. However, he recognized the boy's potential after witnessing Bell's battle with a Minotaur.

FINN DEIMNE

Known for his cool head, he is the commander of *Loki Familia*.

TIONE HYRUTE

Amazon and twin sister of Tiona. She is quite taken with her commander, Finn.

OTTAR

An extremely powerful member of *Freya Familia*.

MIACH

The head of *Miach Familia*, a group focused on the production and sale of items.

HERMES

The head of *Hermes Familia*. A charming god who excels at toeing the line on all sides of an argument, he is always in the know. Is he keeping tabs on Bell for someone…?

TAKEMIKAZUCHI

The head of *Takemikazuchi Familia*.

OUKA

The captain of *Takemikazuchi Familia*.

PROLOGUE **EVIL** IN THE MOONLIT NIGHT

Weak moonlight filtered through the thin clouds that covered the night sky.

With the exception of a few stars twinkling here and there, the dark void overhead felt vast enough to draw earth-dwelling onlookers into its depths.

Most people were already asleep at this late hour.

Toward the middle of the city, the taverns were alive with the sounds of adventurers. However, in this dim residential area they sounded distant.

One girl kept to the shadows as she made her way into one of the buildings on her way to meet with a god.

"Please, Lord Soma. Allow Lilly to leave this *Familia*..." Her voice quivered as she pled.

Lilly's body was hidden by a threadbare robe as she kneeled in front of him, her head bent low. Her round chestnut-colored eyes focused on one spot on the floor.

The deity she was talking to sat quietly in the corner of the room, holding his knees up against his chest.

A cloud shifted in the night sky, flooding the room with moonlight through the open window. The light illuminated a series of shelves lining one side of the room. They held numerous potted plants as well as several bottles of clear liquor. The two figures sat in the private quarters of the home of *Soma Familia*'s god.

Lilly had come here to ask Soma directly for permission to leave the *Familia*.

This was all so that she could be released from the curse of *Soma Familia*—so that she could stand next to Bell and the others with pride. She had seen her chance and seized the opportunity for a personal audience with Soma himself.

Leaving a *Familia*—which entailed the rewriting of the Falna that even then was carved upon her back—required the permission of her god, Soma.

"Lilly knows that this comes without warning, and she apologizes for that and for every other offense she has committed. But please, Lilly begs for your mercy..."

She did not make eye contact or even raise her head.

The girl's small, quivering shoulders indicated just how much fear of her god still remained within her. Lilly couldn't wipe away the memories of Soma's wine, how it twisted her, overpowered her. The one who created it was sitting in the corner of the room.

But the deity did not respond.

He looked like a young man of average height. His body and limbs were slender and almost delicate in appearance. He wore a loose-fitting robe, the sleeves and hem dirty with soil.

Soma sat in the corner, looking at the wall and muttering to himself. "Operational regulation...Penalty...My passion, my reason..."

Soma's long, unkempt hair partially hid his downtrodden face. He seemed to be shrouded in a miasma of depression and despair.

He did not stir, keeping his back to Lilly.

A new voice not belonging to Lilly or Soma filled the room. "Lord Soma is very busy right now. But I'll listen to you, Erde."

A human man appeared next to the deity sitting on the floor.

Glasses perched on the man's chiseled features. His narrow black eyes had an air of intelligence, but the vulgar smile on his lips betrayed it. "I'm rather surprised to see you alive. I was informed that Kanu perished."

Lilly desperately fought back the urge to respond.

Zanis Lustra—the commander of *Soma Familia* and an upper-class adventurer at Level 2.

He had been given the title of Gandharva, the Wine-Guardian. His mind was strong enough not to be manipulated by the Divine Wine; his will could overpower it.

With Soma's notable lack of interest in his own *Familia*, it was not uncommon for Zanis to issue commands in his place. In fact, as the leader—and using the name of their deity for his own purposes—he could manipulate the other members for his own gain. Not unlike the man who'd thrown Lilly into a horde of killer ants, Zanis thought nothing of taking advantage of the weak.

After concealing her own death and making careful plans to sneak into Soma's quarters, Lilly had been found by the one person she absolutely wanted to avoid.

"Come to think of it, haven't seen any of Kanu's buddies around, either...You have anything to do with that?"

The girl answered honestly to the man whose smirk hadn't changed since he entered the room. "...Lilly doesn't know." Her response was curt and to the point. She fought hard to hold her tongue to prevent her own anger and annoyance from coming through. "Mr. Zanis... Lilly is here for a reason. She's waiting for Lord Soma's answer."

"Oh yes, indeed. Let's get back to that." Zanis exaggerated his words and nodded his head much deeper than normal, almost as if he were acting in a play. He slowly and carefully enunciated each of his next words. "Of course, a large sum of money will be required to exit our group. That's the only thing that can relieve Lord Soma's pain—he's spent so much time raising you. He'll want at least ten million vals."

Lilly sat motionless for several seconds.

Her spirit seemed to drain out of her body the moment that she understood Zanis's words.

"What say you, Lord Soma?"

"...It's up to you."

Soma didn't turn or look up when he responded. The deity was little more than a rock in the corner of the room, not budging a celch.

"T-ten million..." Lilly uttered as her face turned pale.

Her own god didn't know her, nor did he respond to her voice. Zanis chuckled darkly to himself as he stared down at Lilly, knowing that any further discussion was useless.

Lilly collapsed to the floor like a puppet whose strings had been cut. Her thin arms managed to break her fall. Slowly but surely, the girl climbed back to her feet.

Her face void of any emotion, Lilly stumbled her way out of the room on shaky legs.

The moment she disappeared from sight, a large figure stood in the doorway in her place.

"Hey, Apollo's guys're out front," said a very unfriendly looking dwarf wearing a large calabash gourd strapped behind his lower back.

"Very good, Chandra. Show them into the small room down the hall."

"Not my job. Do it yourself."

The dwarf named Chandra spoke in a gruff monotone as he turned his back on Zanis, then disappeared down the hall as if to avoid a pointless conversation. The man shrugged his shoulders, more amused than annoyed.

He turned back to face the god in the corner and spoke. "Lord Soma, I will go conduct negotiations. What is your desire?"

"…It's up to you."

Soma was completely uninterested. Zanis smirked, chuckling quietly through his nose.

His eyes seemed to hide a sneer as he walked toward the doorway. Silence fell as soon as Zanis closed the door behind him.

"…"

The god stopped muttering to himself now that he was left alone in his room.

Bluish gray moonlight illuminated the plants and bottles on his shelf. Soma reached out, grabbed a bottle, and flipped open the lid.

He raised it to his lips and drank the bottle dry in a few quick gulps.

CHAPTER 1 THE FURIOUS RABBIT

The stone roads are warmed by the sun overhead on this mild afternoon.

The weather's been nice for several days now; everyone seems to be in a good mood. The city center overflows with happy voices. The wide main street is filled with horse-drawn carts, demi-humans, and travelers in their traveling gear going about their business.

Past these waves of humanity and in the center of the road straight ahead stands a white tower so tall it pierces the blue sky.

"But still, I'm so glad that you and the others made it back safe and sound."

"Sorry to make you worry...And thank you."

I'm outside of one of the bars on West Main, The Benevolent Mistress. I don't know how many times I've apologized and thanked Syr, but I do it once again. I'll never forget the look on her face when I first came to tell her that I'd returned from the eighteenth floor. That smile, the look in her eyes, how her silver hair swished back and forth—everything.

I still can't believe that it's already been three days since we defeated the Goliath and returned to the surface.

It was a week ago today that we couldn't get out of the middle levels and had to go all the way down to the eighteenth. Apparently a lot of people above ground were worried about us. Syr was definitely one of them. While she couldn't come into the Dungeon herself like the goddess did, she sent her coworker Lyu in after us.

I will be forever grateful to the elf who saved my life so many times.

Of course, I'll never forget how happy I was that she would do that for me.

I grimace to hide my embarrassment from the girl smiling right in front of me.

"Has your body fully recovered?"

"Yes. Lord Miach...I received treatment from a friendly *Familia*, and I'm doing fine now."

Thanks to Lord Miach and Nahza's strongest medicine and potions, I was able to recover all the strength and mental power I'd lost over the past three days.

We returned to the surface the day after fighting the floor boss. I've spent the past two days recovering as well as contacting everyone I know to make sure they know I'm okay. I meet them in person, see their relief, endure their anger, and share a few laughs. Actually, Syr was the first person I'd gone to see, so this is the second time I've seen that smile of relief on her face.

The warmth of the sun on my skin and the bright skies are proof that I really did make it out alive. Thanks to that, I can experience the joy of reuniting with people I thought I would never see again. I suppose that the more fear and danger you experience, the happier you are to make it home safe.

I really am back.

Even with all the commotion around me, I can feel my cheeks pulling back into a smile.

"Syr, Mama Mia has asked us to open...Oh, Mr. Cranell. I did not know you were here."

"Lyu."

Lyu emerges from the doors of the bar to call Syr back inside. She says a quick good morning and I answer with a morning greeting of my own.

The hooded cape and battle cloth she wore in the Dungeon are gone, replaced with her bar-waitress uniform. Seeing her dressed like this after fighting alongside the strong and beautiful hooded adventurer feels very weird...There's a big difference between this cute waitress and the warrior I know.

"I'm glad to see you are well. You looked little better than a corpse on our way back from the Dungeon. I was worried about your health."

"S-sorry about that..."

I'd pushed myself way too hard and was half carried back to the surface. The elf shakes her head softly from side to side and finally says, "It's nothing." Her thin, defined lips loosen slightly.

...It's only a bit, but I feel like the distance between Lyu and me has shrunk. Her tone seems slightly more friendly, her expression softer than usual. It's extremely slight, but enough to notice.

It wasn't very long, but the time we spent together in the Dungeon allowed me to become a little closer to her.

"...Bell, you've become friends with Lyu, haven't you?"

"Wh-wha?"

"But it's never all right to sneak a peek, okay?"

"A-all right...!"

She stares me down for a moment, her finger right in front of my nose.

Her stern warning is so intense I can only yelp in response.

When I first came to see her, Syr had already known about the peeking incident...I kind of saw Lyu naked. She fiercely scolded me, but it felt more like a punishment.

I had never seen Syr so angry before. A stern lecture from an older girl was more than enough to make me flinch. It's true that I reaped what I'd sown, but still...

I cringe as a new wave of embarrassment and repentance floods through my body, my face turning red.

"Syr, that was an accident. Please do not blame Mr. Cranell."

"Lyu, how can you be so sure it was an accident?"

"If I had sensed any impure emotion, I would have cut him down on the spot."

—My spirit ices over. I need to do everything possible to avoid repeating past mistakes.

"I heard this from Lyu, but you fought an extremely powerful monster, didn't you, Bell?"

She hits me with that question the moment I get my head back on my shoulders.

"Oh, yes." I manage to get a response out of my mouth as soon as I realize she was talking about the Goliath on the eighteenth floor.

"I also heard you took it down. Is that true?"

"Eh, um, about that..."

I start to deny it, but Lyu suddenly catches my eye. *No need for modesty.* Her gaze overpowers me and my voice shrinks into silence. I still remember her scolding me for looking down on myself at the pond where she was bathing...I stand there for a moment before Syr nods to pass the awkward moment.

"Wow, that's amazing! Bell, you've become such a strong adventurer!"

"Well, I, um..."

Syr excitedly brings her hands together with a clap. All I can do is force a smile.

Receiving all these compliments and praise feels good, and it makes me really happy to see that look of respect in her eyes, but I can't take all the credit.

I truly believe that if someone, anyone hadn't been on the battlefield that day, I wouldn't be standing here right now. I'd happily bet on that.

It's true that I delivered the final blow with my Skill, Argonaut. But if it hadn't been for Lyu and everyone else protecting me, I would've never had a chance to use it. Not only could the floor boss have taken me out, but there were hundreds of other monsters swarming around the battlefield. I had a lot of help, and I'd needed it.

We were only able to seize victory because every adventurer set aside their *Familia* affiliations and worked together.

It was much more accurate to say that we'd *all* taken down that monster.

"One of our regulars has become a famous adventurer! I'm so proud to work here!" She's beaming with joy, like it was her own accomplishment and I'm just some other guy. Her eyes narrow and mouth widens in a smile that makes me feel ticklish, and she continues. "How would you like to throw another party to celebrate? It's not every day that you return from a near-death experience, right? How about this evening?"

She suggests we do something like when I leveled up to Level 2.

I'm really happy to see her so excited but...the shadow of a daunting figure pops into my head. It might be a good idea to turn her down.

"I couldn't ask you to do that, not after all the trouble I've caused... I don't think I'd be able to look Ms. Mia in the face..."

Mia owns and operates The Benevolent Mistress. Apparently she was extremely angry that Lyu left her post to join my search party. She snapped, saying that someone who needed to rely on the help of people outside of their own *Familia* should "quit needing people to rescue 'im."

Just the image of her seething face in the back of my mind makes me recoil in fright.

"Heh-heh, she'll cheer right up if you tell her stories about what happened, you know."

Syr's cheeks flush red as she leans in toward me, a strange smile on her face. Meanwhile, Lyu adds her own opinion in her usual matter-of-fact tone. "Agreed. Mama Mia enjoys tales of bravery."

"What do you say?" Syr asks in a friendly voice. It makes me happy that she feels this way, but unfortunately it can't happen tonight. I shake my head no.

"I'm really sorry, but I'll have to take a pass on that, today. I've already got plans tonight..."

"Oh, you do?"

"Mr. Cranell. Do these plans involve your battle party members?"

My lips spread into a smile as I enthusiastically nod.

It's just as Lyu said, I'm going to celebrate with my friends tonight.

The sun sinks out of sight behind the high city wall, covering the streets in a blue shadow.

Orario grows even livelier as night falls.

Jubilant songs echo from the taverns, and street performers put on shows in the parks and open spaces around the city. Many people have gathered to greet adventurers as they emerge from the Dungeon. Magic-stone lamps light up the night.

One particular block adjacent to South Main is really living it up.

Magic-stone lamps of various colors illuminate the wide road. The lamps themselves are bright enough to rival the stars in the sky. Looking down the street, all of the buildings are tall and each has a unique flair to it. There are bars, casinos, and theaters all over the place, along with other establishments not seen elsewhere in the city. South Main Street is every bit as crowded as its reputation for an entertainment district would suggest.

But I leave all of that behind and go one block over.

I meet Lilly and Welf inside a bar that's lined with all kinds of animal masks, from birds to lions. The three of us sit around the table and clink our mugs together.

"Cheers!"

Smiles overflow around the table like the bubbly foam on the top of our mugs of ale. We aren't the only ones having a good time. *Clink, clink!* Other groups of adventurers at tables around us are starting to enjoy a drink after a hard day's work.

There's a big red sign that looks a lot like a *Familia*'s emblem on the wall that has some kind of insect design. It's the symbol of this bar: Hibachitei, the Flaming Wasp.

Located in a back alley of the business district, this tavern is popular among different groups of adventurers and smiths, Welf being one of them. The bar's claim to fame is a deep red mead. It's apparently good enough that people commute here just to drink it.

Compared to The Benevolent Mistress, this place is rather cramped. I suppose that's because it's on a back street instead of the main road. There are enough tables, chairs, and other obstacles in here to make it difficult to get around. The inside is a little bit dirty and filled with dwarves and men laughing together in loud voices. I can't quite put my finger on it, but there's something different about the atmosphere in here. Syr's place is bright and modern, but the Flaming Wasp feels more like an adventurer's bar.

Some prum girls work their way past us as I share a laugh with Lilly and Welf.

"Congrats on leveling up, Welf!"

"Mr. Welf is now officially a High Smith, yes?"

"That I am…Thanks."

He bobs his head, looking a bit more bashful than usual. But that smile on his lips is all the proof I need to know that he's attained both his goal as well as the pride that goes with it.

Welf had gained enough excelia through our journey into the middle levels and the many battles on the eighteenth floor to level up—going from Level 1 to Level 2. At the same time he acquired the "Forge" Advanced Ability.

Lady Hephaistos updated his status, and the announcement of his rank-up was made this morning. He came straight to my goddess's home to tell us as soon as he found out, a massive grin on his face. From there he went to tell Lilly, and now the three of us are here celebrating it.

Welf is now a High Smith—we can't let this special day pass by without commemorating it.

"Mr. Welf, are you now free to mark your work with your *Familia*'s brand whenever you want?"

"Whenever I want might be pushing it. I'll need Lady Hephaistos's approval along with several of the other leaders before I can use that brand. A weak-ass weapon getting stamped would just sully her name."

Now that Welf has joined the ranks of the High Smiths, he's allowed to engrave the Ήφαιστος insignia on his weapons and armor.

It sounds like he can't do it every time but I bet…no, I'm *sure* that Welf's work will start selling really well. The Ήφαιστος mark has that much influence.

Add in the fact that equipment made by a High Smith is always in high demand, and Welf's reputation as a blacksmith should spread like wildfire. While I'm extremely happy for my friend, I'm also a little sad. "But this means…you're leaving the battle party, doesn't it?"

The main reason that Welf had wanted to join us in the first place was so that he could gain the Forge ability. He's met his goal, so there's no reason for him to stick around. Refusing to let him pursue his dreams would be selfish on my part.

This could be the last time I see him. Lilly is looking a little heavy-hearted, too.

Welf scratches the back of his head. He smirks and looks at us like a big brother of sorts, trying to stop himself from blushing. "Don't look at me like some abandoned rabbit on the side of the road." He swirls the ale in his mug a few times and continues. "I owe you guys. I can't just say 'I'm done, see ya' and take off."

"Huh..."

"I'll join you whenever you call, including for Dungeon crawling. So don't worry," he finishes with a toothy grin.

I blink a few times before his infectious smile takes over. Lilly's eyes curve upward as the three of us clink our mugs together yet again.

We're still a battle party.

"Mr. Welf only joined us two weeks ago...Ranking up didn't take very long at all. Lilly was sure it would take a lot more time."

"Well, I wasn't exactly sitting on my ass before joining up with you two. But yeah, it happened in the blink of an eye...I suppose almost dying five times in the middle levels sped up the process a bit."

"Ah-ha-ha..."

Our conversation joins the din inside the lively bar.

Plates upon plates of many different kinds of food are carried to the tables of the other customers. Grilled ham steaks, fried fish with herb sauce—the smells in here are amazing. I work up the courage to try some of that red mead. Just one sip is enough to send a wave of heat down my throat and warm my stomach. Welf was the one who recommended Hibachitei for our get-together. After sampling some of the food and drinks here, I understand why. This place ranks right up there with The Benevolent Mistress. I wonder which one is cheaper?

Our goddesses were also going to join us tonight. But according to Welf, Lady Hephaistos was rather angry with Lady Hestia—something about Hestia my goddess having "other responsibilities," or something like that...She has to work at her part-time job in Babel Tower, and she's not happy about it. She did her best to give Welf her well-wishes, but the depression on her face was obvious. Welf had grimaced and accepted the congratulations.

"So Bell, you didn't level up?" Welf changes the subject.

"No, not yet," I answer honestly.

My Basic Abilities jumped quite a bit during our four-day trip through the middle levels, but not enough for my Status to go over the top.

"It's more difficult to gain excelia at Level Two than it is at Level One. The same is true for leveling up...But Lilly is sure that Miss Lyu received most of the excelia from the last battle."

Lilly is disguised as a young werewolf girl using her Magic to hide her true identity. The wolflike ears on top of her head twitch back and forth as she talks. I agree with every word she said.

The last battle...The floor boss, Goliath.

We joined forces with the adventurers from Rivira to attack that monster. There had to be more than a hundred of us working together, protecting one another and creating openings for others to attack. However, the Goliath summoned swarms of monsters into battle. Other adventurers took them on so that we could focus on the Goliath alone. There must've been at least five hundred of us, now that I think about it.

All adventurers who take part in group battles are entitled to a share of the excelia gained during combat. Even so, the ones who shouldered the heaviest burden get the largest shares—in this case Asfi and Lyu because they held the Goliath at bay the longest, and Lyu inflicted more damage. I'm sure that she received far more excelia than anyone else.

If Welf and the others hadn't covered for me, bought me time, I would've never landed my last attack. Lyu, however, did almost everything by herself.

Facing down a monster of that size alone to protect her allies and still charging forward...I'm still in awe at what she accomplished. Her heroic deeds are worthy of being immortalized in a book of heroes. Remembering how she moved, the crispness of her strikes, her aura itself still sends shivers down my spine.

"...So, what was it? That Goliath?"

Since the topic seems to be drifting in that direction anyway, Welf asked us directly about the "Irregular" that we encountered on the eighteenth floor.

The three of us lean in close so as not to be overheard by the people around us.

"There is no explanation, other than it was an Irregular...A floor boss appearing in a safe point hasn't happened in this era."

"That bastard was stronger than the rest of them, yeah? It was tossing upper-class adventurers around like bugs! If another one of those things shows up, we'll be wiped out for sure."

"I think you're right..."

A black floor boss. A stronger Monster Rex.

A monster appearing on a floor that it shouldn't have, which sent us spiraling into the deepest pits of despair. Everything about it defied common sense. Simply dismissing it as an Irregular didn't do it justice.

"Lady Hestia seems to know something about it..."

The moment she saw that black thing emerge—she said it had been sent to eliminate her.

The Dungeon was angry that gods were inside.

The gods stayed out of the Dungeon to hide their presence.

Seeing how she had reacted and hearing what she said, I can't shake the feeling that the gods and goddesses have some kind of connection with the Dungeon. Perhaps these all-knowing deities are hiding something.

"Did Lady Hestia tell Mr. Bell anything?" Lilly asks, but I shake my head no. After the battle, the goddess apologized several times but dodged the question whenever I asked her.

She kept acting like it was something that I wasn't allowed to know, and I couldn't fight against her divine will. It made me feel rather anxious.

But she doesn't want to say, or maybe she doesn't need to.

That's the impression I got from her.

Discovering mysteries that lurk within the Dungeon might be our job as adventurers—ours and ours alone.

These thoughts and more ran through my mind as I had stood, slack-jawed, in front of the goddess.

"Welp, that's about all we know, isn't it...How did people take the news?" Welf changes the subject to improve the mood at our table.

We start talking about what happened after the battle and the current situation.

"There was no confusion or panic within Orario because the Guild issued a gag order right away. We are the only ones who know the real story, along with anyone else who was there."

"*Don't say a damn thing* is how they put it..."

"There'd be a pretty big penalty, too. The Guild can really be tenacious."

"Lilly has heard Rivira is back in business on the eighteenth floor. The Dungeon appears to be normal, with nothing out of place."

Lilly's very good at gathering information because of her past as a thief and con artist. She's got a lot better handle on what's happening than Welf or I do.

Apparently the Dungeon and the city of Orario are well on their way back to normal. The Guild's efforts to keep everything quiet must've paid off—after all, the Guild has power over all adventurers because it controls their income as well as managing the Dungeon's resources.

Despite all of that, I wonder if the residents of Rivira really went back. It had been a life-threatening situation, so I'm not sure if they're fearless or extremely motivated merchants, or just crazy...

"Speaking of that, Bell, you all right? I heard the Guild threw the book at you and Lady Hestia. The penalty had to be pretty steep."

"Ah—yeah..."

To be precise, penalties were levied on both my *Familia* and Lord Hermes's *Familia*.

Lady Hestia and Lord Hermes were summoned to the Guild to provide information on the incident. That's when the hammer had fallen.

Completely ignoring their explanations, the Guild declared this incident to be a "Calamity"—a disaster in which gods are directly responsible. Both of them received a stern warning and a harsh penalty.

As for the penalty…It was a fine.

"How much was it, Mr. Bell?"

"Half…Half of our *Familia*'s assets."

"…Ouch."

On the contrary, we'd gotten off easy.

The Guild knew that *Hestia Familia* was extremely young and that we didn't have much in the way of savings. We were only fined a few thousand vals—still quite a bit of money, though.

The item drop left over after the battle with the floor boss, Goliath's Hide, was practically forced onto me during the craziness that followed our victory…It was probably worth enough to cover the penalty. However, I'll never forget the goddess walking slowly to the Guild, carrying large sacks of money, tears dripping down her face as she shuddered her way there.

On the other hand, what Lord Hermes had to go through bordered on tragedy.

Members of *Hermes Familia* are involved in many different fields and had considerably more assets. The amount of money that they had to hand over to the Guild made our fine look like pocket change by comparison. The look on Lord Hermes's pale face dryly laughing still hasn't left my mind. All Miss Asfi did was sigh.

I try my best to smile back at the look of shock on Welf's face after my story.

"…?"

We enjoyed our food after that while being completely surrounded by the loud voices of other customers.

Suddenly I notice that something about Lilly seems off. So I turn to her and ask:

"Lilly…are you feeling okay?"

Thinking back, she hasn't been her usual self all night.

She's listlessly looking at nowhere in particular…What is it? It's like she's desperate not to look at me. She's here physically, but I think mentally she's somewhere else.

"Sorry, Mr. Bell. Lilly spaced out." She responds to the concern in my voice and flashes a smile in an attempt to reassure me that everything's okay. "Mr. Bell's reputation has improved considerably in the past few days. At the very least, the adventurers who witnessed the battle know Mr. Bell's strength."

"Th-that's great…"

That was an obvious attempt to change the subject. I awkwardly nod back at her.

I look over at Welf out of the corner of my eye. He has noticed, too. He's looking at Lilly over the top of his mug. He puts it back on the table and meets my gaze. *Now's not the time,* he mouths at me with a shrug.

Lilly, in her werewolf-child form, swishes her tail back and forth, trying to look energetic. I'm pretty sure Welf's right.

"—Get this, some 'bunny' just got famous overnight!"

A loud voice cuts through the din.

It came from an adventurer sitting at the table beside us.

The prum adventurer, speaking much louder than he needs to, is holding a glass in one hand and sitting at the table with five others.

"That rookie sure got some guts! Don't care if he really is the record holder, it's amazing that people swallow all of his lies! I couldn't pull that act off in a million years!"

His voice has the timbre of a young boy and seems to fill the bar corner to corner. I can feel the eyes of other customers start to focus on us as the three of us glance at the table.

A golden bow and arrow in front of the burning orb…No, that's the sun on their emblem.

All six of the adventurers, including the prum, have that symbol somewhere on their clothing. They're all in the same *Familia*.

The prum leans back in his chair and takes another swig of ale. Our eyes meet and his lips curl upward. "Anyway, I've heard he's extremely good at running away. That must be how he got the level-up—he ran away from that Minotaur until it collapsed from exhaustion. That's a bunny for ya! Quite the talent!"

His tone…it's really dry. Is that contempt?

Prums are known for their big eyes, and this one's no exception.

He keeps talking really loudly, almost like he wants me to hear him. The other adventurers at the table are doing nothing to stop him. In fact, they look thoroughly entertained.

Of course I don't like what this guy's doing…but I keep my mouth shut.

It's better to avoid conflicts between *Familias*. My goddess told me as much the day I joined, and Eina drilled it into my head after that. I have every intention of following their advice.

On top of that, I don't have the anger or the courage to say anything back or do anything about it. Pitiful, I know, but true.

I hear their taunting laughter but I do my best to ignore it and block it out.

The other customers in the bar must be expecting something. I can feel it in their gaze.

"Oh, you know what else? The bunny joined up with two random pieces of riffraff! A washed-up smith and some puny supporter. That party's so unbalanced I'm surprised they can even stand!"

I turn my back to their table and look at Lilly and Welf. *Keh-keh-keh*. The men in their group laugh even harder along with the prum's cackling snicker.

My shoulders twitch.

I can't ignore those words. I can't help but clench my fists upon hearing my friends insulted.

I spin around my chair to face them. Immediately, Welf and Lilly grab my arms.

"Cool it, don't worry. Let 'em say whatever they want."

"Mr. Bell, don't listen to them."

Welf has a cool enough head that he takes another drink from his mug. Lilly sounds like she's scolding me.

It's been a long time since I've felt a red surge of anger that strong. Thanks to Welf and Lilly, though, it's ebbing away, and I manage to control myself.

We're at a bar, and I've been drinking. I might be a little drunk. I tell myself as much over and over, take a few deep breaths, and try to relax.

Then, the prum clicks his tongue in our direction as if he's disappointed that we've kept our tempers in check. His next words take on more of a violent tone.

"I also know that his *Familia* is led by some goddess not worthy of even the slightest shred of respect. You'd have to be pretty weak and stupid to join *a disgraceful deity like that*!!"

—In that moment, sparks burst in my field of vision.

I jump to my feet, my chair flying backward.

"Take that back!" I howl.

Forgetting myself, sound explodes from my mouth.

My ears vaguely pick up the sound of my chair crashing into the ground as I glare daggers at the prum man.

Lilly's staring at me, lost for words. That's how angry I am.

My goddess—the one person in my life whom I hold in higher regard than any other—has just been insulted. Nothing else in the world could infuriate me this much. She is my family, my *goddess*, and this bastard is looking down on her, talking about her like she's trash.

Every person in the bar looks at me in silence. I don't know if the little prum man has lost his nerve, looking at me as I tower over him. There is an unmistakable hint of fear in his eyes.

Somehow, he forces his lips into a sneer and says in a shaking voice:

"S-see? Bull's-eye. Can't bear the shame, eh?"

Whoosh! Blood rushes up into my head all at once.

Overpowered by this wave of emotion, my body moves on its own.

"Don't do it, Mr. Bell!"

Lilly's voice can't stop me now. My hands are yearning for this bastard's throat.

One heartbeat before I could grab hold—a sudden burst of air.

A leg comes flying into my line of sight—*whok*—and buries itself in the prum's face.

"Bmmph?!" The prum lets out a muffled yelp of pain as he and his chair crash to the floor.

A river of blood flows from his broken nose as his eyes roll back in his head and several parts of his body start twitching. He's out cold.

The bar once again falls silent as the man who threw the kick and deprived me of my target, Welf, stands on one leg beside me.

His right foot is still outstretched as every set of eyes in the bar looks his way.

Did he cover for me? Was he just as angry?

I stare at him in disbelief. Welf smirks. "My foot slipped," he says with impudence.

He narrows his eyes and grins at the other adventurers at the table. It's almost as if his actions are a signal.

The prum's friends stand up at once.

"You son of a bitch!"

"Now you've done it!"

One of the adventurers kicks the table, sending it spinning into the air. The sound of shattering dishes instantly echoes throughout the bar, accompanied by the screams of the staff. The adventurers throw everything out of their way in a mad charge toward us. Meanwhile, Welf grins and loosens up his right arm with a few swings of his fist.

It takes me a second to come back to my senses, but I tackle one of them who's trying to attack Welf from the side.

—*Waaa!!* The other customers' voices erupt into a wall of sound. "Why, why is it always adventurers?!"

A fervor sweeps through the confined tavern. Lilly's voice somehow manages to cut through it all as punches and kicks are thrown in every direction.

This is an all-out brawl. All tables and chairs within range are instantly thrust out of the way as we engage the offending adventurers to the delight and incitement of the bar's customers. Mugs and bottles in their hands, they surround our battle in no time.

I bob and weave, dodging and counterattacking in an atmosphere so electric that it lights up the night. Now Level 2, Welf is able to keep all four of the attackers at bay on his own more than once. He must be used to this kind of fight. One adventurer charges at him, but he just smiles before sending the guy flying backward with an impressive uppercut. I move into the fray, duck down to the floor, and sweep my right leg forward. I catch an animal person behind the knee and he falls flat on his butt with a loud "Gah!"

I dip and dive again, dodging even more punches and kicks as Welf and I use a basic formation to overwhelm our opponents, just like a frontline attacker with middle support in a three-man cell fighting monsters in the Dungeon.

"…"

Our audience gets steadily louder as our two-man cell overpowers their four-man group.

However, the last of the prum man's friends chooses this moment to make his move.

He'd been sitting in his chair all this time, calmly drinking what was left in his glass. *Crash!* He throws it to the floor and stands. His movements are swift and glamorous—sure, I'm being distracted and can't watch too closely, but I still notice—as he approaches Welf.

The man grabs hold of Welf's outstretched arm just before it makes contact with another adventurer's face, pulls it back with one hand, and flips him on his back.

"Uwah!"

"Welf?!"

A new wave of rage consumes me the moment I see him land. I charge his attacker head-on.

I throw punch after punch, but he keeps dodging by the slimmest of margins—I catch a glimpse of his pompous smirk between my fists.

Suddenly his body becomes a blur. Just like that, my punches hit nothing but open air.

"—"

I'm very confident in my speed and agility, but it feels like he's trying to show me up. He's laughing at me.

I finally get him squared in my sights and lunge forward, only to feel sudden intense pain just below my chest. My eyes fly open in pain and I realize that he's buried his knee in my gut.

He grabs my airborne body by my shoulder and forces my head up.

His incoming fist fills my vision like an oncoming boulder. Stars explode in front of my eyes.

"Mr. Bell?!"

I fly backward.

The adventurers watching our brawl jump out of the way and I plow into one of the round tables behind them. Lilly's scream mixes with the splintering sound of wood breaking on impact.

My face feels hot. I'm on my back, a piece of the broken table underneath me. Reaching up to cup my bleeding nose, somehow I managed to get my head off the floor.

"That was just a love tap."

He's calmly standing on the other side of the wreckage, looming over me.

He's a tall, kind of lanky adventurer. The man is handsome enough to rival an elf.

His long brown hair is well kept and neatly styled. The man's skin is smooth and white, almost feminine. He's wearing all kinds of accessories over his *Familia*'s uniform, including several golden earrings. Eyes as blue and vast as the sea are focused solely on me.

"That's...Hyacinthus."

"The Sun's Favored Child, Phoebus Apollo..."

"He's Level Three, a second-tier adventurer?!"

Many voices suddenly fill the bar, a whirlwind of shock and surprise. But my ears pick up something that make my fingers go numb.

Level 3—upper-class, second-tier adventurer.

This guy is a full rank above me.

"You're a feisty one, Little Rookie." Hyacinthus—I think that's his name—has a high-pitched voice for a man.

His blue eyes leave me and hover for a moment over the prum man, who's still twitching in his broken chair. He looks the other way, and the bodies of his fallen comrades reflect clearly in his eyes. He's the only combatant who still has the strength to stand.

Lilly rushes over to help me, but I can't climb to my feet even with her support. Welf has made it back to his knees. The man is just

© Suzuhito Yasuda

standing there, looking at us in silence. All of the excited energy that had filled the tavern a moment ago seems to fizzle out in an instant.

The muscles in my face start to tense, blood dripping from my chin as the man fixes his hair.

"You have inflicted injury on my friends. This is a serious offense. We will receive appropriate compensation."

His blue eyes take on a sadistic gleam. I'm sure that's what I'm seeing.

He sneers at me again and takes another step toward me as if to deliver a finishing blow. That's when someone else makes their presence known.

Another splintering jolt hits my ears as yet another table is kicked into the wall.

"!"

Every head in the bar snaps in that direction.

The figure of an ash-colored werewolf man sitting on a chair greets our eyes. His leg is slowly coming down after kicking the table.

"Get lost, small fries, ya don't belong." The werewolf growls as if annoyed and itching for a fight, his facial tattoos rippling.

An anxious stillness spreads throughout the bar. The werewolf's ears and tail twitch, revealing his bad mood.

I know him. I just can't believe it.

—*That guy.*

That night still hasn't faded from my memory.

That incident at the bar that became my motivation to chase after the female knight, the girl who's become my idol.

One of *Loki Familia*'s adventurers, he was there the day I was mercilessly chased around by a Minotaur.

I think his name is…Bete?

"It's your fault that this piss-weak beer started tastin' foul, too. Y'killed my buzz, you repulsive wimps. Get outta my sight!"

He and a few other adventurers around him are all wearing the "trickster" emblem. All the adventurers around stand in awe of the group from the strongest *Familia* in Orario, and in fear of the leader of this particular group, the werewolf.

While much more boorish and harsh than Aiz or the others, he has the same aura of strength. I'm sure the others here have picked up just how dangerous this man is.

Only the handsome man is able to speak, or even remain calm as he shrugs back. "Hmm...How rude. Apparently *Loki Familia* has gotten sloppy. They forgot to put a leash on their dog, of all things."

Bete's amber eyes instantly narrow, his temper flaring as he glares at the man.

"Wanna be torn in half, pretty boy?"

Werewolf and human size each other up.

The tension in here is suffocating. Time stands still before the handsome one breaks eye contact first.

"I've lost interest in this," he says as he turns away. "We're leaving," he tells his companions as he walks toward the exit on his own. The four of them somehow manage to stumble to their feet, lending a shoulder or two to their unconscious prum ally, and follow their leader out the door.

The last of them gone, a tranquil calm falls within the bar.

...Did he just...help me?

Loki Familia forced the other group of adventurers out...For the life of me, I have no idea why Mr. Bete would do something like that.

My mind stops racing and I wipe the dried blood off of my face... Slowly but surely.

The werewolf steps forward; he's coming right toward me.

"Eh?" comes out of my suddenly tight throat, and I'm not the only one. The adventurers who witnessed our brawl waste no time in getting out of Bete's way. My butt's still on the floor as I look up at his imposing figure. He comes to a stop right in front of my feet.

My heart trembles. The feeling of being made into a laughingstock that night rears its ugly head in the back of my mind.

He made me feel like a fool in front of Aiz. I could do nothing, only run away. That despair threatens to take over my mind once again when suddenly I see his left hand reaching down to me.

He's extending his hand—but there's no time to take it. He grabs hold of my collar and forcefully pulls me up.

I can't breathe.

"—Know yer place."

He pulls me up to his face, nose to nose.

The rage burning in his eyes is overwhelming. No sound comes out of my mouth; I have to nod. I can feel the strength pulsing in his fingers. Just keeping eye contact is terrifying.

Then he lets me go, dropping me on the spot. *Thump!* Pain shoots up my legs and into my back as soon as I hit the floor. Mr. Bete's mouth twitches before he turns around and walks toward the door himself, anger emanating from his back. His tail swishing looks like an ash-colored flame in his wake.

The rest of the adventurers in his group quickly jump to their feet. One of them sets some money on the counter as all of them follow him outside.

First the handsome man and his group, then *Loki Familia* leave Hibachitei.

"Are you okay, Mr. Bell?"

"Damn those guys, what were they trying to pull...?"

Lilly sits down next to me as Welf massages his lower back, eyes still on the door.

I nod at Lilly and follow Welf's gaze. The door is still open. I can see the dark back street and even a piece of the night sky. I touch my face and instantly feel pain course through my swollen lip.

The bar staff is already hard at work, throwing away broken chairs and tables and sweeping up the splinters that litter the floor.

We're the only ones left, but none of us knows what to say.

A little time has passed since the brawl at Hibachitei.

Welf, Lilly, and I have made our way to a hidden room under an old church, *Hestia Familia*'s home.

"Ohh, so there was a fight," the goddess calmly says as she rubs medical cream on my face—it's cheap stuff, so anyone in Orario can buy it. My face tenses up whenever her fingers pass over one of my many cuts and nicks.

We're here to explain to her in our own words what happened and heal up at the same time.

We're not hurt *too* badly, but the goddess was extremely surprised to see us covered in bumps and bruises when we arrived. Lilly told her what happened and the goddess seemed to accept her explanation. We apologized to the bar's owner after the fight and told him that *Hestia Familia* would pay for the damages.

"Turns out you're a bit more rambunctious than I thought, Bell. I'm kind of happy about that, but it makes me sad, too..."

"Mr. Bell has been acting like Mr. Welf! Mr. Bell has been behaving more and more like a violent adventurer ever since he met Mr. Welf!"

"Hey, hey, you know that's not true...Wait a sec, there has got to be a nicer way to say that!"

The goddess's gentle fingers glide across my face as we sit side by side on the bed. Lilly and Welf are on the sofa directly next to us. The two of them have been arguing ever since Lilly claimed that only an idiot would waste a potion to recover from a bar fight and began roughly smothering Welf's injuries with the same ointment the goddess is using on me.

Lilly's taken on an aura of superiority ever since we left the bar. "Lilly can't believe this...This'll come back to haunt us...Please consider how worried Lilly is." She keeps repeating herself under her breath.

The goddess listens to what she has to say and does her best to smile at us.

"I'm surprised at you, getting into a fight like this. Then again, you *are* a boy, Bell."

"..."

Her thin fingers are gentle as she rubs more cream onto my face. I feel really bad for making her worry, but I stay silent.

Satisfied with my treatment, the goddess takes her hand away and looks at me with serious eyes.

"However, fights are never a good thing! It's just like what your supporter said. You realize you really got hurt this time!"

I let her finish and then immediately stand up.

Everything that happened in the bar, all the anger, I can't keep it in anymore.

"But those guys—they insulted you!"

This might be the first time I've ever talked back to her. Lilly and Welf freeze and look up at me.

I wouldn't care if they'd insulted me—I can take it.

However, they went after the people I care about—they insulted my *goddess*. She can't expect me to let that slide.

My goddess has given me so much, and that prum man made her out to be nothing more than dirt under someone's boot.

I clench my eyes shut in an attempt to keep tears from leaking out from the rage built up inside me. The goddess looks up at me with unblinking blue eyes.

She just stares at me for a moment before a small smile appears on her lips.

"I'm happy you would get this angry for my sake. But doing so put you in a lot of danger and that makes me much sadder."

The goddess's soft tone is in stark contrast to my body shaking in anger.

"I understand how you're feeling, Bell. If it were the other way around and someone insulted you, I'd be mad enough to breathe fire. But if I got into a fight over it and came back injured like you did today, how would you feel?"

"…I'd want to cry."

"See? That's how I feel. I know it's unfair, but please don't get angry if you hear someone say something bad about me. Gods are happiest when their children are healthy." And then she smiles at me. "Make a joke out of it next time. Something like 'that wouldn't anger my goddess, she's got a big heart' or something like that."

The goddess…*My* goddess's words cool my hot head.

She gently accepts all of my anger and rage, contains it, and helps me let it go.

Her smile unravels the knots of emotion that had built up in my chest.

I fall silent, nod, and apologize. "I'll put up with it next time...I'm sorry."

I look at the floor as I make my promise before looking up at her face. She's smiling from ear to ear—absolutely beaming, like a healthy flame in a fireplace.

Tap, tap. She pats the bed next to her. I do what she's asking and take a seat on the bed. She gently runs her fingers through my hair. I'm starting to blush, but I don't move away.

Lilly and Welf watch the two of us. They do nothing to try and hide their amusement.

A calm, serene mood fills the hidden room under the old, run-down church.

"Lilly's worried about how the other *Familia* will respond. It would be nice if they didn't hold a grudge and come after Mr. Bell."

The goddess had been rubbing my head and shoulders and was about to lean in for a hug when Lilly voices her concern.

Welf runs his hand over his black jacket, looking for damage. He doesn't even look up when he adds, "I started it. Bell should be fine."

"That may be so...but adventurers have a lot of pride. If their *Familia* is concerned about losing face, there might be a problem."

"Hmm, that's a good point." The goddess looks over at Lilly and agrees with her. "Shall I talk to their god to prevent problems down the road?"

"I'm sorry, Goddess..."

I bow a little bit, but the goddess forces a smile. "Oh, it's fine. Do you know what *Familia* they were from?" she asks me.

"Um, I think..." I try to remember everything before the fight started and recall the details. My memory clicks, and I tell her. "...they wore a sun emblem."

Golden emblems bearing the mark of the sun flashed in the moonlight pouring down from the cloudless night sky.

They gathered in a dark alley, away from the light of the magic-stone lamps.

A group of six men made up of humans, animal people, and prums had found their way into one of the countless alleyways in the city of Orario.

"Gimme a break, Hyacinthus. Why do I always have to do the crappy part...?"

"Hee-hee, don't be that way, Luan. You get to be the star."

Hyacinthus grinned at the little man, who still had the well-defined outline of a boot on his face. The rest of the group traded laughs, further damaging their prum ally's ego.

The prum adventurer named Luan had a youthful face. His smooth cheeks twitched in disapproval of the role he had just been assigned.

Hyacinthus's lips curled up into a shrewd grin as he took in the anguish on the prum's face.

"There was some unexpected interference, but we accomplished our goal..."

The noises of Orario's vibrant nightlife were distant.

The handsome young man smiled fully as he mentioned his god by name.

"Lord Apollo will be most pleased."

His golden earrings wavered slightly in the darkness.

Hyacinthus looked up and narrowed his eyes at the brilliant moon, shining in place of the sun on this clear night.

CHAPTER 2
Shall We Dance?

"So then, you have made a full recovery?"

"Yes, I feel great." I smile and nod at Eina.

I had decided to drop by Guild Headquarters the day after the events at Hibachitei.

She and I are sitting in one of the Guild's consultation boxes as I bring her up to speed and we discuss how to proceed from here.

"Do you know how worried I was? I just about had a heart attack when I heard you hadn't returned from the Dungeon."

"I-I'm sorry…"

"…But I'm willing to forgive you. You made it back in one piece, after all."

She flashes a grin.

My cheeks flush with warmth as my eyes are drawn in by her beautiful, refined smile.

She was so happy when I came to see her the other day that she cried. The image of her first tear rolling out from beneath her glasses is still fresh in my memory.

"I can't thank you enough for the salamander wool…It saved our lives."

"Is that right…" She softly smiles at me again, her eyes half closed.

We sit on either side of the desk in silence, regarding each other for a few moments.

Eina coughs under her breath. The atmosphere in here is getting a little awkward.

"Back to the business at hand, Bell…Strictly speaking, I'm not allowed to pry for information, but it was quite dangerous?"

"…Yes."

She didn't have to say anything else for me to know what she was talking about.

It could only be the Irregular's—the Goliath's—appearance in the safe point. The Guild was doing everything in its power to keep the incident in the dark, including forbidding its employees to look into it themselves. So instead of talking about the cause, Eina asks me about the perilous situation.

I slowly nod my head. Looking back at her, she also nods and says, "I see."

I see a flash as she adjusts her glasses—it feels like her emerald-green eyes gaze right through me.

"I would like to offer you as much assistance as possible from here on out. For starters—I'll increase the scope and depth of our study sessions."

"Huh?"

"I was foolish not to inform you about the monsters deeper in the middle levels and the safe point, since I assumed that there was no chance you could possibly go that far. It was my fault you weren't prepared. I won't let that happen again. It's become evident after this incident that it's impossible to predict what you might encounter, and where…Yes, I'll make sure you're ready for anything the Dungeon can throw at you."

Eina has been giving me what she calls personal lessons—more like heavily informative lectures—ever since the day I first registered with the Guild and she was assigned to be my adviser. The Guild doesn't require her to do any of this, so it's all her idea. Thanks to these lessons, knowledge of the Dungeon—monster types and abilities, the layouts of the floors, and so on—has been drilled into my head.

I come to the painful realization that I'm alive today as a result of her aggressive teaching techniques…and now they're going to get more intensive? Both Eina's strict lessons and Aiz's harsh combat sessions could give the ancient Spartans a run for their money.

Eina just grins that same grin as my body shrinks back into the chair, my face drifting backward. "Let's do our best," she says, her eyes smiling at me.

She's really worried about me. I can't refuse her offer.

I lightly return the smile, nod again, and say, "I will…"

"All that's left to discuss are your plans for today."

My heart rate goes back to normal and our conversation resumes. I tell Eina the schedule I have in mind. "Ah...sure. I'm planning to go back into the Dungeon in two days."

"In two days...Is it correct to assume that you're taking a rest?"

"Well, the truth is that Welf...the smith I have a contract with is making some new equipment for me."

I see a spark of understanding flash in Eina's eyes the moment I mention Welf's name and our contract.

We lost a lot of weapons and armor on our trip to the eighteenth floor. My light armor is in bad shape after the battle with the Goliath. While it's still usable, Welf insisted on crafting new gear for me.

The work of High Smiths, those who have acquired the Forge ability, puts the quality of all others' work to shame. This is Welf's first job as a High Smith; he's a bit more excited than usual. I can't wait to see what kind of armor and weapons come out of his workshop.

"In that case, you will resume Dungeon activities once your new equipment is complete, yes? Which floor are you planning on going to first?"

"I think it's best that we start at the thirteenth floor. We might have made it to the eighteenth, but it wasn't pretty..."

Eina gives a few more pieces of advice as she and I work out a few finer details for my battle party's return to the Dungeon.

Our first goal is to completely master the thirteenth floor. Now that Welf's Level 2, it should be much easier to hold our own. Still, we can't let our guard down.

Next, Eina introduces several quests that we could undertake after evaluating my battle party's new balance. Quests are issued by individuals who require items that can usually only be found in the middle levels and below inside the Dungeon.

I'm thankful to Eina for giving me this opportunity to gain valuable experience and accept two quests: one, find the drop item from a specific monster; and two, locate a special mineral found on the thirteenth floor and bring it back to the surface.

Our very productive conversation over, the two of us stand up and leave the consultation box.

"One last thing, Bell. Don't get into fights with adventurers from another *Familia*. I'm sure that Goddess Hestia has already scolded you enough, so I won't say much…"

"Y-yes…"

"But I'll say this much: Nothing good can happen from two groups fighting with each other."

She leans in closer and talks about last night's events. "In the worst case, the entire city of Orario could become a battlefield if two *Familias* fight head-to-head." A chill of fear runs down my spine as I gulp down the air in my throat.

I thought I'd understood how dangerous these fights could be, but the seriousness in her voice makes that threat feel very real.

"…?"

We had just returned to the lobby and I was about to say good-bye to Eina at the reception counter.

I feel someone looking at me from behind. Turning around, I suddenly meet the gaze of two female adventurers in the corner of the lobby. Both of them seem to be looking at my eyes and hair for some reason. They must've been trying to find me, because they're coming this way.

It's about noon. There are usually a lot of adventurers coming out of here at this time of day, and today's no exception. The two women weave their way through the white marble lobby and come to a stop right in front of the two of us.

"Bell Cranell—am I wrong?" the lady with short-cut hair asks in a strong, curt voice.

"Th-that's me." I'm at a loss as to how to respond. Her partner lightly drifts up to me, long hair lightly swishing behind her as she nervously sways back and forth.

"Umm, this…"

She bows forward, her eyes glancing up at me as she holds out a letter.

No, it's…an invitation.

The envelope is extremely fine and sealed with a wax emblem. Ingrained in the wax is *a bow and arrow in front of a sun*.

© Suzuhito Yasuda

My eyes widen in surprise. The shorthaired girl opens her mouth to speak.

"The name's Daphne. That's Cassandra. As you can see, we're from *Apollo Familia*." The lady, Daphne, introduces herself and confirms what I thought.

An emblem that simultaneously inspires images of an archer and a beam of light through the darkness—*Apollo Familia*. These two are in the same group as the adventurers last night at the bar.

Eina leans over to me and whispers in a hushed voice, "Daphne Laulos and Cassandra Illion. Level Two, third-tier adventurers." They must be well-known veterans.

I'm sure both of them are older than me. I picked up on the aura of strength emanating from Daphne right away, but she seems calm and in control. The same can't be said for her friend Cassandra. The air about her is distant, a childlike innocence in her eyes.

I'm pretty sure they were waiting for me, watching all the adventurers come in and out of the Guild from a spot where they could see everything.

I freeze in place, looking at both of the ladies in turn. The one named Cassandra takes another step forward.

"Um, you see, it's an invitation. Lord Apollo is going to hold a Celebration, a-and if you'd like…I-if-if you don't want to, that's okay…"

Slap! Daphne hits the back of Cassandra's head with an open palm and steps in front of her.

"Oww," comes a soft cry. Daphne ignores both the cry and the beads of cold sweat running down my face and shoves the invitation into my hands.

"You must inform your goddess. Got that? You got the invitation."

"…I understand."

Daphne steps away as soon as I get the words out of my mouth. She must not have wanted to waste any time on idle talk, because she motions to Cassandra and turns to leave.

She suddenly stops in midstep and looks over her shoulder, short hair shifting to the side.

"My condolences."

What? I open my mouth to ask, but Daphne doesn't say anything else. She's already halfway into the crowd. Cassandra makes a small bow before taking off after her.

Eina and I watch them go. I look down at the invitation in my hands as soon as they disappear out the front entrance.

That night the goddess and I are at home, just like usual. I tell her everything that happened this afternoon.

"An invitation to the 'Celebration of the Gods'..."

The opened envelope lying in front of her, my goddess sits in her chair as she reads the paper in her hands.

We've just finished dinner. All that is left on the table are two cups of hot tea. The goddess was tired after a long day at work, so I'm washing dishes.

"It's been about a month and a half since Ganesha held one...I imagined someone would organize something soon."

The Celebration of the Gods is a party for deities by deities.

I've heard that part of it is so that the host can brag about their *Familia*'s influence and power, but it's basically a place for the gods and goddesses to have fun. My goddess has participated in at least one of these Celebrations before.

This time, *Apollo Familia* will be hosting a Celebration in two days.

Apollo Familia...I've looked into them myself. They have a good deal of influence as well as many powerful adventurers. One of their battle parties successfully slew the Goliath on level seventeen. The Guild gave them a D ranking.

Compared to our undersize *Hestia Familia*, they are far more prominent in Orario.

"What should we do?"

"We can't ignore it, not with the fight yesterday..."

I feel absolutely horrible. The goddess looks trapped, as though both decisions are impossible.

The brawl with *Apollo Familia* was only twenty-four hours ago. How would it look if we refused their invitation so soon after?

Thinking about it logically, ignoring their invitation would be like throwing mud in their faces.

"Hmm." The goddess's mouth pouts up toward her nose in thought.

I quickly apologize. "This is all my fault, Goddess..."

"No, it's all right, Bell. You don't have to feel that way...The truth is, I don't like Apollo that much."

"Eh? Can I ask why?"

"Ha-ha......A lot happened in Tenkai."

I tilt my head to the side, confused by the change in the goddess's tone.

"Anyway, back to the matter at hand...This Celebration is a little bit different than usual. A bit more interesting," she says while looking at the invitation, a grin on her lips.

I gave her the envelope without reading it myself. What could be so interesting about this Celebration?

I start putting dry dishes away, but my mind won't stop racing.

"It's pretty well decided that we have to participate. Miach and the others probably have their invitations by now. Chances like this happen once in a blue moon, so why don't we all enjoy this together?"

Enjoy this together? I look over my shoulder at the goddess.

This may be a little out of the blue, but Orario is greeting spring now.

The heavy clouds of winter have all disappeared, leaving behind the blue sky as a background for all of the blooming flowers. I've heard that many people come to Orario this season to visit because the weather is very stable. The seasons were beginning to change when I came to the city about two months ago. It could be said that outsiders like me coming into Orario are what make this city so lively.

The air is still crisp in the mornings, but the temperature steadily increases day by day.

Signs that summer is fast approaching are everywhere—but I know that the changing of the seasons isn't why I feel so hot right now.

Rumble, rumble. The wooden wheels of our horse-drawn carriage grind against the stone road beneath me. I run my fingers through my bangs for no reason at all. My palms are moist with sweat.

I can't relax. I don't think my body will calm down until tonight is over, but we have to get there first. I cast my gaze out the window and watch the red-tinted cityscape pass by.

The carriage comes to a stop.

The horses neigh in the background as the door of our fancy carriage opens in front of me. I step outside.

I'm not used to these clothes—wearing a coat with tails feels weird. Even the sound of my expensive shoes clicking with each step sounds like someone else.

My feet finally beneath me, I turn around and extend my arm to the girl behind me.

Lady Hestia emerges from inside the carriage, a joyous smile on her lips.

Just like me, she's wearing extremely formal clothing. She looks even more beautiful and stunning than usual.

"Thank you, Bell. You're pretty good at this escort thing."

"R-really...?"

She's taking long, elegant strides toward me. I'm so nervous that my joints are tightening up. A puppet could move more freely right now.

More and more extravagant horse-drawn carriages arrive every moment. Handsome men and dazzling women wearing some of the most expensive clothing I've ever seen fill the street. But the knockout punch comes from the exquisite manor—no, the absolute *palace*—that's looming over me. I'm trapped in a different world, and even breathing is a challenge.

Today's Celebration hosted by *Apollo Familia* requires deities *to bring one of their followers*, making it a god and human mixer party of sorts.

These parties are called "Celebrations of the Gods" because only gods are allowed to attend. However, this time the host has decided to change things up a bit. The deities want entertainment, and this gives them an opportunity to show off their favorite followers. So there are many adventurers and smiths mixed in with the absolutely flawless looks of their gods and goddesses. Lady Hestia and I are among them.

A farm boy from the middle of nowhere, wearing extravagant clothing and trying his best to look taller...I must stick out like a sore thumb.

I look down at my black coat, wondering if I even belong here. All of my clothes were prepared specifically for tonight, which makes me feel even more out of place.

"You look amazing, Bell. There's no need to be embarrassed," the goddess says calmly as I start to feel light-headed. I don't know if it's because she has an excuse to wear an extravagant dress, but she's in a very good mood.

Her aquamarine dress is lined with many frills and laces; it looks like flowing water as she moves. The focal point of the dress is, of course, her magnificent chest. Honestly, I don't know how to look at her right now.

The queen of a distant land...Well, maybe not that far, but the goddess has achieved a radiant balance between cute and beauty.

"My apologies, Hestia, Bell. Preparing everything for us, including these clothes, must've been difficult."

Lord Miach emerges from our horse-drawn carriage and joins us. Nahza is beside him, her hand resting in the crook of his arm. Of course the two of them are dressed just as formally as we are.

Lord Miach's *Familia* is very poor, so he was opposed to spending money on something like this. He wasn't planning on coming to the Celebration at all until Lady Hestia told him, "It would be good for Nahza to get out and spread her wings once in a while." Lord Miach nodded and eventually agreed. As a thank-you, the goddess and I had paid for their formal attire, as well as hiring the horse-drawn carriage for this evening.

Considering that they give me substantial discounts on high potions and dual potions that normally cost tens of thousands of vals, this was much cheaper.

"Thank you for the invitation, Bell…"

Nahza is a Chienthrope, a dog person. She says hello from beside Lord Miach while our two deities carry on their own conversation.

I've only seen Nahza wear simple clothes, so seeing her in a full dress is very novel, not to mention appealing. The dress itself is a soft red with long sleeves designed to cover her artificial right arm.

"…Do I look nice?"

She lightly pulls the skirt of her dress out to the sides with her fingers and does a little curtsy. I give her a big nod, as big as my stiff neck will allow.

Her eyes are the same as always, half closed. But there's the joy in her expression that I haven't seen before. *Swish, swish.* Her tail happily flicks back and forth beneath her dress.

"Well then, shall we proceed?"

"Sure. All right, Bell. I'm counting on you?"

"Y-yes!" Slowly but surely, I reach out and take Lady Hestia's extended hand.

I turn to the front and am once again overwhelmed by the extravagant palace in front of us. The doors to the front entryway are open. All of us make our way inside, our clothes and shoes sparkling as we pass through the well-lit doorway.

My breath leaves me.

It's a different realm, one that I have no connection to, a world of the night.

If someone had told me when I first came to Orario that I would be able to be a part of this realm alongside my goddess, would I have believed them?

I'd be lying if I said I wasn't excited…but more than that, I'm nervous.

Time stands still as I'm swept up in the luxurious atmosphere around me. I take a small breath before taking my first step into the hallway.

Other guests make their way into the building as well, men escorting the women. Lord Miach and I each take the hands of our partners and join the line flowing deeper into the palace.

*   *   *

The entrance hall is just as ornate as the outside of the building. Golden pillars decorated with hundreds of candles line the hallway. I have to squint my eyes. The soaring style of architecture makes it feel very open. Alabaster statues designed to look like every single god and goddess stand in different areas of the hallway like small shrines.

The hallway leads to a set of equally extravagant stairs. The location of tonight's party is waiting for us at the top: the second-floor ballroom.

The ballroom is already noisy with guests who had arrived before us. And, of course, the ballroom is just as well decorated as everything else. Many chandeliers equipped with magic-stone lamps hang from the ceiling, and long tables with elaborate spreads of food run down the sides and back of the ballroom. There's a balcony beyond the tall, thin windows.

The sun has already set, and no light is coming in from outside. This building is located on North Main, surrounded by the houses of some of Orario's wealthiest residents. That could be why the sounds of the taverns and nightlife feel very far away. This place is so quiet that it's hard to believe I'm still in the same city.

It's amazing that a place that can give you the feeling of stepping into another world exists in Orario.

"Um…That person, I've seen him before…"

"That adventurer has been famous for a while. He's strong, too…I haven't heard good things from other members of his group. They're a bit afraid of him, actually. Be careful…"

I catch glimpses of well-known adventurers as we go into the center of the ballroom. One elf looks like she'd rather be anywhere but here. There's a dwarf whose clothes are too tight, and some sharp, vigorous-looking animal people and Amazons. Humans and demi-humans are intermingling with the gods and goddesses.

Nahza tells me a lot of things as we go, but I'm still overwhelmed by this atmosphere.

"Ah yes, there you are."

"Miach, too! This is a surprise."

"Hephaistos, Také!"

A god and goddess greet us as we make our way toward the corner of the room—and Lady Hephaistos and Lord Takemikazuchi. Lady Hestia rushes out to meet them, followed closely by Lord Miach and Nahza, who smile and give short bows.

"Hey," says Nahza.

"You look well," says Lord Miach. Both sides smile and say hello.

"You brought Mikoto, eh, Také? Thanks for what you did the other day."

"Y-yes, er, n-no! It's nothing…!"

"Who is accompanying you, Hephaistos? I don't see anyone."

"He's a strange one, leaving me here to explore the party on his own."

Lady Hestia expressed her gratitude to Mikoto, the human hiding behind Takemikazuchi's back. The girl who came deep into the middle levels to save me not too long ago is now blue in the face with nervousness.

Her long black hair has been expertly braided and matches her flowing dress. She's physically shaking…I'm glad it's not just me.

She must not be used to exposing her shoulders, because she's huddling in, making them as small as possible. Even the tips of her ears are turning red.

I can relate. I don't blame her for standing there with her eyes flying left and right. Lord Miach and Lady Hephaistos continue their conversation beside us.

"—Hey hey, everybody's here! Let me join in the fun!"

"Ah, Hermes."

I turn around in time to see Lord Hermes practically bound over to our group. He's wearing his usual charming smile, his eyes narrowed.

"Feh." Lord Takemikazuchi doesn't seem to be too happy about this.

Miss Asfi is right beside him, her silver glasses sitting comfortably on her face. "Lord Hermes, please lower your voice…" There's a hint of protest in her tone as she sighs under her breath.

"Why did you come over here? We haven't had direct contact for very long at all."

"Hey, c'mon, Takemikazuchi. Didn't we just work together? Don't leave me out in the cold!"

Lord Hermes slips by the obviously perturbed Lord Takemikazuchi after giving us an energetic greeting.

A few moments later, he's standing in front of me, showing off a toothy grin. "Hi there, Bell! Love that jacket, that's what I call style! And Nahza, wonderful dress!"

"Th-thank you."

"Appreciated…"

"What's this? Got some butterflies in your stomach, little Mikoto? Your cute face is going to waste!"

"C-cute…?!"

Unlike Lord Miach and myself, Lord Hermes is dressed rather casually. He goes around our circle, complimenting everyone from my goddess to Nahza. His eyes twinkle like a kid who's found a new toy when he turns to face Mikoto. He reaches out and takes her hand before pressing his lips onto her fingers. *Poof!* Mikoto's face practically explodes in a deep red blush.

Thud! Smack! Lord Takemikazuchi slaps Lord Hermes in the back of the head at the same time that Miss Asfi drills her heel into his shin.

"Many of us have come out tonight."

"This time the children are with us. Tonight's Celebration promises to be a bit livelier than usual."

Lady Hephaistos and Lord Miach strike up a conversation to try and ignore Lord Hermes's whimpers of pain after he collapses to the floor.

But they're right…This is starting to feel like a party. Even our little corner of the ballroom is starting to get noisy.

I think I'm getting used to this atmosphere, though.

"—My guests! I'm glad to see you've all arrived!"

A loud voice echoes through the ballroom.

Every head around me instantly turns to face the other side of the room.

There is a god standing in front of the opposite wall.

He has blond hair that seems to shine like the sun. The bright and wavy locks glide over one another like early afternoon sunbeams. With a smile that is equally as brilliant, his handsome looks are powerful enough to make me, another male, stand and stare.

He's pretty tall, too, and wearing a crown of laurels on top of his head.

Two very powerful-looking adventurers, a man and a woman, are standing just behind him on either side.

There's no doubt about it. This has to be Lord Apollo.

"An idea came to me about how to make this event special. How do you like it? Dressing up the ones we hold most dear and bringing them to our Celebration—what could be more delightful?"

I can clearly hear the excitement in the voice of our host. Quite a few other gods agree with him, shouting and clapping in approval.

"Seeing so many of my kin and the faces of their beloved children fills me with great joy. Tonight is a night destined to be filled with grand opportunities and new meetings. I have foreseen it."

I step to the side to get a better view, when suddenly—

Lord Apollo's gaze sweeps over the crowd, but then seems to instantly lock on me.

...?

I frown for a moment and look behind me over my shoulder. Lord Apollo doesn't seem to react; he'd already started talking again as soon as I turned back toward the front.

...I might be overreacting because of what happened between me and *Apollo Familia*. That has to be the source of this awkwardness I'm feeling. I should just ignore it.

"The night is young. I have assembled only the finest wines and freshest food. So by all means, wine, dine, and enjoy yourselves!"

He raises his arms high into the air as the last echoes of his voice make their way through the ballroom.

There's another cheer, mostly from the male deities, in response to this. Wineglasses with all sorts of designs carved into their bases are filled and clinked all around me as the party officially gets underway.

"Goddess...Um, what should we do?"

Lady Hestia looks at Lord Apollo the moment I ask her my question. "Mm, I want to settle things with Apollo, but it might be a good idea to wait. He looks a little busy right now."

Of course we need to clear the air after what happened at the bar, but all of *Apollo Familia* is in motion. The *Familia* members are all dressed in their uniforms and are taking the role of attendants for the other guests. Lord Apollo is surrounded by other deities, greeting and talking as he tries to make his rounds. It would be difficult to even say hello at this rate.

Just like Lady Hestia said, we should wait for things to settle down a bit.

"Well, it's not every day that we get to do something like this, so let's enjoy the party. Let's dig into the food, Bell!"

"Ah, sure."

The goddess and I join Lord Miach and the others in their circle next to a table. All of them already have wineglasses in their hands.

"Um, Miss Mikoto. Thank you for everything you did on the eighteenth floor. You did so much to help me..."

"I-it was nothing. Really, I didn't..."

Mikoto must've gotten used to this atmosphere and overcome her nerves. She responds quickly.

Not only was she part of the search party, she also came to our rescue when my goddess was kidnapped by other adventurers. I tell her how grateful I am, but she just lightly shakes her head.

"Do not forget what you accomplished, Sir Bell. Facing down a floor boss under those circumstances and delivering the final blow...It's embarrassing to say this myself, but your strength and bravery left a profound impression on me."

"N-no, I wouldn't have been able to do that alone. Actually, alone I wouldn't have been able to do anything..."

There's an air of nostalgia in her voice, but I can't claim full credit for what happened.

The two of us exchange a few more denials. We smile at each other before we know what is happening.

"...Sir Bell. If you are ever in danger, summon me at any time. My sword shall defend you."

"Miss Mikoto..."

"Captain Ouka and Miss Chigusa would also like to lend you their strength, just as I would."

"Well, me, too...If any of you are in trouble, call me anytime. I'll do anything I can to help." We promise to help each other in the future.

Mikoto's face melts into a smile as we both nod.

She extends her right hand. I feel a wave of shyness rush through me before I reach out and give her a firm handshake.

"If I may ask you a question. I've heard that you grow at an incredible rate. Would you be willing to share some advice?"

"Bell's not completely human. I dope him up with muscle-building pills of my own design every day..." Nahza joins our conversation, clearly enjoying herself.

"Please don't tell stories like that!" I take another look around the room.

I've heard rumors that these Celebrations of the Gods are overwhelmingly strict when it comes to etiquette, but there seems to be none of that here. The gods and goddesses are laughing, drinking, and enjoying themselves. Everything seemed so formal at first, but it turned out to be no big deal.

The only thing left that's making me uncomfortable is this absurdly luxurious building.

"Um, does this building belong to *Apollo Familia*...? Is this their home?"

Asfi answers my question right away.

"No, it is not. This building is under the jurisdiction of the Guild. *Familias* and merchants who require this facility are able to rent it as needed."

Lord Takemikazuchi opens his mouth to speak. "I only know of one god who prefers to hold Celebrations at home, and that's Ganesha. Most of us wouldn't think of inviting other *Familias* directly into our base of operations."

"Everyone's always looking for something to give them an edge. It's impossible to keep secrets from this many of us all at once." Lord Miach adds his own explanation. I understand and nod back.

Lady Hephaistos and Lady Hestia are standing next to our conversation, their eyes scanning the room.

"This Celebration has a different feel to it. Many gods who don't normally participate in these events are here tonight."

"Yeah, Apollo has some unique ideas..."

I take a look around the room for myself.

I see a lot of smiling faces and pause a moment to take in the atmosphere, but there's something else on my mind.

"Excuse me...What's Lord Apollo like?"

"Oh? Are you interested, Bell?"

Lord Hermes turns to face me. "Yes," I say as I make eye contact.

His orange eyes smile back at me as he takes a step closer.

"He's an interesting one. I've known him since we were in Tenkai, and even now I haven't gotten bored of him. That guy has provided us with millennia of entertainment."

Huh? I feel my eyes pop open. I wasn't expecting that answer...

"Anyway, he's rather frisky. Even though he's not an adventurer, we still gave him the title 'Phallus the Passionate' because it fit him so well."

Ph-Phallus?

Why would they do that...? I have no clue.

"He's quite the persistent lover boy—wouldn't you say, Hestia?"

"How should I know?!"

My goddess has her back to us, sampling the food—more like stuffing her face—when she snaps at Lord Hermes's playful verbal jab. She immediately dives back into the food, shoveling it into her mouth a little more vigorously.

Lady Hestia said that she doesn't like Lord Apollo...Did something happen?

"Also, he is extremely...tenacious."

"Huh?"

I flip my head back around to face Lord Hermes.

I'm just about to ask what he meant by that, when suddenly—

Waaaahh! A wave of sound comes from all directions simultaneously around me. It drowns out my question.

"Would you look at that... The big cheese has arrived." Lord Hermes sounds surprised once he finds the reason for the commotion.

I follow his eyes—and instantly find the source of everyone's excitement.

All of the attention in the ballroom is focused on one giant animal person and the silver-haired goddess standing beside him.

"Who's that...?"

"That, Bell, is Lady Freya. I'm sure you've come across the name *Freya Familia* before?"

I lightly nod my head yes. It's a lot to take in at once.

Freya Familia—they're just as powerful as *Loki Familia*. It wouldn't be a stretch to say that those two groups are the heads of the Labyrinth City in terms of strength and influence. Even newbie adventurers have at least heard about both *Familias'* bravery and deeds.

So that silver-haired goddess is the leader of that *Familia*...?

The Celebration's mood instantly picks up upon Lady Freya's arrival. She's just that beautiful.

Silver eyes and a well-defined body line, her large breasts and thin waist are hidden behind a dress that looks like it was woven in heaven itself. She takes one step forward, and all eyes in the room lock onto her. Another step and the gazes follow. She's quite a ways from me, but I'm already hot under the collar.

I've never seen anyone so alluring...

"—Huh?!"

Without warning, Lady Hestia's twin black ponytails shiver out of the corner of my eye. But this other goddess is just so dazzling...

Lady Hestia's face emerges from the table, takes one look at Lady Freya, and then glances at me with wide eyes.

As if understanding everything in a flash, she jumps toward my shoulder.

"Don't you dare look at Freya, Bell!"

"Bwuh?!"

"Any child who sees a Goddess of Beauty will get brainwashed by her charm!"

Coming in directly from my side, she almost knocks me off my feet.

I somehow manage to regain my balance with the goddess draped around my neck, forcing me to look away.

A Goddess of Beauty—it's common knowledge.

A deity who is beauty incarnate, with the ability to entrance gods and mortals alike.

It looks like the goddess wasn't kidding. Almost everyone around me is slack-jawed, staring at her. Man, woman, it doesn't matter. They're just standing there, as if their spirits have left their bodies.

Mikoto and Nahza are fighting hard against Lady Freya's influence. Nahza's eyes are clenched shut as she shakes her head back and forth. Mikoto has turned the other way, but her entire face is blushing. Only Asfi seems to be holding her own. She's looking out in the middle of nowhere, like a daydreaming kid.

"First Ganesha's Celebration, and now this one…Freya never comes out in the public this much."

"H-how do you mean?"

I hear Lady Hephaistos whispering as I struggle to free myself from Lady Hestia's grasp and ask for clarification. It's Hermes who clears things up.

"Lady Freya usually stays in her room on the highest level of Babel Tower, rarely showing her face in public. Many of the gods here come to Celebrations just for a chance to see her with their own eyes."

She doesn't show her face in public…Well, yes, it'd be difficult to go anywhere if you get that much attention just by stepping outside. Lady Freya might like to be among us, but I'm sure utter chaos happens every time she tries.

Looking at how people react to her now, I don't blame her for staying up in the tower.

"—"

That's when her silver gaze falls upon me.

She stops walking and turns in my direction…and smiles.

Ker-tap, ker-tap. The heels on her shoes echo as she approaches. Everyone in her path makes way, backing out as if pushed by some unseen force. Lady Hestia stops struggling for a moment and watches the silver-haired goddess and her massive attendant walk right up to us.

"So you're here, Hestia. Hephaistos as well. First time since Denatus, I believe?"

"...Freya, what are you doing here?"

Lady Hestia lets go of me and squares her shoulders directly in front of Lady Freya the moment the other goddess extends a friendly greeting.

"I'm glad to see you are looking well," says Lady Hephaistos next to my goddess. Lady Hestia looks like she's trying to hold back a torrent with a cork.

"I merely came to say hello. It's a rare chance to see so many familiar faces at once, so how could I not make my way here?"

The words roll off Lady Freya's tongue as she glances toward the small mob of male gods that have assembled around her.

All of them seem to melt as her silver eyes pass by. Lord Hermes is weak-kneed, a dumbstruck look on his face. Lord Takemikazuchi is blushing a light shade of pink and clears his throat with an "ahem." Lord Miach bows and compliments her by saying, "You are quite beautiful this evening."

Not a heartbeat later, the heels of the expensive shoes that belong to their female followers find their way to the toes of the male deities. "Gah?!" "Uwoh?!" "Nuah?!" come their yelps of pain. I take a step back.

Once again, her silver eyes alight on me.

Air leaks out of my mouth as those silver spheres draw me in. Lady Freya's cheeks pull back into an even deeper smile.

She leans forward, extending her arm, and strokes the side of my face.

"—Tonight, will you make a dream of mine come true?"

"—Dream on!" Lady Hestia roars at Lady Freya right in front of me. She slaps Lady Freya's hand away, her eyes burning with rage. "What are you getting excited for, Bell?!"

"S-s-sorry!"

"Listen up! That goddess is nothing more than a dragon that devours every man within reach! A rabbit like you wouldn't last two seconds!"

"Yes…!!"

The goddess is overwhelming. My body shrinks away from her without even thinking. It's almost like she's unleashing round after round of Swift-Strike Magic, forcing me back.

Her twin ponytails are sweeping out behind her like they're trying to express just how dangerous the other goddess truly is.

But Lady Freya is laughing to herself. "My, my, how disappointing."

I think she's enjoying my goddess's reaction…Then she steps away and says, "I seem to have upset Hestia, so I'll take my leave. Until next time."

She turns her back on the still-infuriated Lady Hestia. "Ottar," she calls to the animal person beside her and starts walking. I stand in awe of her follower—a boar man standing more than two meders tall—as the two of them make their way into the crowd. I watch them go, my eyes following the fluid motions of Lady Freya's hips.

My body cools down the farther away she gets. Finally, the last lock of her silver hair disappears.

"—Not here two seconds, and that vixen's already showin' me up."

The storm has passed. A new voice cuts through the calm.

It's coming from the other direction.

It catches me off guard. I spin around and—receive the biggest surprise of the night.

"Loki?!"

"Yo! Itty-Bitty! See ya learned how t'wear a dress. You're actin' so grown-up, I could bust a gut!"

Lady Hestia yells at a goddess with vermilion red hair who's dressed in a man's suit.

And standing beside her…

A radiant girl with blond hair and golden eyes, wearing an elegant dress.

"…?!"

My eyes go wide and my face burns.

Her dress a light green, Aiz looks slightly embarrassed standing just a little ways in front of me.

"Just when did you get here?! You're not the type to sneak in!" demands Lady Hestia.

"Shut up, idiot!! Two floppin' boobies stole my entrance, got that?!"

It sounds like Aiz and her goddess Loki only just arrived. Everyone was so preoccupied with Lady Freya that no one noticed.

Lady Loki is in a sharp man's suit, and Aiz wears a form-fitting dress. It almost looks like some high-ranking nobleman's daughter with her bodyguard, which is the complete opposite of reality.

My body feels hot again, but it's not going away this time.

I can't take my eyes off her. A princess from one of my old picture books has come to life in front of my very eyes.

Her pale green dress is open in the front and in the back, completely exposing her delicate, feminine shoulders. Sparkling beads and various other decorations are sown in as accents in several places on the dress. I have no doubt that her goddess was in charge of the design and Lady Loki had no problem spending a large amount of money to show her affection for Aiz. The finishing touch is the long, silky gloves that extend all the way past her elbows.

Part of her golden hair is tied with a ribbon behind her head. The rest of it is flowing gracefully down her back.

Her angelic face and thin neck, supple breasts making just the right amount of cleavage, thin waist and fluttering dress...

This is not the adventurer, the knight Aiz Wallenstein that I know.

The heat overtaking me right now is different from before—my heart didn't sing when I was taken in by Lady Freya.

My body is throbbing, refusing to move.

"Ah..."

"...!"

Aiz lifts her face and we make eye contact. Neither of us can say a word.

I feel my face blush as she quickly looks to the floor, her hands together in front of her stomach as her shoulders lightly twitch up and down.

Shff, her body swishes back and forth under Lady Loki's shadow.

S-so cute...!

"...Ehh?"

"Ouch?!"

My goddess buries the toe of her shoe deep into the side of my shin. Is it that obvious how I'm feeling? Does my face betray me?

"Ohh, so this is Itty-Bitty's kid..."

I grab my leg and fight back the tears when suddenly I feel Lady Loki's eyes on me.

Her vermilion eyes carve right through me. Every single muscle in my mouth and throat tenses up. She doesn't even blink. Is that a hint of annoyance? Well, whatever it is, it's making me uncomfortable.

After a few moments...

"Nah, this kiddo does nothin' for me. My Aiz is so much better it's like comparin' heaven 'n' earth!"

Her words crack like a whip.

I know that Aiz is out of my league, but that hurts a lot.

I almost lose my balance, feeling light-headed, when I catch a glimpse of my goddess's face. Her cheeks are trembling.

Suddenly, she turns to face Lady Loki head-on.

"Just like before, you know you can't win in an argument, so you have to brag about your child this time?! So predictable, it's painful to watch!"

"—Oh yeah?!" A vein suddenly pops out of Lady Loki's head.

"Anyone can see that my Bell is much cuter than your Wallenso-mething! So charming, just like an adorable little rabbit!!"

"Ya hit yer head, moron?! My Aiz is a hundred times cooler than that puny bunny!!"

An angry bragging contest breaks out.

The two goddesses trade verbal blows with reckless abandon. Lady Hephaistos sighs to herself, whispering, "Here we go again..." Lord Miach has an empty smile on his face. Nahza and the rest just watch, their mouths slightly open.

As for me, I'm absolutely horrified. They hate each other. All of the warmth in my body suddenly fizzles out, plunging me into despair.

The insurmountable barrier between men and women in different *Familias*...There can be no better example than this.

The two of them are practically growling at each other, and other deities are starting to take notice. "Hey, look, it's round two!" "Now this is entertainment." "Check that out." Gods and goddesses are gathering around us. Aiz and I have reached our limit. Both of us step forward and try to calm our goddesses down.

Both of them are breathing heavily, eyes filled with flames of rage. Luckily, Lord Hermes steps in and we finally get them under control.

"…Humph. Itty-Bitty just spoiled my good mood!"

"That's my line!!"

"Ohh? Aiz, we're leaving!"

"Bell, so are we!"

Lady Loki grabs Aiz's wrist as Lady Hestia takes hold of my hand. Both goddesses storm off in different directions, pulling us with them.

I take a quick look over my shoulder. Aiz is looking back at me. Our eyes meet for a brief moment.

If only I'd said something, if only I'd heard her voice…As I watch her get farther and farther away, I can't help but feel I've lost my chance.

How pathetic. I have neither the guts to break away from the goddess's grasp, nor the courage to approach Lady Loki. Aiz turns away, her delicate shoulder blades flashing for a moment from beneath her hair. She's so distant now—is this how things are going to be from now on? Once again, reality has made itself clear. The amount of time I was able to spend that close to her on the eighteenth floor was really special.

More and more people are gathering around Lady Loki every second. Finally, I tear my eyes away from her as the painful reality of my mediocrity sinks in.

I give up hope of getting a chance to speak with her and join my goddess as she moves to another side of the ballroom.

After that, Lady Hestia introduced me to her divine friends and acquaintances as we walked several circuits around the party. It's not easy to introduce yourself to a god, but somehow I'm able to overcome my nerves and string words together.

Two hours have passed since we arrived at the party, and I need a break.

I move away from the group of people, alone, find a quiet spot, and lean against the wall to avoid bothering anyone.

"Whew..." A tired sigh escapes my lips.

I'm absolutely exhausted.

I take a look out over the party. The bright chandeliers hanging from the ceiling light everything up like a work of art.

The attendants are hard at work carrying even more extravagant food out to the tables and passing out richly colored wine. Elegant music starts to play, but I can't tell where it's coming from. Almost as if on cue, the middle of the ballroom floor opens up for dancers, but I can still see Lady Hestia and Lady Loki arguing in the other corner of the room.

It still feels weird being here...

I can't help but feel that way watching these beautiful men and women partner up and start dancing.

This is a sparkling world of beauty and status. Completely different from the world I was in yesterday.

Maybe it's because I'm alone, but I feel more and more like I don't belong, like I'm sticking out. The unfamiliar environment keeps me feeling uneasy.

It's pretty close to how I felt when I first started crawling the Dungeon.

If I have a few more chances like this in the future, maybe I'll get used to this world, too.

But I can't picture that happening.

"..."

I leave my spot against the wall and try to find an escape.

I don't have to walk far. One of the tall windows was left open and I step outside.

Cool air envelops me the moment my foot hits the cement balcony.

A starry night opens up above my head. I take a look around the black abyss and see a faint glow coming from the closest Main Street. A soft breeze tickles my skin.

All of the stress and tension that had built up start to melt as I take a few breaths of fresh air.

My mind is clear.

"...?"

I walk out to the ornately carved hand railing and hear some strange sounds coming from below.

Looking out over the green lawn decorated with a fountain and many trees, my eyes find two human-looking figures.

Isn't that...?

This must be a garden of sorts, and probably part of the building itself. The edge of the property is lined with tall trees, enough to remind me of a wooded area. There, in a dark spot where the lights from the Celebration can't reach—

The handsome man from Hibachitei, the one who beat me so easily...Hyacinthus and a man I've never seen before are talking.

What are they doing out here...?

"Tomorrow morning at the earliest...According to plan...We will handle the timing...Is that clear, Zanis?"

"Yes...About the money..."

I can't make out all of their words. My body moves on its own.

Concentrating with all of my might, I focus my ears—enhanced by my Status—on their conversation.

They're quite a ways from the balcony, but I can also make out their lip movements. With that, plus snippets of their voices, I get a general idea what they're talking about.

Zanis...?

That must be the name of whoever Hyacinthus is talking to.

I know it's not nice to eavesdrop, but I lean a little farther off the balcony.

When suddenly, *shff*, Hyacinthus and the other man look my way. I instantly freeze as I watch their eyes scan all the balconies on the side of the building.

"Bell?"

"!"

A voice comes from behind me and I spin to face it.

Lord Hermes is standing next to the window that leads to the balcony. The Celebration is still in full swing behind him. I look over my shoulder back to where the two men were just a moment ago.

Hyacinthus and the man are nowhere to be seen.

"What are you doing out here?"

"Ah...Nothing really."

Lord Hermes walks out to meet me at the hand railing.

I was eavesdropping, but I can't exactly say that to him. I wish I could've heard more of their conversation, and I try my best to reassure myself that it was nothing important.

"...Oh well, it doesn't matter. Here, drink up."

"Th-thank you..."

Lord Hermes has one glass in each hand and holds one of them out in front of me. I take it and thank him.

Only once I get it to my lips do I realize it's just water. Honestly, I didn't want any more wine, so I'm grateful.

I look at Lord Hermes with questioning eyes, as if to say *why are you out here?* He takes a swig of the wine in his own glass and grins at me.

"We never did have a chance to chat. Sorry I'm not one of those cute girls inside, but may I join you?"

His joke makes me smile and I nod at him. "Of course."

I quickly fix my posture and meet Lord Hermes in the center of the balcony.

"You and Hestia just keep making progress. I've known who you are for a while now, but after seeing what you can do on the eighteenth floor, you can count me as one of your fans."

"I-I'm not that great..."

Seeing Lord Hermes come out here was a little scary at first, but there's something about his friendly smile that eases the tension in my shoulders. He compliments, teases, and jokes as the two of us get settled. Lord Hermes is by far the best oral tactician I've ever met.

Muffled but beautiful music makes its way from the ballroom's dance floor through the window in front of us. The gorgeous tones fill my ears as Lord Hermes and I start talking like friends.

"Say, Bell. Why did you become an adventurer?"

© Suzuhito Yasuda

Lord Hermes leans against the hand railing as he asks me the question.

The muscles in my mouth tighten up. What am I supposed to tell him? "I came to meet the girl of my dreams in the Dungeon!" "I couldn't give up my childhood dream of becoming a hero!" It's getting embarrassing, repeating the same answer over and over.

I scratch my head and think about it for a moment before finally making up my mind.

"My grandfather...The man who raised me said this before he passed away...'Orario has everything you could ever want. If you wanna go, go.'"

"Oh?"

"Orario has money and, um, I could meet lots of cute girls, fulfill any dream...He told me that joining a beautiful goddess's *Familia* and being part of a big family was more than just a possibility."

"—Ha-ha-ha-ha-ha-ha-ha!"

Lord Hermes tilts his chin toward the night sky and laughs from deep within his belly.

I look at the red-faced deity who's clutching his stomach and doing his best to calm down.

"'You can be a hero. Go, if your will is strong enough.'...Those were his words," I say.

It wasn't a demand; it was up to me to decide.

I was still very young, but I clearly remember Gramps saying all of that only once.

That's the reason I came to Orario. That's why I wanted to be an adventurer.

After my grandfather's death, I thought about everything he'd ever said. It didn't take me long to make my choice.

I wanted the warmth of a family.

The one thing I craved ever since childhood—and reinforced by my bond with Gramps—was to meet the person who would make that dream come true.

So I came to Orario, my soul filled with visions of becoming a hero.

Even as I talk with Lord Hermes, flashes of the life I once knew bubble up to the surface of my memory. I look at the floor of the balcony and relive every single one of them.

"...Your grandfather sounds like he was very amusing."

"Yes, he was. He made every day entertaining."

I try to stifle the grin on my lips. The word "amusing" describes my grandfather so well that I just can't help it.

Lord Hermes looks at me like he's going to flash yet another smile. Bringing the wineglass up to his lips, he tilts his head back and downs the rest.

"So then, you spent your entire life in the town where you were born until you came to Orario?"

"Yes. A small village in the middle of the mountains...So, there is still so much I don't know."

Lord Hermes's expression softened the moment I admitted to how little I understood about the city. I have to admit, this is pretty embarrassing.

He looks at me, orange eyes twinkling under long, thin eyelids.

"Well then, do you know of a god named Zeus?"

Then he asks me about a god I've never heard of.

"Lord Zeus...No, I don't. Is he well known?"

"Oh yes. He *used to be* the leader of the most powerful *Familia* in history, starting from the day we first arrived in Orario."

That was unexpected. My eyes wide open, I look back at Lord Hermes, giving him my full attention.

"A-aren't *Loki Familia* and *Freya Familia* the most powerful..."

"Now they are, sure. But it wasn't that way until very recently. Fifteen years ago, to be exact."

Fifteen years ago...My lips go to repeat his words, but no sound comes out of my mouth.

Lord Hermes starts talking again.

"Until Loki and Lady Freya claimed control themselves, Zeus and a goddess named Hera were the top dogs in Orario. The current arrangement came to be when Loki and Lady Freya took them down and banished them from the city."

"...Lord Zeus's and Lady Hera's *Familias* were defeated in battle?"

"That's true, but not in the way that you're thinking. You see, the shift in power all started with a failed quest."

It sounds like he's about to get to the juicy part of the story.

Lord Hermes holds out his hand and sticks up three fingers.

"This world has burdened Orario with the Three Great Quests."

My eyes focus on the three fingertips in front of me.

"During the era that you children call Ancient Times, three monsters with incredible power escaped from the Dungeon—the quests are to eliminate them."

"Eh...So then, that means..."

"That's right, they're alive. These ancient monsters that burst out of the Dungeon are still out there."

I gulp down the air in my throat.

"Ancient Times"—That means these monsters have survived for more than one thousand years. This is incredible.

Judging by the way Lord Hermes is talking about them...I don't think they're related to the monsters Nahza told me about, the ones that escaped the Dungeon and reproduced on their own on the surface.

"This should be obvious, but the Dungeon provides adventurers in the Labyrinth City with the perfect training ground. As citizens of Orario, they have the obligation to the rest of the world to dispose of the monsters that emerged from beneath their feet."

No other city can rival Orario in terms of pure power and influence. This is directly due to the Dungeon, a place where monsters continuously spawn and provide adventurers with nearly limitless opportunities to level up. Aboveground, monsters and humans are much weaker, meaning that adventurers have a very difficult time acquiring excelia—and chances to level up are hard to come by. I've heard that the strongest adventurers in other cities are only Level 2, rarely making it to Level 3.

That's the real reason that Orario is considered to be the center of the world, this source of absolute power.

"Fifteen years ago...Zeus and Hera were at the height of their power. Their *Familias* were home to the most powerful adventurers in history, and they set out to challenge the three ancient beasts. First, the Terrestrial Tyrant, Behemoth, then the Ruler of the Sea, Leviathan, were defeated.—And last..."

Lord Hermes puts down two fingers in turn. He raises the last one up to his face.

"The last one, the Black Dragon, was too strong and wiped them out."

I finally remember to blink.

"The B-Black Dragon...It can't be—is that the One-eyed Dragon?"

"That's right. You know about it?"

Oh, I know. I know.

I met that living embodiment of death and despair in the pages of one of my books when I was a kid.

The epic tales of heroes from the Ancient Times immortalized in the pages of the labyrinth's scripture, the *Dungeon Oratoria*. It's a cruel and merciless monster that appears in the book's final chapter.

The bravest of the heroes sacrificed his own life to cut out one of the beast's eyes, forcing the Dragon King to retreat into the clouds.

Words have left me, but with Lord Hermes's story replaying in my mind I manage to grunt an affirmation.

The living scourge, living legend, the living end.

This creature that appears in many heroic tales and legends of old is not just a work of fiction, but *alive*...I'm absolutely stunned.

"Both Zeus's and Hera's *Familias* lost their strongest followers in the battle with the Black Dragon, leaving them weak and vulnerable. And now we're back to where we began. Loki and Lady Freya teamed up to force the two high-ranking scrappers—no, their biggest rival deities—out of the city."

Lord Hermes smiles again and shrugs his shoulders.

"It was just a sign of the changing times. Even the Guild, which had supported them through thick and thin for generations, didn't protect a feeble Zeus and Hera."

Lord Hermes goes on to say that it might be better to say the Guild couldn't protect them.

"That's the fall of Zeus and how the Orario you know came to be."

"…"

"The peoples of the world still yearn for the completion of the last of the Three Grand Quests, the slaying of the Black Dragon. As a citizen of Orario, you will have a part to play."

Lord Hermes sums up his point while grinning at me as I stand frozen in place.

He just explained how the once powerful and famous *Zeus Familia* and the fate of the city of Orario were intertwined.

Sure, I grew up in a little village in the middle of nowhere. But it's painful to realize just how clueless I was. This world seems peaceful at first glance, but there's a disaster waiting to happen hidden in the shadows.

Where is the Black Dragon now, what's it doing, there's so much I want to know…But as one young and inexperienced adventurer, I don't have the right to know those details. There's not much reason to.

But at the very least, the ones closest to that Dragon in power are—the warriors belonging to the two most powerful *Familias*.

"…Um, Lord Hermes?"

"What is it?"

"Lord Zeus and Lady Hera…Can I ask what happened to them?"

I have a feeling he won't tell me anything more about the Three Grand Quests, so I ask him about the banished gods instead.

He looks at me for a very long moment before flashing a grin and closing his eyes.

"That's a tough one. The idea that they would return to Tenkai sounds pretty convincing, but no one really knows what happened to that good-natured old man. He might be out scouring the globe for new heroes, or he could be hiding in some shack, wallowing in despair. Knowing him, he could be traveling to the ends of the earth just to see what's there…That's more likely."

"I-I see."

"Are you curious?"

I look away and say that I'm not really interested. For some reason, I can't give him a direct answer.

Hearing that those two deities were chased out of the city makes me think.

If for some reason I was drawn into a battle for power and my side lost...Lady Hestia and I...Would we be banished, too?

I can't ignore this and assume that it's someone else's problem. It's a little scary.

"Well, our chat went a little long. Sorry to take so much of your time, Bell."

"N-no, it's all right. Thank you for talking with me."

Our conversation over, Hermes gives me one of his charming smiles. Suddenly the atmosphere on the balcony changes completely.

Lord Hermes cocks an eyebrow after I thank him.

"Say, Bell, are you not going to dance?"

"Eh?"

"Take a look inside. See?"

I follow his gaze and, sure enough, the center of the ballroom is sparkling, alive with movement.

"That grandfather of yours told you, didn't he? That Orario has enough gorgeous women and beautiful ladies to turn the world green with envy? This is your chance to enjoy it."

"Eh? Um...what?"

Oh no, it's that grin. I've seen Lord Hermes make that face before.

He puts his arm around me, guiding me to the window. The corners of his mouth are so far back, I'm surprised his teeth haven't hit his ear.

"L-Lord Hermes, I don't know how to dance, so don't worry about me. I'm happy enough just being here...!"

"What happened to your spine, Bell? So now, what's your type?"

He tightens his arm around me, grinning hugely.

Completely unable to move, I have no choice but to look at the women scattered around the ballroom. There's an absolutely gorgeous goddess dancing in the middle of the floor, her dress fluttering around her. A little ways back, an elf is being invited to dance at this very moment. A sleek catgirl is enjoying the cuisine at a table off to the side. More and more young women come into focus as I look from corner to corner and back again.

I fight back the burgeoning heat coming from under my eyes. The only thing I know for sure is I can't look at her, anywhere else is okay *but not at her*...But that plan backfires.

My eyes manage to find a streak of blond hair amid the lights and decorations of the ballroom—I find Aiz right away.

And, of course, Lord Hermes notices.

"Oh-ho! The Kenki, eh? You don't mess around."

"No! I just, um...!"

The words stop coming out as my face starts to boil, turning beet red.

Lord Hermes looks at me in silence. Then without warning, his eyes light up, accompanied by another toothy grin.

"—So that's how it is...I see, I see."

"Uh, uhhh..."

The deity nods and looks at me with that cheek-splitting smile plastered on his face.

He knows. He just figured everything out; I can see it in his expression. My whole body feels like it's on fire.

He saw right through me like it was nothing. I look away, unable to maintain eye contact, and throw my head back, resigning myself to misery.

At the same time, "All right, that settles it!!" Lord Hermes sounds much more excited than he did a minute ago. "I'm no God of Love, but that doesn't mean I can't make sparks fly!"

"Why are you talking so loud?!"

But Lord Hermes doesn't respond to me. Instead, he grabs my hand and pulls me back into the ballroom. He takes long powerful strides straight toward Aiz.

"Wh-what are you doing?!"

"Taking you to your dancing partner, obviously! The Kenki, who else?"

My heart jumps into my throat.

"I can't, it's impossible! There's no way!"

I repeat myself over and over, getting louder and louder as Lord Hermes pulls me through the ballroom. But he's not listening.

Like hell I can ask her. Even if I did, there's no way she'd accept. But above all else, our goddesses would never allow it to happen!

Lord Hermes turns around and gives me one of his classic "manly" smiles. Perhaps one of my objections finally made it through?

"Leave it to me. I've got a plan."

That said, he takes off at a brisk pace with me in tow.

Perfectly crafted melodies from the musicians fill the dimly lit ballroom. The magic-stone lamps on the chandeliers have been turned down, leaving the dance floor illuminated by moonlight.

Lady Hestia and Lady Loki are still arguing in the back corner. Aiz is standing just behind them. I bet that anyone who extended a hand to her was immediately driven away by her overprotective goddess under threat of the wrath of *Loki Familia*. I doubt anyone has even said hello.

She's just standing there, watching the goddesses go at it and wondering if she should step in.

Lord Hermes finally releases my hand and walks over there.

Finding a brief opening in Lady Loki and Lady Hestia's argument, he puts on the air of a gentleman and bows in front of her.

"Oh my, how exquisite you are on this night, Kenki! May I, Hermes, have this dance?"

I see him thrust his hand out to her. My mind is racing on so many levels.

Aiz's face goes pale as she stands, motionless, in front of the god. Unsure of what to do, she tries to catch the eye of her goddess, Lady Loki. Unfortunately for her, the argument between the two goddesses is still in full swing.

A few long heartbeats later, Aiz looks back to Lord Hermes and opens her mouth. She's probably going to refuse, but before she can…

"Oh, goodness no! How could I have forgotten something this important?! I just remembered!"

Lord Hermes turns away, his hand over his face. It feels like I'm watching an actor on the stage more than anything else.

I blink several times, my eyes nothing but little dots on my face. Aiz isn't moving. I don't think she's even breathing.

Clap! Lord Hermes brings his hands together as if he's just gotten an idea. He looks back over his shoulder before spinning to face me.

"It is an embarrassment as a god, and as a man, to not be able to honor my own invitation—Bell, take my place."

My jaw drops to the floor. Aiz looks light-headed.

Both of our eyes are as wide as they can go.

"Huh, what's going on…?"

"You understand, Bell? My reputation is at stake, so don't let me down."

Every muscle in my body suddenly tenses. Then, Lord Hermes winks at me.

The whimsical god has just forced me to play a part in some kind of scheme—did Lord Hermes just give me an opportunity to ask Aiz to dance? He's willing to take the heat from the goddesses?

Then a wink makes me realize what had just transpired. Lord Hermes was with us on the eighteenth floor as well as in the town of Rivira. He seems to believe that since Aiz and I know each other, she won't refuse my invitation.

Lord Hermes grins and walks away. Aiz and I are alone, staring at each other.

"…"

"…"

The distance between us unchanging, we stand in one spot, staring into each other's eyes.

My body's getting warmer and warmer. I make up my mind.

I can't waste the chance that Lord Hermes gave me. But more than that, I can't walk away from the confused girl in front of me. The shame of abandoning her would be unbearable.

But…how do I ask her to dance?

A storm is raging in the back of my mind, sweat pouring like rain down my face and hands—that's when Lord Miach appears at my side.

I look back toward Aiz and see that Nahza is standing beside her.

The two of us watch with wide eyes as Lord Miach and Nahza step toward each other.

"My lady, would you care to join me for a dance?"

Lord Miach extends his hand to Nahza and gives a respectful bow. She smiles and puts her hand in his.

"Gladly."

The two walk, hand in hand, to the dance floor.

Aiz and I watch as an example unfolds right in front of us. Lord Miach and Nahza grin back at us, thoroughly enjoying the moment.

Ba-dum. My heartbeat fills my chest.

The two of them went out of their way to help me; I can't just stand here anymore.

Aiz is looking right at me when I take my first step.

Tap, tap. The sound of my footsteps cuts through the other sounds in the room. I gradually approach her, the distance between us disappearing.

I come to a stop an arm's length away and meet her gaze.

"Can I...*May* I—have this dance?"

I quickly look down to hide my bright red face.

I extend my left hand, my heart rate increasing every second.

I sneak a peek at her face...Aiz, clad in that beautiful dress, is smiling at me.

"...Gladly."

I feel the weight of her hand in mine. Summoning up every ounce of courage in my body, I close my fingers around hers.

The two of us turn toward the dance floor, holding hands.

I hope she can't feel my pulse through my fingers; my heart's beating like crazy. Doing my best to keep my breath steady, the two of us find an open spot in a ring of dancing couples. I slowly loop my right arm behind her and put my hand on her back as she lightly places her left on my shoulder.

Now all I need to do is listen to the beat, watch the others, and try to dance.

"Uwah—"

"Nnn—"

We're not in sync at all.

I stumble; she trips. We're fighting just to keep our balance. Aiz is first and foremost a knight, so dancing might not be her thing. But then again, I'm a man and yet I'm failing to lead. This is pitiful.

Thump. Aiz's head hits me square in the chest. If I don't do something soon, this'll be a complete disaster. But what? A wave of cold sweat escapes from every pore in my skin.

"Calm your mind. Do not try to lead by pulling her with your arms."

"!"

Another couple comes close to us just as Aiz and I are trying to find our feet. It's Lord Takemikazuchi and Mikoto.

Mikoto is blushing again, but Lord Takemikazuchi's precise movements guide her effortlessly around the floor. They step toward us, and Lord Takemikazuchi and I are back to back as he whispers more advice into my ear.

"Relax your shoulders. Take your eyes off your feet and look ahead."

"S-Sir Bell. The battle is not lost as long as you don't step on your own feet."

Lord Takemikazuchi guides Mikoto right past me. A new bead of sweat rolls down my cheek as I desperately try to decode their instructions.

Aiz is listening, too. Our feet start to line up.

"You're adventurers—look at each other. Discern each other's movements with your feet and communicate with your eyes. No techniques are necessary, only advance and retreat."

Lord Takemikazuchi's words echo over and over in my mind. Just for a moment, it feels like I'm back on the city wall, training with Aiz.

I desperately try to read her attacks, figure out where she is coming from, and defend. How would she follow, what is she aiming for? It all comes down to that first step and moves on from there.

I look into her eyes, glistening in the moonlight. I'm not sure who breaks down first, but we suddenly smile.

—Right?

—L-left, please.

Uneven at first, then slowly but surely, then finally we move in unison.

We don't need to speak; our eyes and subtle movements do all the talking.

Lord Takemikazuchi smiles. He must think we're okay on our own now, because he and Mikoto glide away to another part of the dance floor.

"*—Whaaaaat?!* What in th' hell d'you think you're doing, Aiz?! Leggo of me, Itty-Bitty! I said, hands off—!!"

"Huh? What are you sayi—*whaaaaaaa*?! Wait, *Bell*—!"

Two loud voices reach my ears from the corner of the ballroom. I catch a glimpse of two raging goddesses from the corner of my eye. Seeing Lady Hestia's hair flare out like that makes my blood run cold.

But at that moment, Lord Hermes points and Miss Asfi's dress flutters through the air.

"—Hold them back, Asfi!"

"I take no responsibility for the consequences..."

""Ngggh!!""

Thin, feminine arms wrap around each of the goddesses. The two deities get yanked from view. Looking back at Aiz, she's just as speechless as I am.

"...Ottar. Tell me, is it possible to unleash a horde of Minotaur here right now?"

"It is not, Lady Freya..."

...Why is my spine tingling?

"This is my first..."

"Huh?"

"This is my first time dancing..." I watch Aiz's lips move. We are about the same height, so talking face-to-face is easy. "I always wanted to try, when I was little..."

"R-really?"

"Yes."

That's unexpected.

It feels strange, but a smile grows on my face. I can feel my lips loosening with each passing moment.

"So I'm happy...Thank you."

She shyly glances down, then looks back up at me with a beaming smile.

For a moment, she looks like an innocent child instead of the hardened warrior I know. I lose myself in the sparkles of her golden eyes.

The mask of refinement and grace she always wears is gone, replaced by the smile of a little girl.

Maybe, no, *definitely*—*this* is the real Aiz Wallenstein. Not the warrior.

"...!!"

I'm pretty sure I'm smiling.

I'm so happy, I wouldn't know if I were making a weird expression.

She smiles back, her gaze slightly trembling. My hand on her waist and hers on my shoulder, we join the ring of couples and dance a waltz.

Her golden locks flow in perfect time with the music.

Our steps slightly better than before, we spin in place, matching the other couples on the floor.

All the beautiful people and perfect clothes sparkle in the moonlit ballroom.

The magic-stone-lamp chandeliers give the illusion of a starry night as she and I dance, the moment feeling like a dream.

The dance over, Aiz and I find Lord Hermes and the others standing close to the ballroom wall.

I lead Aiz as far as I can until finally I let go. I can still feel her fingers, delicate and warm, in the palm of my hand. My head is somewhere in the clouds, but Aiz sighs as all of her muscles relax at once.

Lord Miach, Nahza, as well as Lord Takemikazuchi and Mikoto smile at the two of us. I don't think I've ever felt this shy in my life, but I need to show them my gratitude.

"Um, thank you so much, for all of your help. You, too, Lord Hermes..."

"Glad to be of service."

He grins at me before opening his mouth to continue. However, he immediately closes his mouth again and sticks both hands high into the air.

"At least I can die knowing you're happy."

" *"Hermes!"* "

Two goddesses cloaked in auras of fury appear directly behind Lord Hermes.

Snatch! Two arms suddenly pull him off his feet and drag him into the corner. *"Gyaaaaaah!!"* A scream of pain cuts through the air. The color drains from my face.

Lord Hermes's "execution" complete, Lady Hestia charges toward us like she were shot out of a cannon. *Bang!* Aiz goes flying from my side.

"Bell! You're dancing with me next!"

"Aiz, yer hittin' the floor with me! No refusin'!"

Lady Hestia grabs both of my hands with vigor. The look in her eyes is terrifying. Aiz isn't doing much better. Lady Loki practically has her in a bear hug.

All of my muscles stiffen at once, making my body stand up straight at the speed of light as I hold out my hands.

I force a smile. There's no way I can refuse her—

"—Guests, are you enjoying the Celebration?"

Lord Apollo, the host for the evening, appears in front of our group.

A handful of his uniformed followers spreads out behind him as he squares his shoulders.

Wait a minute, why did the musicians stop playing? It's eerily quiet in here.

"It brings me great pleasure to see you are indulging. That lets me know hosting this Celebration was worth it."

All of us stop moving, frozen in place as other guests make their way toward us. There's a ring around us in no time at all and Lord Apollo is at the center.

The god wearing a crown of laurels locks his eyes on Lady Hestia as soon as he finishes his general greeting.

"Much time has passed but...Hestia. It appears my children have caused you some trouble."

"...Yes, and mine you."

Lord Apollo smiles, but my goddess is eyeing him suspiciously.

First and foremost, we need to settle this. Lady Hestia takes a deep breath as she figures out the exact wording she wants to use.

However, the god doesn't give her time.

"*My precious child was critically injured by your boy.* I demand compensation."

He takes a step forward and makes his claim.

I tilt my head in confusion, my nerves getting the better of me. Lady Hestia, on the other hand, becomes furious.

"That's an exaggeration! My Bell was hurt, too! You have no right to *demand* anything!"

"My dear Luan came home so beaten and bloodied that day I had to hide my eyes...My soul wept in his presence!"

Lord Apollo puts his hand on his chest like an actor trying to be overly dramatic before spreading his arms open wide. He points out his other followers, all of them crying as if on cue. A figure emerges from behind them. "Aah, Luan!" Lord Apollo cries as he rushes to his side.

Luan...that's the prum from the bar...His entire body is wrapped in bandages, like some kind of ancient mummy. He groans in pain as he works his way forward with Lord Apollo's aid.

"It hurts, everything hurts..."

"B-Bell…! You didn't do this, did you…?"

"I didn't, I didn't!"

I yell at the top of my lungs, trying to reassure the visibly shaking goddess next to me. This is way over the top!

"Additionally, I have heard that it was your boy who initiated the fight. There are many witnesses. You are not talking your way out of this."

Swish. The god raises his arm and wiggles his fingers as if beckoning someone forward. Forward they come, all at once. Many people come to the front of the crowd, forming an even closer ring around us.

Witnesses…The other customers at Hibachitei? I don't remember seeing any of them, but all of them in turn say they were there and side with Lord Apollo. The strange thing is, they all grin at me right after doing so.

Were they paid off? Were they really there?…Either way, this is no coincidence.

I'm starting to get a really bad feeling about this.

"Wait, Apollo. It was my child who made the first move. Surely Hestia does not deserve all of the blame."

"Ah, Hephaistos, what a beautiful friendship you have. But you need not stick your neck out for her. It is clear as day that Hestia's boy is the one who sent your child to do the dirty work."

Lord Apollo quickly dismisses Lady Hephaistos's claim, adding that she could ask any of the witnesses present for the full story. The goddess's good eye, the one not covered by a bandage, narrows.

He's trapped us in some kind of elaborate blame game, saying who did this and who didn't do that. Unfortunately, Lord Apollo has brought a large number of supporters with him. His argument is much stronger.

"One of my beloved followers was badly wounded. I cannot accept this lying down. The reputation of my *Familia* is on the line…Hestia, will you not take responsibility for his actions?"

"Enough already! Like hell I'll accept that!"

I watch Lord Apollo's face contort after Hestia's refusal—into an evil visage.

The corners of his lips curl upward into a dark expression unfit for a deity.

"Then you leave me no choice! Hestia—I declare a War Game!"

My goddess is just as flabbergasted as I am.
—"War Game."
It's a staged battle between two *Familias* with a strict set of rules. Each deity deploys their followers like pieces on a board game and sends them into battle in a test of wills.
In other words, followers fight a war for their god.
The victorious deity steals everything from the defeated. The winner receives the right to order the loser to do anything. Normally, they take all money, property, and even *Familia* members for themselves.
One of Eina's more recent lectures flares to life in the back of my mind. It's not long before I'm completely speechless.
Hestia Familia, just me and my goddess, against an upper-mid-level *Familia* like *Apollo Familia* in a War Game?
That's not even funny.
"Apollo's done it now—!" "What a bully..." "Actually, I'd like to see that!"
Voices erupt all around me as soon as Lord Apollo makes his declaration.
The gods and goddesses are always looking for entertainment, and this seems to have piqued their interest.
The ring of people around us voices their support for Lord Apollo. The goddess and I are surrounded on all sides. I scan the crowd and catch a glimpse of a silent Lady Loki and briefly meet the gaze of a very concerned Aiz.
"Should my side prevail...I demand you surrender the boy Bell Cranell to me."
Those words practically knock Lady Hestia off her feet.
"*What?!*" My eyes snap back to Lady Hestia in time to see her whip herself into a frenzy. "This is what you were after all along...!"

I'm so confused—what are they talking about? I look back and forth between the two deities over and over again.

A horrifying smile filled with greed appears on Lord Apollo's face. "—It's *unfair*, Hestia. You keeping such a cute boy all to yourself..."

Zing!

Every hair on my body stands on end. The color drains from my face.

Lord Apollo's penetrating gaze bores right through me.

Never before in my life have I felt such a powerful sense of foreboding. The goddess told me a little while ago that Lady Freya would "devour" me—now I think I understand what she meant by that.

"You vile pig...!!"

Lady Hestia casts her infuriated eyes on Lord Apollo as if he was the root of all evil. The deity just glares back at her.

"Harsh, Hestia, very harsh. We sang the melodies of love once. I even offered you my heart back in Tenkai, now didn't I?"

"Lies!! All lies!! Don't get the wrong idea, Bell!! This airheaded creep wouldn't leave me alone, and I shot him down right away! Do you think a goddess as young and pure as me would accept an offer from a perverted bastard with standards like that?!"

"O-of course not...!!"

The air around Lady Hestia is pulsing, the heat from her red face pushing me back.

So that's the reason why she doesn't like Lord Apollo—he asked her to marry him. Lady Hestia's energy must've just run out. "Haaah, haaah." Her shoulders heave up and down as she wipes sweat off her chin.

But I get it. I understand.

Most likely, Lord Apollo is attracted to those who look like my goddess...or me. Man, woman, it doesn't matter to him. Once he sees something he likes, he'll stop at nothing in his lustful pursuit.

Apollo Familia...Now that I think about it, all of the members of his group that I've seen fit that description: young, innocent-looking men and women. The staff here, Daphne and Cassandra when they gave me the invitation...even Luan the prum has the same kind of cute features.

Passion that has gone too far, burning bright like the sun.

—*Phallus.*

A god whose desires carry him to comical lengths...That's Lord Apollo.

"Starting the fight at the bar, everything that happened, it was all part of your plan, Apollo...! Everything was to steal Bell away from me!"

Realizing she's trapped, Lady Hestia glares at each of the deities who had thrown their lot in with Lord Apollo for sheer entertainment. What few allies we have are in disarray. Nahza and Mikoto are looking around in confusion. Lord Miach and Lord Takemikazuchi are frowning, silently watching the events unfold, powerless to stop it. Lady Hephaistos sighs, massaging her temple. Lord Hermes is standing right next to her, grimacing alongside Miss Asfi.

We're isolated, alone. My head starts spinning as I desperately look from face to face, and I happen to spot Lady Freya quietly sipping from her wineglass. We lock eyes for a moment.

"Hestia, what is your answer?"

"I have no obligation to accept, now do I?!"

The goddess turns her back on Lord Apollo when he asks for her response.

If this really does escalate to a War Game, *Hestia Familia* doesn't stand a chance. I would have to take them on myself.

Lady Hestia outright rejects him.

"Are you sure you won't regret this?"

"Hardly! Bell, we're leaving!"

Lady Hestia's eyes flash at the smirking Lord Apollo as she grabs my wrist.

"So dull..." Several deities voice their disappointment as they step aside, allowing us to pass. Honestly, I don't think they want to be the one to get in Lady Hestia's way right now. She may be small, but the fury emanating from her is terrifying. We leave the ballroom and walk down the stairs.

"—"

A handsome young man is standing right next to the exit. We make eye contact.

Hyacinthus's cold stare burns itself into my memory.

"..."

The goddess pulls me past him, but I look back over my shoulder.

I watch as the palace of the building and the follower of that deity shrink into the distance.

It's almost like they're telling me that this isn't over.

CHAPTER 3 **OUTBREAK**

The sun has risen on the morning after the Celebration of the Gods.
Hestia updated Bell's Status in their *Familia*'s home, a hidden
room beneath an old church. The two of them were busily preparing
for the day.

Bell Cranell

Level 2

Strength: C 635   Defense: D 590->594

Utility: C 627   Agility: B 741   Magic: D 529

Luck: I

Magic

(Firebolt)

• **Swift-Strike Magic**

Skills

(Heroic Desire, Argonaut)

• **Charges automatically with active action**

It went up a little...

Bell slipped a potion into his leg holster as he held a sheet of paper
in his left hand.

He looked over his Status one more time, his gaze trained on his
Defense, which had improved since his return from the Dungeon.

He hadn't set foot belowground since the battle with the Goliath
on the eighteenth floor five days ago. A full two days had passed
since the brawl at Hibachitei. The hit he took from Hyacinthus
during the fight that day was strong enough to earn excelia and be
reflected in his Status.

His Level 3 wasn't just for show. Bell scratched the back of his head as memories of that embarrassing sequence of events floated to the surface.

"That jackass. War Game this, War Game that..."

At the same time, Hestia had just changed into her uniform. She'd been muttering curses under her breath since the moment the two of them arrived at home last night. She closed the closet door, sat down on the sofa, and called out to the boy.

"Bell, please be careful. I doubt he'd be stupid enough to try anything today, but some of his followers might try to pick another fight."

"I-I will..."

Bell lightly nodded at his goddess's warning.

Apollo Familia was in the midst of a grand scheme to steal Bell away from her, and she would have nothing of it. Updating Bell's Status, despite his lack of dungeon crawling, was one of the countermeasures she was using to prepare for their next stage. Of course, they didn't have many options, but she felt it was necessary to do everything she could.

"Promise me, Bell—promise me you'll run away at the first sign of danger. Never travel alone, and always stay in areas with lots of people."

"I will."

"And for the time being, it might be a good idea to work with Mikoto and her group. Také knows what's going on, so they should allow you to join their battle party."

Bell took his goddess's words to heart. He had heard from both Aiz and Lilly many times that ambushes were common in the Dungeon. He knew that he couldn't be too careful.

The boy had equipped the armor that was still damaged from the battle on the eighteenth floor of the Dungeon. He was wearing his old boots in place of the greaves that had been completely destroyed. Hestia Knife and Ushiwakamaru strapped firmly to his lower back, Bell stood in front of the door, ready to reenter the Dungeon.

"Bell, both of us are going to Babel Tower anyway, so let's go together?"

"Yes, good idea."

Hestia smiled back at the boy. She was due to work a shift at one of *Hephaistos Familia*'s shops in the tower. Bell opened the door and led the way up the staircase that connected their room to the surface.

The short staircase was dimly lit and lined with dusty, unused bookshelves. Bell listened to Hestia's footsteps as he pulled back the segment of wall in the back of one of the church's old storage rooms.

Emerging from the narrow room, the boy took a look around. The worn-down place of worship still had an altar at the back, but weeds of all shapes and sizes were growing out of the floor. The ceiling, or rather the roof, had many holes that let through beams of late-morning sunlight. Bell paused for a moment to look at the blue sky through one of the larger ones and resolved to find the time to make this place look a little better.

...*Magic?*

Bell had just started walking forward again when his senses tingled. He looked up.

It was the slight ripple in the air produced when mages were either in the middle of their trigger spell or casting Magic. It was very faint, but since Bell was not a magic user himself, he didn't know what it was for sure.

He took another look around, much more quickly this time. He caught a glimpse of Hestia emerging from the narrow storeroom. The two exchanged awkward glances, heads tilted to the side.

Sensing danger, Bell motioned for the goddess to stay inside and took a step outside of the doorless entryway.

"—"

Then, the moment the sun's rays touched his face in front of the ruined old church—

Countless figures emerged on the roofs of the surrounding buildings.

Eyes glared down at him from every angle. The figures had created a perimeter around the front of the church. They were carrying bows and staffs.

—*Apollo Familia.*

A cold sweat covered Bell's body the moment he identified the emblem of the sun engraved on their armor.

All weapons were drawn the moment Bell came into view. Archers drew back their arrows, magic users stood ready with only the last line of their trigger spell left unsaid. The whole city block was inundated with magical energy, an unnatural breeze cutting through the morning stillness.

A male elf with half of his face hidden by a scarf raised one arm as if he were in charge of this team of adventurers. Bell's body took over—sprinting back inside.

He made a mad dash for Hestia, still standing in front of the storage room. Bell swept the surprised goddess off her feet and drove toward an old congregation room behind the altar in the back of the church.

Not even a moment behind, the elf thrust his arm down—and a deafening explosion followed.

The seventh block of Orario lay just north of West Main Street.

Many citizens lived in this area sandwiched between West Main and Northwest Main. The loud explosion caused this quiet little block to erupt in chaos.

"What's going on?"

"A fire, meow?!"

"It's morning, have your fight later, meow…"

Employees of the The Benevolent Mistress, the human girl Runoa and the catgirls Ahnya and Chloe, ran out of the building and onto the main street. People were already out, stopping and staring at the dark pillar of smoke rising only a few streets away.

© Suzuhito Yasuda

"Those are the booms of battle, meow."

Chole's ears twitched as she watched the plumes of smoke rise. This was no kitchen fire—only spells could make explosions that loud and smoke that thick. Soon the echoes of another salvo rang out and even more smoke rose into the sky. The girl's sharp eyes instantly spotted black figures running on the rooftops before they disappeared behind another building.

"Could this be...?"

"Two *Familias* having at it, meow?"

"Been a long time, meow."

Other people in the street also came to the same conclusion and immediately ran for cover.

In a city with as many *Familias* as Orario, disputes among the groups were not uncommon. Despite being in broad daylight and right beneath the Guild's nose, many of them had experienced an outbreak before. So, none of them wasted any time in getting clear of the area.

Horse-drawn carriages swerved into wide U-turns and citizens fled in fear as Syr and the rest of the employees of The Benevolent Mistress made their way out onto the street. The one exception was the owner, Mia. She simply threw back the curtain of her window and stuck her head outside.

The pillar of smoke had worked its way up into the clouds.

"The *Familias* living around here...Do you think they're after ol' White Head, meow?"

"Quiet."

Runoa scolded Ahnya for her lack of tact.

A pair of silver eyes filled with worry watched the smoke billow out overhead. A basket was in her hands, filled with food for a boy who had yet to arrive to pick it up.

Another explosion, closer this time. The basket shook in her grasp.

"..."

Lyu, the last of the employees to arrive on the scene, turned to look in the direction of the blast.

Waves of magical energy reflected off her sky-blue eyes.

The explosions' shock waves overlapped and compounded one another.

The old church collapsed under a barrage of Magic attacks and arrows laced with explosive powder.

The crumbling statue of an ancient goddess that had decorated the deteriorating structure above the doorway fell to the ground and shattered.

"?!"

The wooden door at the back of the church flung open so fast it fell off its hinges.

Bell emerged from the new opening along with a suffocating cloud of smoke. Clutching Hestia tightly against his chest, the boy stumbled as he made his way through the debris. He looked over his shoulder as soon as he regained his balance.

All that was there to greet his eyes was a burning pile of rubble. All that was left of home.

"—SHYAAA!"

"?!"

He didn't have time to mourn. The next wave of figures jumped down from above.

A group of animal people brandishing shortswords and daggers landed on the ground, surrounding the two fugitives as if they had been waiting for this very moment. Shifting Hestia to his left shoulder, Bell withdrew the Hestia Knife with his right hand and deflected an oncoming blade.

Block, dodge—his already damaged armor received fresh scars as Bell weaved his way around the attackers and back into the cloud of smoke.

The attackers froze, not sure how to proceed. Sensing their hesitation, Bell used the smoke as cover and found his way into the closest back alley.

"BuAHH!"

Hestia coughed hard the moment they emerged from the cloud of smoke.

Bell wrapped his right arm around her legs, completely ignoring the ash coating his face. He took off as fast as he could in an effort to get away from their pursuers.

—*They set a trap?!*

In broad daylight, in the middle of the city!

Apollo Familia's merciless attacks sent a fresh wave of fear coursing through Bell's mind.

This wasn't an ambush in some dark corner of the Dungeon. Their enemy openly invaded their territory on the surface with an all-out attack.

Since the War Game was rejected, had they opted for the real thing?

Had *Apollo Familia* officially decided that *Hestia Familia* was their enemy?

Had they thrown all formalities to the wind, even ignoring the Guild's impending retribution?

Bell's mind was spinning, each of these questions adding to the turmoil. When suddenly—*If the worst happens, the entire city of Orario will become a battlefield if two* Familias *fight head-to-head—* Eina's words came to the forefront of his thoughts.

Bell realized he was now officially involved in a battle of *Familias*.

"Bell, who are they...?!"

"*Apollo Familia!*"

The two yelled at the top of their lungs as Bell charged through the three-meder-wide back alley.

Hestia rested her chin on Bell's left shoulder and looked up at the smoldering pyre in the distance.

"Th-that monster...?! Destroying my and Bell's love nest...!"

"Eh?!"

Hestia's choice of words caught him off guard, but there was something much, much more to it.

Bell took another look for himself—he had no place to return to; the one place he called home was gone. That fact shook him to his very core.

"Bell, they're in front of us!"

Bell had the look on his face of a child lost in the streets, his eyes moistening. Hestia's voice snapped him back into the present.

Looking forward, he immediately spotted a group of five adventurers at the other end of the alley. Each had weapons drawn, blades faintly flashing in the dim light. The boy made a hard right onto another street to avoid them.

The sounds of hundreds of footsteps echoed through the back alleys, the voices of the attackers called out to one another—"He went this way!" "Over here!" From the right, from the left, from behind, from ahead, they could hear their enemies surrounding them.

Bell's face contorted in frustration. He couldn't engage them in combat while carrying Hestia in his arms.

His only option was to escape their net. Choosing the narrowest path, Bell willed his legs to go even faster. Just beyond that—

Ten archers appeared, standing on the roofs that lined the path. "?!"

Five on each side, the team of elves and animal people already had their glinting arrowheads pointed in his direction.

Bell glared at them. Hestia's gasp filled his ears, but she didn't take another breath.

The boy leaned forward, kicked off the ground, and focused solely on the end of the path. Sprinting straight ahead, he was able to avoid the volley of arrows loosed at him from both sides.

"He got away?!"

"The hell are you doing up there?!"

Bell tore through the path, every inch the rabbit that had become his reputation. Not a single arrow hit its mark. Angry yells and the sound of footsteps on shingles filled the air as Bell managed to put more distance between them.

—*I'm completely surrounded!*

The hunters had caught up to him, running parallel to his position on the rooftops.

The city block was completely inundated with enemies—far too many to evade or overcome. The full force of *Apollo Familia* was overwhelming.

Despite knowing these paths like the back of his hand, he would never be able to get away. Bell bit his lip when he realized that no amount of speed was going to get him out of this. Even still, he ran with all his might, turning and looping his way through the intricate backstreets.

"Bell, that's a dead end!" Hestia shrieked as she held on for dear life.

Indeed, the side of a house completely sealed off the end of this road.

Even though they were trapped in a cul-de-sac, Bell increased his speed.

"Goddess, hold on tight!!"

Hestia's mouth opened, but no sound emerged. Her eyes shot open as the air pressure pushed her even tighter into Bell's chest.

The wall was fast approaching until Bell slammed his foot into the ground—and took to the air.

"Uu—WAAAAAAAAAAAAAAAAAAAAAAAAAAAAAAAAAA AAA!!"

A great leap.

Using the incredible increase in strength and speed provided by leveling up, Bell managed to clear the eight-meder wall.

Bell's trajectory arced only slightly as Hestia's scream reverberated behind him. Only the tips of his right toes made contact with the roof of the house, but it was enough. His left leg slung forward and he landed with a soft thud just as Hestia ran out of breath.

Free of the claustrophobic confines of the backstreets, Bell enjoyed the feeling of the morning breeze through his hair and the blue sky above. He scanned his surroundings, taking in the roofs of expensive houses and catching a glimpse of the Pantheon to the north.

My only choice now is to hide inside the Guild…!

They were the highest authority inside Orario. None of his attackers would be able to lay a finger on him there once he got inside.

The solemn Pantheon, that was Bell's only escape route. He had to take it.

"You should give up."

"!"

Bell spun around to face the voice that came from behind him.

Standing on the same roof and accompanied by another battle party of adventurers was Daphne. Cassandra, wearing a long skirt-style battle cloth, was among them.

Daphne stood tall, unblinking even as her short hair danced in the breeze.

"Lord Apollo chases any child he likes to the ends of the earth. At least until he has them."

"...!"

"It was the same for Cassandra and me. He chased us from the moment he saw us. City to city, country to country...Until we resigned ourselves, he was always there. It's just a matter of time now. It's merely a question of sooner or later." Daphne revealed a piece of her past mixed with a warning.

She had been in his shoes, so she could sympathize. Hestia's face turned sour.

"I didn't think he was this clingy...!"

Daphne's story made Hestia realize what was really going on. Apollo was taking away all of Bell's options one by one. She was instantly filled with regret, and her dislike of the passionate god turned to utter hatred.

—*He is extremely...tenacious.*

This time, it was the words that Hermes shared with him at the Celebration that flared up inside Bell's head.

"Surrender? You're going to be my ally soon, so I'd rather not get rough."

"...I refuse."

Tap, tap. Daphne hit the palm of her hand against the swords strapped to her waist a few times. Bell shook his head no.

Bell declined her offer and took a few careful steps back. Hestia sighed in his arms.

"Should've expected that. Okay, then—sic 'em!"

Daphne drew her sword at the same moment she gave the order

and pointed directly at Bell. Three of her team moved as one, charging straight for the boy.

However, Bell turned his back to them and ran across the rooftop toward the Guild.

"Our target is slippery. Have Lissos's team cut them off!"

Another one of her subordinates nodded and took off in another direction. Daphne withdrew a dagger and threw it straight at the fugitives.

Bell's ears alerted him to the danger. Showing no fear or panic, he rotated his right shoulder into position to intercept the white blade. *Shing!* The weapon didn't penetrate his armor, but the impact threw him off balance.

The team of three attackers saw their window and moved in.

"...! Goddess! I have to fight!"

"O-okay!"

Bell regained his footing and turned to engage. At the same time, he cradled the goddess against his left side and pinned her there with his arm. Hestia suddenly blushed. If the circumstances had been any different, this would have been her favorite moment in history.

Bell whipped his now-free right hand around his back and grabbed the Hestia Knife. Their opponents arrived a heartbeat later.

"Uwah?!"

Bell swatted away the oncoming sword with his knife before spinning and intercepting a spear coming in from the side. He side-stepped a slice, dodged a stab, ducked under a sweep. He avoided their attacks by the narrowest of margins.

The oncoming adventurers' formation and movements were extremely well timed, with the next attack about to hit just as the previous one was avoided. They were a well-trained and highly experienced team.

Amid all of his dodging and spinning, Bell suddenly realized that they were preventing him from making any progress toward the Guild.

At this rate...!

He wouldn't be able to escape from them with Hestia hanging onto him.

There was no hesitation in Bell's movements.

Locking eyes with Hestia for a moment, he passed her the knife. Bell thrust his right arm skyward at the same moment that Hestia caught the hilt of the weapon in midair.

His three assailants all happened to be above him at that moment. Bell shouted.

"Firebolt!"

An electric inferno burst from his palm.

Three bursts of his Swift-Strike Magic sent all three adventurers flying backward.

Exposed skin burned and armor charred, the attackers landed painfully on the roof, shrieking in pain.

Daphne was taken by surprise, but her reaction was swift.

"Cassandra!"

"Going!"

The last remaining member of Daphne's team stepped forward. Cassandra raised her staff.

With a quick trigger spell, suddenly healing magic had been cast.

"?!"

The adventurers reeling in pain from their burns were surrounded in a soft blue light. Their injuries were healed right before Bell's eyes. Mere seconds later, the three climbed to their feet with anger in their eyes.

Cassandra—the presence of a healer added to Bell's frustration as he stared her down.

A healer made a battle party complete. Their teamwork was exactly how a *Familia* should fight.

Realizing he was outclassed and outmatched, Bell felt his blood run cold.

"Ugh—?!"

Even more figures appeared on the rooftops around him in addition to Daphne's team.

The next round of arrows and throwing knives forced him to jump back down to the street.

"Quite the escape artist...but this is all pointless. He should give up," said Daphne under her breath as she watched Bell run from her vantage point on the roof of the house. She looked more sympathetic than angry as the boy's white head disappeared around the corner.

She was not like Hyacinthus and the others who cherished their leader. Daphne had a much less favorable opinion of Apollo due to having been forcefully conscripted into *Apollo Familia*. However, he was her family now and treated her well. She would follow his orders; she felt it was her duty. At the same time, he was much friendlier toward the ones he favored—and her god tended to favor young men.

Now that very same god wanted Bell. Although she pitied him, she would not turn her back on her god's wishes.

"Um, Daph, don't you think we should stop...That might be better."

A voice came from behind her. Cassandra, the only one left on the rooftop other than her, cautiously got her attention.

Cassandra shared a similar fate as hers. The two of them had stood by each other for a long time because of this connection. Daphne's friend was standing still, fidgeting with her waist-length hair and looking up at her.

"Stop what?"

"Chasing after that boy...We mustn't trap the rabbit."

Daphne sighed at Cassandra's mysterious warning.

"Another dream?"

Daphne asked even though she knew the answer. Cassandra's eyes grew wider as she vigorously nodded up and down.

The long-haired girl was gifted with prophetic dreams. Unfortunately for her, no one ever took them seriously. That included Daphne.

Daphne believed that Cassandra's almost random and thoughtless words were the result of her upper-class upbringing in the days before Apollo.

After all, all sheltered girls had dreams of their own as well as time to be lost in the curse of their "magical allure." It was almost laughable.

"Cut the crap and let's get moving."

"Wh-why, why won't you *believe* me?"

Daphne frowned. She didn't want to put up with this now. But she knew if she didn't at least ask, the girl would get even more annoying. Daphne cocked an eyebrow and looked at Cassandra.

"Fine. What did you see?"

"Errumm...A bloody rabbit jumped over the moon and swallowed the sun..."

Daphne laughed through her nose.

"Indeed. Dreams need to have a certain level of absurdity."

"*Daph!*"

"Enough. After him."

Daphne ran in the direction in which Bell had disappeared, with the still-muttering Cassandra close behind.

Central Park was located where all eight main streets met in the center of the city.

Welf, a brand-new greatsword over his shoulder, and Lilly, disguised in her werewolf form, stood beneath the imposing shadow of the white tower, Babel.

"...Isn't he running a little late?"

"Yes, Lilly thinks so, too...Mr. Bell has never been this late, and would send a message if it were to happen."

Welf and Lilly were fully prepared to reenter the Dungeon. Weapons sharpened and backpack full, they were waiting for Bell's arrival.

Many parties of adventurers made their way through Central Park around them.

"Those weird blasts are still going off...Am I the only one with a bad feeling about this?" The man voiced his concerns as he tightened his grip.

"..."

Bell's new knife was wrapped in a white cloth in Welf's hands. Lilly remained silent.

They were waiting for Bell at Babel's west gate, which directly faced West Main. The first explosion happened several minutes ago and had yet to stop. The sounds were unnatural, very similar to those created by Magic. Citizens and adventurers alike poured into Central Park from the main roads. The usually quiet and mundane park was coming alive with fear and panic. Lilly anxiously watched all of the people pouring in from West Main.

The crowd of people had grown to the point where they could hear snippets of conversations.

"Apollo's men! They're attacking someone, starting a war!"

"They're after *Hestia Familia*—chasing after the Little Rookie!"

Lilly and Welf instantly locked eyes.

"Let's move!"

"Right!"

The two didn't stop to pick up more information from the traumatized citizens about the battle that had been raging since midmorning as they made their way through the crowd.

A moment later, they knew where they had to go when a flash of violet lightning appeared over the seventh block of the city.

"Has Lady Freya made a move?"

Two figures looked down from the roof of the tallest building situated close to North West Main, a little ways removed from the destructive game of cat and mouse.

Hermes surveyed the battlefield with great interest. He turned to face Asfi as soon as she joined him and she asked her question.

"No, *Freya Familia* is only observing the situation."

"Is Lady Freya planning to stay out of this one?" Asfi adjusted her white cape as she spoke. Hermes brought his hand to his chin, muttering to himself in a soft voice.

The odds were stacked heavily against Bell. The boy was tasked with trying to escape as well as protect his goddess in the face of an all-out assault—he was outnumbered more than one hundred to one.

Whether Freya had a reason for staying put or she considered this some kind of a test for Bell, Hermes did not know.

His best guess was that she derived some kind of pleasure watching the ever-changing boy react to a challenging environment. She had done the same thing less than a week ago; he was there.

It wasn't hard to picture Freya rejoicing in the boy's "glow," which was no doubt growing at this very moment.

"How should we proceed?"

"By taking it easy."

Hermes's eyes were back on the chase. He responded to Asfi's question without looking at her.

"I'm the one and only Hermes, you know? I am and always will be an observer."

He wanted to see Bell's story unfold and follow it to the very end with his own eyes. The charming god looked back over his shoulder and grinned at his follower.

Asfi didn't say anything, only sighed as she pictured the many problems she would have to solve in the near future.

"I need a better view. Asfi, help me out."

"Yes, sir..."

The two of them jumped to the next rooftop, following the sounds of battle.

"Argonaut is on the run!"

Meanwhile, at *Loki Familia*'s home on the northern edge of the city...

Tiona had just returned from gathering information on the streets. Other members of the *Familia* gathered in the common room to listen to her report.

"Tiona, is that true...?"

"No doubt, *Apollo Familia* is running around in circles, trying to corner him!"

Aiz arrived in the room in time to hear the Amazonian girl's first report. In turn, the girl relayed all the information she'd picked up in town.

The blond girl's face was blank, but a small anxious twinge of worry filled her eyes as she looked off into the distance.

The dwarf, Gareth, and the elf, Reveria, sat on a sofa in the room and dissected the situation.

"Been a long time since this many people were fighting in the city."

"*Apollo Familia* doesn't appear to be concerned with the Guild's punishment for their actions."

The sound of footsteps belonging to other members of their *Familia* rained down from overhead. Everyone knew something big was happening outside.

"Speaking of which, where is Loki? Wasn't she just here?"

Tiona's twin sister, Tione, posed a new question for the group. Bete answered her with a very disinterested tone.

"Said there was somethin' worth watchin', already gone, the dunce..."

"...All gods have their vices." She responded in kind.

"Aiz, don't get any strange ideas."

"Finn..."

Aiz had ignored the conversation going on around her and anxiously stood up from the sofa. Finn noticed and immediately stepped in front of her.

"The situation is completely different from the eighteenth floor. Please, do not try to aid *Hestia Familia*."

The commander of *Loki Familia* stopped Aiz's train of thought in its tracks.

Aiz was a high-ranking member of the *Familia*. She couldn't strike out on her own. *Loki Familia* had no reason to assist Bell.

Worse, an attempt to do so would cause an even bigger problem. Should an influential group like *Loki Familia* become involved in the scuffle, the consequences could be catastrophic.

"I know this is difficult, but Loki forbade us from interfering. We need to let things play out for now."

"Okay...I understand."

Finn's penetrating gaze overtaking her from below, she lightly nodded at the prum.

Aiz walked over to the window as the commander issued more orders to other members of their group.

Looking past her reflection in the glass, Aiz watched the ominous black cloud spread over the city.

Bell ran as fast as he could.

Hestia firmly in his arms, he weaved his way through the backstreets in a desperate attempt to escape the net his enemies had set for him.

"Sorry!" he yelled as he jumped over a group of townspeople who hadn't evacuated in time.

"Th-there's more...?!"

Bell focused forward as soon as Hestia's warning reached his ears.

Two of them stood at the end of the street—no detours, no escape.

Bell slowed down only enough to let the goddess safely out of his arms and onto the ground before drawing both knives and picking up speed again.

"?!"

"Uwah?!"

The two adventurers weren't expecting Bell to attack. However, the boy charged at them with both blades flashing menacingly in his hands. He was on top of them before the adventurers could defend themselves. Targeting the joints and their armor, Bell made quick work of the would-be hunters.

Memories of his battles with well-armored killer ants in the Dungeon flashing through his mind, Bell reached out and took Hestia's hand. The deity had done her best to keep up.

"I'm so sorry for...slowing you down...like this...Bell...!"

The young goddess was out of breath but forced an apology out of her throat. Bell squeezed Hestia's hand as they ran together in an attempt to reassure her.

"This isn't your fault, Goddess!"

One of the absolute laws of the land was that a mortal cannot kill a god. Only other gods had that ability.

Should the deity receive a life-threatening injury, their divine power would instantly activate and heal them completely. Unfortunately, activating Arcanum was against the rules of the gods themselves. They would be sent back to Tenkai as punishment.

Should Apollo capture Hestia and kill her, Bell would be left behind as a "free" adventurer, able to join any other *Familia*. If both of them were captured, Apollo would be able to use Hestia as a bargaining chip. Choose to join *Apollo Familia* and Hestia can remain on Earth; refuse and she'd be sent back to Tenkai and he'd be forced to join.

In any case, Bell could not let the hunters capture Hestia. He had to protect her and keep moving.

A lot of them are Level 2…but!

Bell hit a group of archers with Firebolt before they had a chance to release their arrows. Taking advantage of their surprise and injuries, Bell dashed in close and took out all three in the blink of an eye.

Bell could hold his own against Level 2 adventurers. He was confident he could take them one-on-one, and that he had the Agility advantage.

He could deal with them as long as he wasn't pinned down from too many angles at once. A vague plan forming in his head, Bell found the angle where the enemy net was weakest and charged through. At last, there was hope.

"B-Bell, they can't defend against your Magic. Isn't that our best option? You can take them down one after the other!"

"No…well, I don't want to use that if I can help it…"

Bell wanted to keep collateral damage to a minimum, especially since his Magic involved fire. The Western block of Orario was mostly a residential area. If he turned it into a sea of flames, there was no doubt in his mind he would be exiled from Orario no matter how things turned out. Of course, it was always an option in a pinch, but he couldn't overdo it.

His Swift-Strike Magic gave him the ability to turn the tables at a moment's notice, but he couldn't count on it in the middle of the city. "...?"

The hunters running on the rooftops had individual roles. Some doubled as lookouts and roadblocks to set up advantageous situations for the higher-level attackers.

The sea of enemies around him making Bell slightly dizzy, his ruby-red eyes noticed an emblem on one particular adventurer.

A crescent moon and a wineglass...?

It was not the emblem of the sun worn by members of *Apollo Familia*. This was another group entirely.

The small flicker of hope that had appeared was suddenly snuffed out. There was more than one enemy *Familia*?

Another flashback: the garden last night.

What he had seen from the balcony on the night of the Celebration...

Bell could see the two figures clearly in his mind. A moment later—

Thud! Something landed right behind him.

"—"

A menacing aura more powerful than anything he felt overtook him.

Ba-dam, ba-dam, ba-dam. His pulse echoed through his body.

Bell's instincts instantly screamed, *Don't show your back to this one!*

The boy's head whipped around. The cold smile of a handsome man was waiting for him.

His battle cloth was mainly white. A longsword and a shortsword hung from his waist, their hilts sticking out of the white cape draped around his shoulders.

Apollo Familia's field general, Hyacinthus, bent his knees into an aggressive stance.

"?!"

The man charged at the same time that Bell shoved Hestia into the opening of another side street.

His advance was too fast to follow. All Bell could see was a long rouge blade shining with flaming providence—a flamberge.

The boy managed to draw the Hestia Knife in time to intercept the blade, but the sheer force of impact knocked him off his feet.

"Bell?!"

Hyacinthus denied his opponent a chance to recover and charged forward.

Bell managed to catch a glimpse of the incoming weapon and rolled out of the way, barely dodging the tip of the blade as it hit the stone-paved street beneath him. Jumping back to his feet, Bell withdrew his other knife, Ushiwakamaru, from its sheath and rushed to counterattack.

Hestia's screams echoed through the back alley as she watched the battle unfold. The two locked blades after only a few seconds of combat.

"I commend you for making it this far, Bell Cranell. I bestow you the honor of facing me—rejoice!"

"Dahh?!"

Hyacinthus spun out of the lock and went back on the offensive. Two knives and one longsword clashed over and over at high speed, sparks flying.

Hestia had fallen silent, her eyes trembling as her ears were overwhelmed by constant metallic echoes. Bell knew there was no escape from this enemy; he had no choice but to engage him head-to-head.

This particular backstreet was very long and narrow. Bell was continuously pressed deeper and deeper down the street in an effort to dodge the oncoming attacks. The true onslaught had begun.

"—"

Bell's right arm was flung out of the way by the rouge blade's vicious sweep. By instinct, the boy used that momentum to bring his left arm forward.

The two locked eyes, never blinking. Attacker and defender traded places back and forth instantaneously. Hyacinthus took an aggressive step forward, thrusting his blade directly toward Bell's chest. The white-haired boy sidestepped just in time and knocked the sword away with one of his own weapons.

Or at least he thought he had. The tip of the sword suddenly connected with his still-outstretched arm. Blood spewed from the wound instantaneously.

"So that's how it is. You win with speed."

Hyacinthus's grin made Bell's eyes shake with fright.

Bell was wielding two knives, while his enemy had only one longsword. He should have had the advantage. But somehow every one of his strikes was either deflected or blocked outright. Hyacinthus moved as if he knew what was coming. None of Bell's attacks were getting through.

He wasn't fast enough to win this contest of Agility.

"?!"

Hyacinthus's white cape suddenly flashed in front of the boy's face. Bell's reaction to the next attack was delayed by just enough to create an opening for attack.

The rouge blade arced through the air and came down hard from above. Bell crossed the blades of the Hestia Knife and Ushiwaka-maru to stop the weapon just above his head.

The two knives pressed against the flamberge, and the combatants stared each other down through the cross they formed.

Click, click, click. The blades shook as their masters tried to press forward. However, the longsword was gaining ground despite Hyacinthus using only one hand.

"You can't hold it against me for hating you, stealing Lord Apollo's love as you have…but if that is his will, then I will personally force you into our glorious *Familia.*"

His Strength was overwhelming.

Bell saw his own fear reflected in the eyes of his smiling foe.

—Level 3.

Bell's thoughts turned to the moment that they first met. The "fight" at the bar where he was unable to defend himself.

Bell pushed off the ground, focusing all of his strength into his arms and neck, and managed to force the rouge blade upward. Bell glared at his assailant.

"UHH—AAAHHHHHHHHHHHHHHHHHHHHHHHHHHH
HHHHHHH?!"

Bell roared with all of his might as he knocked Hyacinthus's weapon to the side.

The handsome man took a quick step back to gain some distance. Now was Bell's chance and he wasn't going to waste it.

Tensing up every muscle like a bowstring, he launched his body forward—an arrow yearning to hit its target.

"HAAAA!!"

Top speed.

The stone pavement shattered beneath his feet as Bell kicked off the ground. He poured everything he had into this one attack.

This Rabbit Rush, a double-bladed onslaught of high-speed slashes.

He engaged Hyacinthus with a merciless avalanche of strikes. A storm of sparks erupted around them.

"—Slow."

However.

Hyacinthus didn't flinch, still grinning.

"—"

Arcs of violet and crimson light continuously pummeled the handsome man.

Every single one of the countless strikes was blocked, just like before. Nothing got through his defense.

The Hestia Knife cut nothing but air, and Ushiwakamaru was stopped in its tracks. Neither one of the blades could make it past the heavily decorated flamberge. Its blade glowed with the intensity of the sun with each swipe. Each impact hit with the veracity of flame. The metal sang out with a high-pitched screech and was accompanied by a shower of sparks every time it hit the Hestia Knife and Ushiwakamaru with incredible force.

It was a special blade, the Solar Flamberge, that only the leader of *Apollo Familia* was allowed to carry.

It moved so fast that Bell's eyes couldn't follow, only track the afterimages in its wake.

"Civilized rabbits do not howl."

Bell saw Hyacinthus smirk just before the man's entire body became a blur as he picked up speed.

He felt the impacts before he saw them.

The crimson light of Ushiwakamaru's blade was redirected out to the side at the same moment that the violet Hestia Knife was knocked backward. The blur in front of Bell's eyes seemed to flow, a truly beautiful technique—both of Bell's arms looped around his body as if swimming through the air. He couldn't breathe, and time seemed frozen in place.

Before his eyes could blink, the flamberge slashed from below.

His body's reflexive retreat wasn't fast enough this time. Bell's breastplate was sliced clean in half. The tip of the longsword met flesh, carving its way through skin, muscle, and bone alike in one long, graceful slice. Extreme pain shot through Bell like a wildfire.

—He was hit.

His eyes managed to catch a glimpse of the rouge blade on its top swing.

Suspended in midair and bleeding profusely, Bell didn't have time to dwell on what had just transpired. Hyacinthus was on top of him once again.

"Gah?!"

The hilt of the man's weapon connected with Bell's cheek in a sideways swipe. Jumping forward, Hyacinthus raised his right elbow and brought it down hard.

The elbow hit Bell square in the throat, making his body flinch. He couldn't even yell out in pain before the man's fist buried itself in his gut—and was followed up with a spinning kick. Momentarily blinded by his opponent's boot, the next thing Bell saw was the sky as his back hit the stone pavement.

Hyacinthus came out of his spin, keeping close behind. The man's golden earrings jiggled as he landed.

"B-Bel...?!"

Hestia's scream became an inaudible sound before she could finish his name.

Bell's body didn't move. He looked like little more than a bloody corpse lying in the street. His chest wound was deep, the still-flowing blood forming a small puddle around his body. Even his face was stained red. At long last, one shaking hand grabbed ahold of the top of the stone. His body lurched to the side as Bell tried his best to sit up.

Hestia was stunned speechless at the sight of her bloodied and broken follower in defeat.

"Ah, gahhh, uwh...?!"

"Still conscious, I see."

Bell's vision was blurry as he willed his upper body off the ground. Tears welling up in his ruby-red eyes, he looked up at Hyacinthus.

This was—a second-tier adventurer.

Hyacinthus was an authentic Level 3 adventurer. He didn't depend solely on his superior Status; his technique and strategy were top notch. This was completely different from facing a monster in combat—there was no time to plan or even use Magic. Trying to charge his Argonaut Skill would be downright suicidal. There was no way Bell could win.

He was outmatched, plain and simple.

As an adventurer, Hyacinthus was in a completely different league.

The feeling of being slammed into the mud in defeat overtook him. Rivers of tears flowed out of his eyes.

Bell had no words as the physical pain and mental anguish raging within him expressed themselves on his face.

"Such a horrendous face, so unlovely...Just what does Lord Apollo see in you?"

"Whuh?!"

Hyacinthus stood over Bell, taunting him before mercilessly kicking him in the ribs.

Unable to defend himself, Bell's body rolled farther down the street before sliding to a stop in an open intersection.

"Stop this at once!"

Hyacinthus did not respond to or even look at Hestia as he approached Bell.

"I have sworn my body and soul to him. Only I am worthy of his affection...The rabbit shall be captured."

The man's words were laced with jealousy as he crouched down in front of the boy.

"…Can't have you causing a fuss. You'll be healed no matter what I do to you, so a few severed tendons won't make much difference."

Smiling like a man possessed, Hyacinthus rotated the flamberge in his left hand and pointed the tip at Bell's face. Fear flashed through the boy's eyes.

Hestia was running to his aid, but she wouldn't make it in time.

The rouge blade flicked upward and was about to swing down onto Bell's shoulder when suddenly—

Several arrows pierced the stone pavement where Hyacinthus had been standing just a moment ago.

"What?"

He had dodged the sneak attack by the skin of his teeth. Bell and Hestia were just as surprised by the sudden turn of events.

All three of them looked to find where they came from. In the distance, a little ways off of West Main, was an old, run-down bell tower. It was very faint, but there was the shadow of an archer holding a longbow on top of the roof.

An extremely long-range attack executed with pinpoint accuracy—

"A sniper?" Hyacinthus muttered to himself. "Chienthrope…"

Hyacinthus narrowed his eyes just as the next round of arrows was released.

"This is why I despise upper-class adventurers…"

Nahza frowned as she watched Hyacinthus dodge every one of her arrows.

Drawing rounds of arrows from the quiver attached to her waist, she continued her barrage in an attempt to support Bell from afar.

She was quick to comprehend what *Apollo Familia* was trying to do, and she immediately grabbed her weapon, came to the top of this tower, and located Bell. *Miach Familia*'s former third-tier adventurer was a skilled archer whose accuracy was second to none.

She was so far away from Hyacinthus that a normal person wouldn't have even seen a human outline, let alone be able to come within a celch of hitting the target.

"Bell, run..."

As if her plea had been answered, Bell staggered to his feet just as she was whispering to herself. The boy grabbed Hestia's hand and the two raced down another street. Hyacinthus started to give chase but was cut off by Nahza's next round.

The man looked straight at her, eyes burning with fury. She fired yet another arrow, aiming straight for his chest. Without missing a beat, the rouge longsword knocked the arrow harmlessly out of the air.

He must've given up pursuit for the time being, because as soon as the arrow hit the ground, Hyacinthus took off in the opposite direction. Nahza saw his white cape swish as her target disappeared from sight.

"Too many enemies..."

The dog person turned her attention to the other shadows pursuing Bell on the rooftops and proceeded to take them down one by one. It was like dispatching individual bees in a swarm, with no end to it.

From her vantage point, Nahza roughly estimated that there were at least two hundred adventurers pursuing Bell.

Tossing an empty quiver aside, Nahza equipped a new one.

She was firing so many arrows that she didn't have enough time to watch them hit their targets. Instead, she listened for the distant yelps of pain and soft thuds as the hunters fell from the rooftops.

"Lord Miach, please hurry..."

A solitary bead of sweat worked its way down her anxious face.

"Bell, are you okay?!"

"I-I'm f-fine..."

Bell's breath was shallow and ragged as he responded. Hestia was on the verge of tears.

Hyacinthus had inflicted considerable damage; the boy's entire body was in pain. It'd taken every high potion he had to close the wound in his chest. They ran with everything they had, putting one foot in front of the other in a desperate attempt to gain some distance. However, Bell couldn't keep his balance and needed Hestia's help to stay upright.

His body may not have been moving as well as he would've liked, but luckily his ears were at full strength. They picked up the sound of the spell coming from not too far away.

"?!"

"Magic?!"

Hestia noticed, too. Sure enough, there was an elf mage directly above them holding an outstretched staff.

Using that particular building's architecture to shield herself from Nahza, the mage had been lying in wait while casting an enchantment. What's more, her hiding spot was out of Firebolt's range. Bell and Hestia immediately took off in the other direction, but it was too late to completely escape the imminent blast.

A lightning spell with a particularly long range flashed right behind them.

"—?!!"

The hair on the back of his head singed, Bell hugged Hestia in close as the two hit the street and rolled.

Bell did his best to shield Hestia from the blast, but the lightning magic carved its way into the surrounding buildings and ground. Everything around them was instantly blown to pieces; the air was inundated with smoke.

"Lissos, I have them!"

"Superb! Send word to Daphne!"

Bell's and Hestia's ears were ringing, vision hazy as many footsteps rushed in to surround them. The first figure to appear on the other side of the thinning smoke was an elf wearing a scarf that covered his mouth—the same one who had led the attack on the church. This time he was accompanied by five more adventurers.

Lissos, a rather handsome elf even by their standards, glared at the two fugitives and said, "Chests to the ground, now."

Bell rolled over to protect Hestia, his dirty face locked on the elf—then, a new group appeared on the scene.

"Huh...?"

"This game of yours looks like fun. We'll play, too."

Six figures appeared behind Hestia and Bell, a party of adventurers.

Watching the party move to confront their attackers, Bell's eyes were instantly drawn to the large man leading them. He was none other than *Takemikazuchi Familia*'s captain, Ouka.

Next to him was Chigusa, brandishing a spear of her own. Mikoto was standing tall, ready for battle.

"Imbeciles...Do you not realize you are threatening members of *Apollo Familia*?!"

"Oh, that's what we came here to do."

"We refuse to sacrifice our bonds of friendship when allies are in need!"

Ouka answered Lissos's enraged warning by drawing his greatsword. Mikoto accentuated his sentiment with a few words in her own high-pitched voice.

The two factions stared each other down. *Apollo Familia* and *Takemikazuchi Familia* drew weapons and shouted battle cries as they prepared for combat.

"We made it in time...!"

"M-Miach?!"

Both groups charged in, trying to land the first hit, when suddenly Miach emerged from the backstreet, trying to catch his breath.

Hestia was first to notice his presence and raised her head to greet him. The god looked down and nodded with a short "Ah."

"I requested the aid of *Takemikazuchi Familia* when the explosions first rang out. Are you all right?"

"Y-yes."

"Miach, friends like you are just so...!"

The deities smiled at the look of surprise on Bell's face and the gratitude radiating from Hestia's eyes.

Nahza had been operating independently while Miach joined Ouka's battle party on the way out here.

"Unfortunately, we cannot linger. Leave this fight to them. You, Bell, get moving."

"Wha...but—"

"Listen to me. This battle will not end until your safety can be guaranteed. You must understand this."

Bell hesitated. In that moment, more loud voices announced the arrival of yet another group.

More hunters. Reinforcements.

Bell struggled for breath as Miach looked at him with pleading eyes.

"Now, go!"

"...Sorry about this, Miach!"

Hestia climbed to her feet. Bell fought back the pain and nodded.

The two made it to the entrance of the closest back alley. Bell took a quick look over his shoulder at Mikoto's group, locked in fierce combat. The fact that others were now involved in this mess weighed heavily on his heart.

At that moment, Bell understood what a conflict between *Familias* truly implied.

As soon as one group made a move, others would be forced to meet them in battle—it becomes a quagmire. Combat would become more intense as time wore on. Bell was convinced, rather forcefully, that no *Familia* was going to pull any punches.

"That's the city wall! They forced us all the way out here...?!"

Hestia looked down the back alleyway, running as fast as she could while supporting the injured Bell.

The imposing curtain of rock that surrounded the city loomed over them. Hestia guessed that, based on their distance from the wall, the two had been forced all the way to the very western edge of the city.

They met up with a monumental roadblock and hadn't been able to plan their escape. In their desperation, they'd gone in the complete opposite direction of the Guild.

"Over here!"

"…?!"

They were surrounded by the sound of enemy footsteps in no time.

The hunters had to use the architecture for cover against Nahza's arrows. But now, they caught up to Bell and were ready to attack.

Three figures jumped over the top of Bell, their shadows blocking out the sun.

"—You want a piece of this?!"

"?!"

A new black figure launched itself from one of the side streets, colliding with the three hunters in midair. Holding a greatsword in his left hand, the figure sent two of the hunters hurtling to the ground with one sweep.

Additionally, a golden arrow plunged into the cheek of the hunter the figure had missed, and he fell to the street just short of the boy and his goddess. The black figure landed a moment later, delivering a kick that sent the final hunter careening into a wall.

"…Still breathing, Bell?"

The figure's long black jacket furled as the red-haired figure turned to face him.

"Welf?!"

The young man rested the greatsword over his shoulder as the two comrades made eye contact.

"Mr. Bell!"

Lilly emerged from the shadows and rushed to join them.

Reloading the bow gun strapped to her right arm, Lilly called out her friend's name.

"Supporter, too…"

"Why…why are you here…?"

"We were worried about Mr. Bell and Lady Hestia, obviously!"

"Everyone's talking about a 'rabbit hunt' around town. Word travels fast."

Lilly, still in her werewolf form, stopped right in front of a very surprised Hestia as everyone exchanged information.

The two newcomers were stunned by Bell's appearance. Exposed skin covered in dried blood, an enormous scar crossed his chest where his breastplate should have been. What was left of that piece of armor hung loosely below his chest. Lilly flung her backpack to the ground and instantly withdrew three vials—a high potion she had purchased from Nahza for their Dungeon trip and the two dual potions. Wasting no time, she shoved all three of them into Bell's hands.

"Thank you, Lilly..."

A searing pain coursed through Lilly's heart as she looked at the weak smile on Bell's battered and beaten face. *How cruel*, she thought as the boy winced. Her eyes trembled as if she could see herself in his position.

Bell uncorked a vial of dark blue liquid and did his best to overcome the twinges of pain as he chugged it down.

"We can't stay in one place. We need to move, now." Hestia turned to face the others when she spoke.

"Lilly thinks she understands the situation...This is all a result of that night at the bar?"

"No, that's part of it. This is all part of Apollo's plan."

Lilly asked the question as the four of them took off. Hestia answered her right away.

Whether it was all true or just some elaborate prank, everything that Bell knew was on the line. Lilly nearly tripped as that information sank in.

"Yo...We've got company!"

"!"

Welf, who was leading the way, spotted more figures up ahead. There were three in the front with a few more joining them from behind.

Bell's and Hestia's faces tensed up, but it was Lilly who urged them forward.

"Please proceed to the Guild!"

"We'll clean up here and be right behind you! Don't worry about us!"

Bell knew by the number of oncoming enemies they wouldn't have a chance, but Welf waved him off. Lilly locked eyes with Hestia, pleading her to go.

"We're counting on you!" she said with a reluctant nod and grabbed Bell's wrist.

"Cover me, Li'l E!"

"Of course! But will Mr. Welf be okay on his own?!"

Bell and Hestia went down a different side street as Welf and Lilly rushed to meet their enemies head-on.

Welf cocked an eyebrow at the prum girl as if annoyed by her concern.

"Well, I'm a hell of a lot stronger now—"

The first three hunters rushed in.

Both hands clamped firmly on his greatsword, Welf swung his weapon low and brought it arcing forward into a full swing.

His wide-eyed opponents were too slow to dodge the oncoming blade and were flung backward to a chorus of their own shrieks of pain.

"—so I'll be fine!"

"...Being strong is all well and good, but clear a path!"

The airborne hunters spun and flipped over Lilly's head and landed behind her.

Lilly hid just how thankful she was for Welf's Level 2 and yelled a stern warning instead.

The enemy reinforcements arrived a moment later and immediately engaged them in combat.

"This guy's movin' better than the others!"

Welf and Lilly fought back against a party of Level 1 and Level 2 adventurers. Welf quickly dispatched the weaker opponents as Lilly drew the only upper-class adventurer's attention away from him with arrows from her bow gun.

Welf spun like a top as he got into position and landed a blow that launched the upper-class adventurer straight into the wall behind them.

"Mr. Welf! Out of the way!"

"Huh?! You, you can't be serious…!"

Lilly withdrew a fist-size pouch from her backpack and threw it into the oncoming ranks of the next wave of hunters.

She covered her nose with her sleeve even before the pouch reached its target—a morbul.

Welf's face went pale as he ran in the opposite direction. *Poof!* The pouch exploded on contact with the street surface, inundating the narrow back alley with a thick cloud of green powder.

"GYYAAAAAAAAHHHHHH!!" Tormented roars erupted only moments later.

"If you're gonna use that, tell me first!"

"Lilly did! Mr. Welf didn't clear a path, so she did!"

Pinching their noses shut with one hand, the two argued as they raced to escape the expanding putrid cloud.

Despite being safe in the knowledge that no enemies could overtake them from behind, they engaged one wave of hunters after another as they attempted to catch up with Bell and Hestia.

"...There's a ton of these guys!"

Welf yelled out in frustration as yet another wave moved to attack him the moment he'd finished off a different foe.

The young man took a look around—there were enemies coming from every angle. A whistle suddenly pierced the air. Had Bell and Hestia been found? However, these hunters didn't react. Lilly took a quick look around.

"Are they...listening to a different commander?"

Upon closer inspection, she realized that their formation was much different and not as crisp. Their movements were not planned and had an air of desperation to them.

Theirs was a net that relied solely on numbers. The two allies came to a stop as a wave of hunters moved to cut them off...Welf stared them down, tightening his grip on his sword. Lilly, however, froze in place.

"Ehh? Wha...why are they—?"

"Hey, what's with you?!"

Lilly's arms hung limp as she stopped fighting and stared at the body of a human lying in the street. The emblem on his armor bore a crescent moon with a wineglass. She grabbed her left shoulder out of reflex.

Nausea overtook her; sweat coated her body. She shook her head back and forth, mumbling, "That's not possible, that's not possible…"

It was the emblem that stopped Lilly cold in her tracks—*Soma Familia*'s emblem.

Her chestnut-colored eyes trembled with fear the moment the image of Divine Wine under crescent moon came into view.

"?!"

Coming back to herself, she scanned the surroundings. Welf was currently fending off a large animal person using his weapon as a shield; an Amazon was jeering at him from the rooftop next to a very sinister-looking dwarf with an arrow sticking out of his back. Lilly couldn't help but feel that she had seen all of them during the time of her life that had become distant.

Lilly came to the conclusion that the reason for the overwhelming numbers was that another *Familia* had joined forces with Apollo.

That's when she spotted the thin man wearing glasses who was barking orders to the other adventurers.

"Li'l E?!"

Ignoring Welf's call, Lilly took off at a sprint. Deactivating her magic behind a pile of wooden boxes, she climbed them and stepped onto the roof.

"Mr. Zanis?!"

"…Ah, I thought you'd be here, Erde."

The leader of *Soma Familia* didn't seem the least bit surprised when Lilly appeared before him, and he grinned at her.

The human man and prum girl stood face-to-face on the flat rooftop of the house.

"What…what do you think you're doing?! Why are you helping *Apollo Familia*?!"

"They asked for it. Even forked over a large sum of money in exchange for our promise to join their fight against *Hestia Familia*. Lord Soma gave his approval…Well, he left it up to me."

Without a doubt, out of all the groups in Orario, *Soma Familia* would be the easiest to bribe.

Their god, Soma, was only interested in his hobby, and he cared nothing for power struggles and politics. His approval could be easily bought with money to fund his expensive pastime.

Most likely, *Apollo Familia* had set up an arrangement with their new partner before they put the plan to capture Bell into action.

"Is Mr. Zanis insane?! Doing this for money...*Apollo Familia* may be ready to accept the Guild's penalty, but *Soma Familia* was already on thin ice! The Guild won't let this go!!"

Soma's negligence concerning the well-being of his followers had been brought to the Guild's attention, and fines had been levied against him. Even now, the Guild was keeping a close eye on his *Familia*. Once the fact that they willingly joined the battle that was turning Orario into a war zone came to light, it wouldn't be surprising if the entire *Familia* was exiled from the city. It was as if Zanis had pointed the Guild's wrath right at himself.

Lilly yelled over and over that they had no reason to attack *Hestia Familia*, that their actions didn't make any sense.

"No, we have our justification."

Zanis laughed off Lilly's accusations as he stood with his hands behind his back.

"Justifi...cation?"

"That's right. *Soma Familia* has a reason to fight *Hestia Familia* even without the request from Apollo."

Zanis calmly stared down at the girl. Lilly frowned back at him. The man narrowed his eyes, a thin smile on his lips as he raised his chin without breaking eye contact. "Do you not know?" he asked with a sneer.

"No idea at all?" he asked again.

"—It can't...be."

The color drained from her face as one possibility came to mind. Then, Zanis confirmed her worst fears.

"That's right. *It's you, Erde.*"

The man leaned closer to her as he lowered his chin.

"Our irreplaceable friend and comrade was stolen from us by swindlers. The time had come for us to exact revenge with justice on our side."

Lilly's knees went weak.

They were using the fact that Lilly was still technically a member of *Soma Familia* as an excuse to join the assault on *Hestia Familia*. This fact protected them from the Guild as well as gave them an escape route to avoid any penalties.

That was the true power of a contract with the *Familia*. If they were able to prove that one of their members was still bound to their god but working for the benefit of another, it would be next to impossible to punish their actions. No matter how much Lilly would try to explain the circumstances, the voice of the *Familia* would win out.

Lilly was another reason that Bell and Hestia were in danger.

"I, too, believed you to be dead until very recently...That is, until I happened to hear the story of one man at a bar."

"A-and that is...?"

"Just the exploits of the Little Rookie on the eighteenth floor, and the little prum supporter who tagged along with him."

Lilly cursed her own carelessness.

She always used her magic, Cinder Ella, to take the form of a werewolf child while on the surface. However, she deactivated the magic while in the Dungeon to preserve her mental strength. Now, because of the events on the eighteenth floor, the group of adventurers there that day not only knew her true appearance, but also that she was in a party with Bell. What's more, that information was spreading.

Zanis must have acquired this information before receiving the offer from *Apollo Familia*. Once money was offered, he seized his opportunity.

"Do not fret, Erde. I will assure Lord Soma of your innocence in this matter. *Hestia Familia* is completely in the wrong."

She'd warned them. Lilly had warned Hestia and Bell that *Soma Familia* would one day seek revenge. That day had arrived.

The flames had reached them...That was how Lilly felt. She'd made a horrible mistake. Her past was a wildfire just waiting to ignite. What's more, she'd fanned the flames to the point of a raging inferno.

This was all her fault.

"The evil ones who tricked you, used you, and profited off you shall receive a fitting punishment. *Apollo Familia* will crush them into oblivion."

Lilly felt dizzy, the rooftops spinning around her. Her whole world was crashing down around her.

She was a plague, infecting everything and everyone she cared about. Her body trembled as memories of the nice old couple and their flower shop flashed before her eyes. *Soma Familia* had destroyed it, and she was the only reason they had ever found that flower shop at all. A storm of grief and guilt raged inside her tiny heart, threatening to work its way up her throat and into a scream of self-loathing.

She opened her eyes and looked out over the battlefield.

Nahza had been chased from her perch on top of the bell tower, *Takemikazuchi Familia* was pinned down on all sides a few blocks away, and Welf continued to trade blows with the hunters just below her. All of them were in danger right now because of *Soma Familia*.

She had been foolish.

Lilly should have never strayed anywhere near Bell and the others.

—It was absurd to believe that her plague would never reach them, that their warmth and generosity wouldn't be destroyed by the flames that followed her.

Eyes glistening with tears, Lilly's neck gave out and her head slammed into her chest.

"Please..."

"What?"

"Please leave Mr. Bell and his friends alone..."

Lilly pleaded with Zanis in a weak, trembling voice.

She raised her face to look at him. There was no life in her eyes.

"Lilly will return to Lord Soma. So please, stop this...Please leave them alone."

It was simple math.

If *Soma Familia* was using Lilly as a justification to participate in this fight, then all she had to do was take herself out of it. If surrendering to Zanis would reduce the amount of hunters pursuing Bell, it was more than worth it.

Members of *Soma Familia* were completely under the spell of the Divine Wine, soma. Its appeal had attracted hundreds of adventurers into her *Familia*'s ranks. But if they weren't there, if she could find a way to convince them to leave, then Bell and the others might have a chance.

She knew it was highly unlikely he'd accept her offer, but she had to try.

Zanis stared at her for a moment, enjoying the look of desperation on her face, until finally pompously nodding back.

"Why not?"

Lilly was shocked at his sudden approval, and also a little suspicious.

Zanis pressed his glasses up against his face.

"Actually, the situation is getting quite dangerous. *Apollo Familia* already paid a decent sum of money upfront, so now might be a good time to call it quits."

The corners of his lips arched upward as he continued.

"But most importantly, *I* need you."

Lilly's eyes shot open. This new information caught her off guard.

Maybe she wasn't just an excuse to get money; maybe there was some truth in Zanis's claim.

What could she, a useless weakling who'd brought about the destruction of everything she cares about, be needed for? As long as Zanis kept his promise, she had no choice but to follow his orders.

"Stand beside me. I will give the signal to retreat as soon as you do."

Zanis reached inside his jacket and withdrew a small flare gun. Lilly did not respond, silently doing what she was told.

The man smiled with satisfaction, raised the flare gun to the sky, and pulled the trigger. A ball of sparkling light instantly shot high into the air.

Many of the adventurers in the seventh block of Orario stopped fighting the moment they saw the arc of light. Just as Zanis had promised, the members of *Soma Familia* started to withdraw.

"Hey! Li'l E!"

With roughly half of his assailants leaving the area, Welf finally had enough time to call out to his ally from the street below.

Lilly took a step toward the edge of the roof and looked down at him with listless eyes.

"Come, Erde."

"Yes..."

Lilly nodded as she turned around at the sound of Zanis's command.

Welf looked up at the two in disbelief. The man turned on his heel as Lilly said her final good-bye.

"Lilly's returning to *Soma Familia*...She won't cause any more trouble. Please tell Mr. Bell."

"The hell are you saying?! I can't look Bell in the eye and say that! Get back here!"

"Lilly's sorry...Farewell."

She gave one last bow before following Zanis.

The prum girl disappeared from Welf's line of view.

"What the hell does she think she's doing...?!"

He tried to pursue them, but unfortunately he met up with a group of *Apollo Familia* hunters and was forced back into combat.

"Dammit!" he screamed at the clouds. There was no choice but to give up the chase.

Bell and Hestia had lost count of how many hits their bodies had absorbed. The tally had just increased by yet another.

With all the hunters' arrows, the spells of magic users, and upper-class adventurers wielding every weapon imaginable, neither of them had time to catch their breath. For some reason, their pursuers had been yelling at one another for a while now—*Apollo Familia* was starting to get desperate and had ramped up their assault.

The two fugitives had made it back to their old neighborhood. It was oddly still, all residents having already evacuated. Once again the sounds of war distended on this normally peaceful block.

"...Firebolt!"

Bell released his Magic into a worn-down stone building that had been empty for years.

The flaming lightning bolts ignited the debris inside the building, creating yet another explosion of smoke. Bell used it as cover to escape the eyes of his pursuers and took off in a completely different direction.

"Ha-haa...!"

"...Bell, this way!"

Hestia grabbed the boy's hand and guided him off the main road as Bell fought back pain just to inhale.

She found a drainage canal that ran beneath the street level. Leaving the backstreet, they found the closest stairwell and raced down to the water level. It wasn't long until they reached the city sewer's entrance.

"Are you okay, Bell?"

"I'm so sorry, Goddess..."

Bell leaned against the wall before sliding all the way down to the ground and offered Hestia an apology. Hestia shook her head before looking around to find their escape routes. They were beneath what could have been a very large bridge, open on both ends with water flowing behind them. She guessed that the water must be running deeper into the city. The street-level landscape was visible at the other end.

Although they couldn't see them, they could hear the yells and hurried footsteps of their pursuers coming from just outside. Praying with all their might that they remain hidden, the two talked in hushed voices.

"Can you still move?"

"...I'm fine. I can."

Bell used the last of the potions he'd received from Lilly in order to recover from at least some of the damage he had taken. Hestia watched his staggered breathing with remorseful eyes. Without warning, a booming voice erupted from the other side of the wall.

"Are you listening? Bell Cranell!"

Hyacinthus's voice.

Hestia sat shoulder to shoulder with Bell. The boy clenched his eyes shut.

"Wherever you hide, wherever you run, we will find you! This game of hide-and-seek is meaningless!"

The man's proclamation filled the air around them. Hyacinthus must've been standing in a high place, because the echoes reverberated in every direction.

"On land or in the Dungeon, it doesn't matter! Your days of peace are at an end!"

Bell gulped as he understood what the man's words meant.

Even if by some miracle they escaped the hunters' net and made it to the Guild, Apollo would pursue him for the rest of his life. They would attack him on sight in the city, in the Dungeon, or wherever else he tried to go.

The boy was feeling the full power of an influential *Familia* dedicated to accomplishing a goal.

Just as Hyacinthus said, the chase would not end until there was a clear resolution. He would never be able to live a normal life.

"..."

Hestia sat silently next to him. Bell was in shock from the realization.

The goddess's eyes narrowed, her mind made up.

"—Bell, please listen."

Hestia moved in front of him, crouching above the boy's outstretched legs and looking him in the eyes.

The ruby-red spheres looking up at her, she let it all come out.

"Since Apollo is serious about this, there is no future for us here. We have two options: fight a battle we can't possibly win—or run away from Orario."

"...!"

Hestia ignored the look of shock on the boy's face and continued. She knew the boy comprehended their situation.

"I'm willing to go anywhere as long as you're with me. It doesn't matter if we're being chased all the time. I'll run alongside you until they give up."

Hestia's resolve was unyielding.

She would miss the friends she had and the peaceful days she'd spent living in the city. But as long as Bell was with her, she didn't care where they lived. That was clear as day.

Leave Orario with the goddess and live somewhere far away...?

Hestia held her hand to her chest, trying to steady her beating heart as she waited on the edge of her seat for Bell's response.

In truth, running away might be the only real option for Bell and Hestia.

It was the same for the other *Familias* that came out on the losing end of these battles...Just like Hermes had told him about Zeus, leaving Orario was the only way.

Bell thought about it.

Just the two of them, he exploring the wonders of the world with Hestia.

Listening to the wind blow through a forest, sitting on top of a hill under the blue sky, feeling a sea breeze on his face while exploring a port town.

She'd be wearing a one-piece dress and a fancy hat, he'd be carrying the bags from that day's shopping. They'd walk down the street, smiling.

Such warm, inviting thoughts.

How wonderful would this journey be? Living a new dream?

It was possible; the two of them could have this future.

But...!

His heart might have been swayed by Hestia's words, but images of all the people he'd met in the city suddenly surged through Bell's mind.

People he'd laughed alongside. All the girls who had shared smiles with him.

All of his days as an adventurer, all of the chance encounters—he remembered everything.

I—

A new image took over his heart.

The start of it all, meeting the knight with blond hair and golden eyes.

The side of her face, blond locks flowing. His heart couldn't leave that behind.

"..."

Hestia's expression gradually disappeared as if she were reading the boy's thoughts like a book.

Her lips tensed as she reached out and grabbed ahold of both of the boy's hands.

The deity asked the surprised human a question:

"Bell, do you love me?"

Bell's voice cracked in confusion.

"Huh?!"

"This is important."

Blushing a light pink beneath her eyes, Hestia kept talking.

"If you say you love me, I'm ready to do anything. If I believe your words, all other petty emotions mean nothing and I can do anything you ask! I can fight!"

She squeezed his hands.

"I love you very much, Bell! You're just so cute, I can't help it. I want to live with you forever, always be by your side...I don't want anyone else to have you."

Her fingers shook.

"What do you think about me?"

Then she asked her question again.

Now blushing profusely, Hestia once again locked eyes with Bell and looked at him with all seriousness.

Bell, too, had turned bright red. But he had no clue what the goddess was trying to say.

"I-I revere you..."

"That's not what I'm talking about!"

Bell's shoulders drooped as Hestia yelled in his face.

The explosions, footsteps, and shouting were still raging around them. Despite that, Bell's mind raced as he tried to figure out what she was asking, what the goddess wanted to hear. What did she mean by the word "love"?

Hestia's eyes quivered as if something important had just broken inside her. Something so important that they might not be able to continue as deity and follower.

Desperately holding onto her last shred of hope, Hestia saw Bell's lips open to speak—

Ka-booom!

"?!"

The shock wave from an explosion at the entrance to the sewer overtook them.

Bell quickly forced his body up to shield Hestia from the debris. A moment later, the outlines of mages and adventurers appeared in the cloud of smoke.

"Found them! In the sewer!"

"After 'em!"

"?!"

Their pursuers had found their hiding spot. Bell jumped to his feet with Hestia in his arms and took off once again.

The white-haired boy made a beeline for the exit on the opposite side of the tunnel.

"Not once, but twice...You've gotten in my way for the last time... you *bastards!*"

Hestia's rage swelled up within her, morphing her face into a hideous visage. Bell took his eyes off her in fright.

Explosions went off in her eyes.

"Now I'm angry! Bell, I've had enough of this!"

"Y-yes?!"

"Southwest—go southwest!"

Bell didn't dare do anything else. Hestia had never barked orders before.

He made a hard right, diverging greatly from the path to the Guild in the west. Even here, Bell tore through the back alleys and side streets. None of their pursuers were expecting this turn of events and stumbled before adjusting their own trajectory.

"…"
…
"…"
…

They raced forward in silence. Bell was secretly relieved that their previous conversation had been left unsettled.

Perhaps Hestia felt the same way. Rather than bring it back up, she shoved her red face deep into his chest.

Bell could feel her shaking in his embrace, much like his own.

Going southwest, as Hestia had instructed, was surprisingly easy.

The enemy's net was so much thinner than before, but the two of them didn't even have to engage enemies in combat to escape it. Crossing West Main, the two entered Orario's sixth district, located between West Main Street and Southwest Main Street.

Hestia guided Bell through streets filled with startled onlookers until finally arriving in front of a rather ornate building.

"Wait, isn't this…"

A gate of tall iron bars protected the entrance to a well-maintained and flourishing garden. A stone structure stood in the middle of it all. A large emblem hung on the gate, a bow and arrow eclipsing in the sun. Bell couldn't speak; only a small grunt of surprise escaped his mouth.

Hestia had led him to *Apollo Familia*'s home.

"We're not here to take over, out of the way! Shoo! Shoo!"

Several guards approached Bell and Hestia as they attempted to open the gate, spears at the ready. Hestia simply brushed them aside, glaring at each of the guards in turn. Suddenly, their path was clear.

Even more members of the *Familia* were standing outside the stone building, as if to demonstrate how many reserves were still waiting for orders to deploy. Once again, Bell was taken aback by yet another demonstration of military might.

Many sets of eyes watched the two fugitives make their way through the center of the garden. All of them wore the same look of anticipation. *Creak!* The joints on the front door sounded as Apollo emerged.

"My, my, Hestia. What are you hoping to accomplish, coming all the way out here like this?"

The deity walked down the front steps of his abode, his perfectly polished teeth sparkling in the sunlight. Hestia watched him descend, fury emanating from her eyes.

Apollo made his way through his army of adventurers, the young prum Luan at his side. The two came to a stop directly in front of Bell and Hestia.

Hestia's aura of pure hatred made Bell and Luan uneasy, looking anywhere but at the goddess. Their faces glistened with a cold sweat. The two deities, on the other hand, didn't even blink as they faced each other.

"...Prum boy, that glove, please."

"Eh...Um, sure."

Hestia's tone didn't allow for dissent. Luan nodded and removed the glove from his right hand.

Hestia snatched it from his grasp and in one clean motion slapped it against the side of Apollo's face.

" "?!" "

Snap! The reverberation of cloth on skin filled the quiet garden.

Hestia used every muscle in her body to deliver the blow; even her twin black ponytails flew through the air as her arm finally came to a stop. Bell and Ruan watched in stunned silence.

Despite the red blotch on his cheek, Apollo's grin never changed. Hestia took in a deep breath and yelled with everything she had.

"Fine! You want a War Game, you're gonna get one!"

Bell saw the corners of Apollo's lips curl upward.

"All of the divine witnesses know it shall come to pass—my friends, a War Game!"

Doors and windows of the stone building flew open the moment Apollo raised his arms. Gods and goddesses emerged one after another.

"YAAAAAAAHHHHHHH!"

As if they'd been waiting for this moment, even more deities jumped down from the trees or appeared from behind bushes in the garden.

Bell, Luan, and all the members of *Apollo Familia* who were on standby didn't know how to react. They looked around with wide eyes as the garden suddenly came alive with divine voices.

"Get this cleared with the Guild!"

"Will need to open an emergency Denatus! Everyone's invited!"

"This is so exciting—!"

"Been a long time comin'!"

A sudden whirlpool of excitement enveloped the humans. The gods were starving for entertainment and now there was going to be a show. Loki's voice was right in the thick of it as the deities started to organize the War Game.

"It's settled, then. The finer details of our Game will be decided at Denatus. The day shall be announced later...Let's enjoy this, Hestia?"

Apollo sneered at Hestia without the faintest hint of fear or anxiety amid the chaos around them.

Apollo turned his back on her and went back inside his abode with Luan in tow.

"G-Goddess..."

Bell watched the god ascend the stone steps, his body frozen in place. Even his voice lacked substance.

The difference between the groups in terms of numbers and resources was astounding. This was a fight that couldn't be won. Visions of the tragedy that was about to unfold flared up in Bell's mind.

Hestia turned to face him with vigor.

"Bell, one week."

She looked up at her follower, the boy's face getting paler by the moment as she continued.

"I will find a way to delay the War Game for one week."

"Huh...?"

"During that time, Bell, become as strong as you can. Stronger than any of the people who attacked us today—become stronger than ever! You can do it!"

Hestia was betting everything on Bell's potential, the Realis Phrase skill.

Bell looked into his goddess's eyes. There was no shadow of doubt. She completely believed in him, and that was terrifying.

"Bell! Lady Hestia!"

"Welf?!"

Welf came through the iron gate in front of *Apollo Familia*'s home. The young man had followed Bell's pursuers and then heard the commotion coming from this location to find them.

"Li'l E went back to…No, no, was taken back to *Soma Familia*."

"?!"

"The other guys got in my way, couldn't help her…I'm sorry."

This unexpected news left Bell and Hestia reeling in shock.

How? Why now? Was she safe?—Bell's spirit ignited, question after question burned through his mind. But it all came down to one thing: He had to rescue her. He needed more information; he needed to talk to Welf.

However, Hestia's hand wrapped itself around his elbow before he could take his first step toward the redheaded man.

"Bell, do as I say."

"B-but–?!"

"I swear to you, I will rescue our supporter. So please—have faith in me."

Hestia cut off Bell's attempt to argue.

The goddess believed in her child; all she asked was that he believe in her.

Bell's veins burned with adrenaline, but the look in Hestia's eyes cooled the flames. The muscles in his tense body relaxed until finally…he chose to believe.

All of the emotions that raged through his mind just a moment ago now at ease, he nodded.

"Bell, please give me my knife before you go."

"Here."

"Welf, I apologize, but I'll need your strength to rescue our supporter."

"No need for apologies. I'm ready for anything."

All instructions given, Hestia looked up at Bell one more time.

"The rest is up to you. Now get moving."

"Yes!"

With that, Bell dashed from the noisy garden in front of *Apollo Familia's* home as fast as his feet could carry him.

There was only one week.

He had until then to get stronger than his enemies—stronger than Hyacinthus.

The Status on his back felt hot as he ran. Fatigue, mental strain—none of that mattered to him anymore. He set a course for the tall tower in the north where the Sword Princess was waiting.

CHAPTER 4 **THOSE WHO GATHER**

The news that a War Game would be held spread like wildfire among the gods.

Of course the adventurers and citizens of Orario couldn't help but notice the jubilant and high-spirited deities all around the city. It was no time at all before every living thing on the surface of the Labyrinth City knew what was going to happen.

Something else transpired just mere moments after Hestia and Apollo's announcement had been made official.

"That's it, that tower has to be…!"

Bell had left *Apollo Familia*'s home at a dead sprint and worked his way through a city much more active than usual. Weaving through unfamiliar territory, he arrived at the northernmost block. One month ago now, he trained with her on top of the city wall. Doing his best to remember the landmarks she taught him, Bell desperately searched to find the building she called home.

The white-haired boy practically flew down North Main Street, furiously pumping his arms in perfect rhythm with his strides. The side streets webbed out around him; his eyes desperately scanned for something familiar.

He turned into one side street filled with decorative houses and well-known structures. Bell kept his eyes on the rooftops, trying to find the one that was higher than the others. A few more turns and suddenly he found himself outside *Loki Familia*'s home, the Twilight Manor.

"You there, halt!"

"State your business!"

"Let me talk to Aiz…Let me talk to Aiz Wallenstein!"

A man and woman immediately blocked the intruder's path at the entrance to their home. The boy pleaded with them to allow him to meet with Aiz.

The male guard took a look at the frantic boy's face, his eyebrows sinking lower and lower as he started to connect the dots.

"You, Little Rookie...? What's the big idea, trying to meet with her?!"

Bell's white hair and red eyes must have tipped him off. The guard immediately came to the defense of his ally, trying to protect her from this outsider. However, Bell couldn't afford to back down.

The boy asked the guards many times to let him see Aiz, but he couldn't explain himself. The guards' voices grew steadily louder and angrier as the boy's pleas became more and more desperate. It didn't take long for other members of the *Familia* to make their way outside.

"...!"

A group of twenty adventurers emerged from the building that was built like a wall of spears with several towers reaching out to the sky. They spread out just behind the two guards, ready to defend their home against the intruder. Bell's situation had just become that much more perilous.

The new arrivals started shouting threats, calling him "pitiful," "shameless," and "reckless," among others...They already knew that *Hestia Familia* would be taking part in the War Game and believed he wanted to convince Aiz to join the fight—a fox recruiting a tiger for her claws. They would do everything in their power to drive him away. Their desire to protect their ally quickly turned to anger—how dare he use her for his own gain?

Fear consumed the boy's body as he took a step back out of reflex.

He knew full well that what he was doing was shameful.

But he was unwilling to turn his back.

He only had a small window of time to get stronger, to overcome the gap that separated him from his new enemy. The only way he knew to become stronger than Hyacinthus in time was to learn from Aiz once again. Just like how she had made him strong enough to take down a Minotaur.

The fact that Lilly had been kidnapped was still eating at him inside. Instead of rushing to save her, he was standing out here getting yelled at. Every moment he wasn't making progress to rescue her or getting stronger felt like an eternity.

"Let me see Aiz!" he pleaded with the mob again, bowing over and over. Every muscle in his face was squeezed to its limit.

"What's all this?"

A voice cut through the chaos.

The mob of adventurers immediately fell silent. Bell stopped moving, his eyes glued forward.

A top-class adventurer, the Amazonian girl Tione Hyrute, walked out onto the lawn. As was normal for her race, she wore clothing that exposed a great deal of her wheat-colored skin. Her long black hair swished back and forth over her shoulders and down her back as she approached.

The mob quickly parted, allowing her to pass. She walked directly up to Bell.

One of the guards leaned close to whisper into her ear and explained everything that had happened so far. The Amazonian girl's eyes flashed at Bell.

"Be gone from here. I cannot allow this mockery to continue."

"...?!"

Tione showed no sympathy. She had delivered the will of *Loki Familia* in place of their leader, Finn.

Her tone was cold and her stare showed no willingness to listen. Bell cowered in her presence. She crossed her arms, aura unyielding and overwhelming. A moment later, she grabbed both of Bell's shoulders and pushed him away from the front entrance.

"W-wait! Miss Tione?! Please, just hear me out...!"

Bell was forced to step backward to stay upright. Her strength overpowered him in no time as Bell was driven farther and farther away from his last hope.

His body shook, trying to push forward, when Tione leaned in close.

"—Turn right from here and go two blocks down that street."

"!"

Her voice was quiet so as not to be overheard by the onlookers.

Tione ignored the look of shock on Bell's face and gave him one last shove into the street.

Her face might as well have been carved from stone, emotionless as she stared at him for a long moment before turning her back. Bell watched her long black hair dance behind her, unable to move or speak. The Amazonian girl walked swiftly back through the mob and into the building.

At long last, Bell's muscles started to respond. Slowly at first, he backed away from *Loki Familia*. Feeling the angry glares of the adventurer mob, Bell backtracked down the same street that he had come...The boy took off running the moment he was out of sight.

He followed Tione's directions, running through a dim back alley with his heart racing and fighting for breath. One block, two blocks and—

"Ah! Hey, Aiz! Argonaut's here—!"

"Aiz?! And—Miss Tiona?!"

Standing there to greet him were none other than the saber-wielding Aiz and the other Amazonian girl, Tiona, with some kind of large sheath resting over her shoulders.

Bell froze in surprise, but Tiona greeted him like a friend as the two girls walked up to meet him.

"We saw you from the window, Argonaut. Some kind of magic-stone lamp went off in Aiz's head, and we asked Tione to meet you."

Tiona went on to explain the other side of the story.

Aiz had figured out immediately what Bell was doing when he appeared at their front door. The look in his eyes told her that the boy wanted another round of training. However, they couldn't allow the mob to see her, so they sent Tione outside to deliver a message.

Whether she wanted to help out her friend or she was just along for the fun, Tiona was completely on board with the idea.

"...Aiz, is this okay?"

Bell took a very cautious step forward as he spoke.

She had no reason to teach him anything, Bell was asking for a huge favor. Since their *Familias* were not working together, she'd be doing this on her own as well as face the consequences it might bring.

Bell's words hung in the air for a moment, tension rising. Finally, Aiz gave him her answer.

"I cannot fight for you or alongside you...You have to do your best, and then..."

"Yep, yep! This is your fight, Argonaut!"

Tiona interpreted Aiz's vague words before—*whoosh!*—pointing her finger right at him.

Bell broke out in a cold sweat. Aiz continued.

"I think it would be wrong to...abandon you."

"Aiz..."

The look in the girl's golden eyes made Bell's heart melt. Completely ignoring the sudden change in mood, Tiona jumped back into the conversation.

"This is *fine*, no *problem*. If Aiz whips Argonaut into shape, the War Game will be more entertaining! Loki'n all the rest'll be thrilled for sure!"

Bell could only grimace at the thought. If the difference in power between him and *Apollo Familia* wasn't so staggering, their fight would be more fun to watch. Aiz looked at the Amazon and lightly smiled.

"But for me, *Apollo Familia* is going about this all wrong. Way over-the-top, dirty, I just can't stand it..."

Tiona's cheek twitched for a moment before she looked at the boy and grinned from ear to ear.

"So I'm gonna help you, too, Argonaut!"

"Wait, so that means..."

"Yep! You're stuck with me, too!"

Bell looked at Aiz, unsure what to say. She nodded back to him.

Getting over the shock of this turn of events, Bell wasted no time in showing his appreciation to the girls.

"Really, I can't thank you enough..."

"Relax, relax, it's nothing! Let's go, time's a-wastin'!"

"Yes."

Bell swore to himself right then and there that he would find some way to repay them for their kindness. He was in their debt.

Tiona was so excited that she thrust her large apparatus straight up, a childish smile on her face. Bell and Aiz followed her down the backstreet.

Their destination: the same place they'd trained before—the northwest city wall.

Bell's training under two top-class adventurers was about to begin.

The Guild officially approved the War Game between Hestia and Apollo almost immediately.

At the same time, preparations began all around the city.

However, no one was busier than the Guild employees. They had to find a way to allow both sides to unleash their full potential within the rules of the game while posing no danger to the citizens of Orario. The combatants would need supplies, directions, and most of all a stage on which to conduct the War Game. It could start any day; there was no time to waste. They also had to accommodate the wishes of the gods.

There wasn't a soul in the city, adventurer or otherwise, who wasn't waiting with bated breath for the conditions of the War Game to be announced. In the meantime, all they could do was prepare.

"—Is Hestia still not here today?!"

On the thirtieth floor of Babel Tower in the center of Orario…

Apollo had reached his breaking point.

Many gods and goddesses had gathered around a circular table in the center of the web of high pillars that supported a lofty ceiling. The rules and style of the War Game were to be decided by the two participating gods as well as the observers—in order to squeeze every possible ounce of entertainment out of the event—at this Denatus meeting.

Three days had passed since the assault on *Hestia Familia*.

Apollo had become irritated that his opponent refused to show her face. She excused her absence by claiming to be "sick" for the past few days. Despite her assertion that she was not physically well enough to take part in the meeting, it was clear as day that she was stalling for time.

Apollo angrily paced around his chair, insisting that she was concocting an escape plan. The moment he finished his rant, the doors to the tall chamber swung open.

"Sorry I'm late. I apologize for keeping you waiting."

Although her words were polite, she didn't sound the least bit sorry. Miach strode in beside her.

What's more, she showed no remorse for keeping the Denatus at a standstill. Apollo scowled at her.

"You're very late, Hestia. How do you plan to take responsibility for delaying Denatus to this extent?"

"It's not my fault I got a fever after being chased around the city by your followers. For a while there, I thought I was a *goner.*"

Hestia once again brought up her health to circumvent Apollo's complaints. Miach sided with Hestia, backing up her claim.

"Yes, she was in dire straits."

"Yah, yah, Itty-Bitty's a moron, but enough burnin' time. Can't we get goin'?"

Loki was leaning back in her chair, one eyebrow raised and hands behind her head as if she were out of patience as well. All of the deities returned to their seats and the discussion finally got under way.

The first order of business was for Hestia and Apollo to sign the necessary paperwork with everyone present as witnesses.

"Once I'm victorious, I claim Bell Cranell."

"..."

"I want to make that perfectly clear. There will be no petty excuses or far-fetched assertions after everything is over. Should Hestia win, she's free to demand whatever her little heart desires."

The possibility of defeat didn't seem to cross Apollo's mind. He wanted only one thing: ownership of Bell Cranell and his immediate transfer into *Apollo Familia*. Hestia remained quiet. The deity in charge of keeping notes for the meeting responded with an "All right, then" as he recorded their terms.

Next up, they needed to decide how the War Game would be fought.

"One-on-one, the best of our *Familias* settle everything. Wouldn't that be exciting?"

Hestia didn't even look at Apollo as she made her suggestion from her spot at the round table.

"It could be held at the Coliseum for everyone to see. The final battle right in front of our eyes. How could anyone not be entertained?"

"I agree. Watching all of Apollo's children attack Bell one after the other sounds rather boring."

"I second the motion."

Apollo's hostile gaze first fell on Hestia and then to her allies, Miach and Takemikazuchi.

Quite a few heads around the table started to nod, seeing the logic in her reasoning.

"What say you, Apollo?" "That's the *Ox Killer* you're fighting!"

"A strong opponent in a one-on-one duel, sounds good to me."

"..."

The deities around the table grinned in Apollo's direction. They were on no one's side; they simply enjoyed watching Apollo's reaction.

The blond deity wearing a crown of laurels put on a calm face before grinning once again.

"The only reason that your *Familia* isn't larger is entirely due to your laziness, Hestia, when it comes to recruiting."

"Muh…"

"You can cry all you want about your lack of children, but that's no reason for me to have to accommodate."

"Grrrr," Hestia growled under her breath as Apollo pointed out that the size of the *Familia* was completely under the god's control.

It was true that Hestia wanted to always be alone with Bell and had never tried to increase the size of her *Familia*.

"In the interest of fairness, why don't we draw for it?"

Unable to defend her position, Hestia remained silent as Apollo suggested a different solution. "Sure," came the voice of their transcriber as he pulled a box out from under the table and placed it on top.

Each of the gods in attendance wrote how they would like to see the War Game be played on a sheet of paper. The papers were collected and put into the box. Of course, Hestia wrote "DUEL" in big, bold letters and shoved her paper into the box.

All that was left was to decide who would draw.

"I can't trust anyone who has sided with Apollo."

"...The feeling's mutual. I won't accept a paper drawn by Miach or Takemikazuchi."

Hestia and Apollo issued their conditions in curt, sharp tones.

In that case...Both of the deities looked around the table, their gazes stopping on one god in particular.

" "Hermes" "

"Ehhh...Seriously?"

Hestia's and Apollo's voices overlapped as they said his name in unison.

Shocked by his sudden selection, Hermes forced a smile without thinking.

"My dear friend, I leave it in your hands."

"I'm counting on you, Hermes."

Apollo, who had known Hermes since their days in Tenkai, solemnly nodded. Hestia looked up at the charming deity with trusting eyes.

This happened because Hermes had always taken the stance of the go-between and had never taken sides in these situations. "Looks like I gotta," he said in a deflated voice, accepting the role thrust upon him by the other two deities. He stood from his chair and made his way around the table. Every set of eyes in the room followed him.

"Please be gentle..."

Hermes whispered to himself as he slowly lowered his hand into the box.

Hestia was on the edge of her seat, unable to breathe as Hermes withdrew one sheet of paper and unfolded it.

Hermes's face went pale as he paused, an empty smile on his face as he opened his mouth to speak.

"Castle Siege."

—*Slam!* Hestia drove both of her fists onto the table, teeth clenched.

"Fa-ha-ha-ha-hahaha! This decision was reached fair and square. This is final!"

Apollo's roar of laughter echoed throughout the chamber.

Whether on the attack or defending, this style of War Game required a large number of warriors. Most likely, Hermes drew the paper written by Apollo himself. "That's Hermes for ya." "Can't wait!" The other deities reacted to the decision, chatting amongst themselves.

Hermes looked up at the ceiling in disappointment while Hestia's face turned red, shaking in anger. Apollo, on the other hand, was in a very good mood.

"It's impossible to defend the castle with just one person. So I concede the attacking role to Hestia."

Apollo was all smiles as his words were recorded.

Hestia's molars were halfway into her tongue out of frustration as the worst possible outcome had come to pass. Her shoulders started to droop…"Excuse me, may I have the floor?" Hermes spoke up.

"Apollo, this puts Hestia at an extreme disadvantage…It's completely unfair. And I'm sure many of us here will get bored watching it."

" … "

"Therefore, I would like to propose outsiders be allowed to participate in this battle."

Hermes's proposal to allow members of other *Familias* to join the War Game in order to even the numbers made Apollo frown.

"…Hermes, I know what you're trying to do: playing something off like it's no big deal while at the same time forcing me into a corner. Don't think for a moment I'll let it happen."

Bringing up their rough relationship in the past, Apollo forced a smile of his own as he tried to stop Hermes's plan in its tracks.

Apollo declared that he wouldn't accept such a ridiculous proposition.

"All participants in the War Game must be contractually bound to a *Familia* directly involved, that's the rule. The presence of other *Familias* on the field of battle would only disgrace the gods at war."

"Well, that's not wrong."

"Also, should a top-class adventurer choose to join Hestia's side, that would put me in danger. I happen to know that Hephaistos is rather friendly with Hestia as well."

Apollo continued his response to Hermes as he looked at all of the gods around the table in turn.

Hephaistos's followers were recognized not only for their skills as blacksmiths but for their exploits on the battlefield as well. Their goddess took one look at Apollo, folded her arms, and said, "I would do no such thing."

Apollo sneered back at her, unwilling to take her at her word, when—

"My, my, Apollo. Are you frightened?"

"Freya..."

The silver-haired goddess had been sitting quietly in her chair up until now. A small smile bloomed on her lips.

"Are you afraid to fight more than one enemy at a time?"

"Don't take me for a fool..."

"So then, you don't trust your children? Is that the extent of your love for them?"

The deity with the power to control love itself took a shot at the pride of the god who loves too passionately. Apollo's jaws clenched together, strong enough to make them cry out under the pressure. Sure enough, a large group of male deities sided with Freya and voted to allow the addition of outsiders. The Denatus instantly shook with fervor.

—*So Freya is interested in Bell.*

While the silver-haired goddess's words set off alarm bells in Hestia's mind, this was not the time or the place to voice them. If the Goddess of Beauty's actions would make even the slightest difference in Bell's predicament, she had to accept them with open arms.

Perturbed by this turn of events, Apollo gave in and agreed to accept *one part* of Hermes's suggestion.

"...Fine, then. There may be one outsider. However, that outsider must belong to a *Familia* outside of Orario."

You monster! Hestia's lips formed the words, but no sound came out as her shoulders fell.

Disregarding sheer numbers, the average strength of a *Familia* located in Orario was much higher than that of the *Familias* residing outside its walls. Most of that was due to the fact that Orario's top-class adventurers were just too powerful.

There were more than likely a few *Familias* operating close to Orario with adventurers above Level 2. The difficult part was making contact with one of them and negotiating some kind of deal before the start of the War Game. It was a next-to-impossible task.

There were no objections to Apollo's conditions. The new rules were added to the War Game as is. Even Freya didn't try to interfere.

The blond-haired god looked thoroughly pleased with himself as he glanced over at a silent and despairing Hestia.

"We can't be usin' just any old castle, so let's get the Guild in on this. We can work out the date then, too. Shall we call it a day?"

Loki called an end to the Denatus. Chairs scraped on the floor as the deities made their way out. Apollo took his time, sneering at Hestia before disappearing through the exit.

Hestia could do nothing but glare back at him. She let out a long sigh as soon as he was out of sight. Soon, only Miach, Takemikazuchi, and other friends of hers remained in the chamber.

"Sorry about that, Hestia. I kind of put you in a rough spot."

"No, Hermes, it's not your fault."

Hermes was the first to approach Hestia and offered his own apology. She shook her head no. No matter how much she didn't like it, the decision had been reached using a fair draw. It was a miracle that an outsider would be allowed to participate. It was all thanks to the fact that the gods and goddesses were thirsty for a good show, and Freya, that her side was given some favoritism during the meeting.

All of the rules were in place, so Hestia made up her mind to do everything she could with the pieces she had. Her eyes burned with the desire to find a way to win.

Mentally flipping a switch, Hestia turned her attention to the other matter that needed to be resolved.

"So tell me, Hermes, did you find out where our supporter is being held?"

She hadn't been standing around doing nothing while feigning illness for the past three days. She had tapped every resource she could to find out what happened to Lilly after she was taken by *Soma Familia*, including asking Hermes for his cooperation.

"In fact, I did. That is to say, Asfi did. It looks like little Lilly was taken to Soma's storage facility."

"A wine cellar?! Not their home?"

"That's right. Soma bought a big building just for storing his wine. Guess his home wasn't big enough."

Hestia doubted his words, but Hermes was serious.

The deity continued to relay the information.

"It's located in the southeast, close to Daidaros Street. Apparently the security is pretty tight, tighter than their home. Upper-class adventurers are crawling all over the place."

"..."

"I'm sorry, but I'm going to keep my children out of this. I won't ask them to fight...What will you do?"

Hestia's head snapped up in response to Hermes's question.

"I'm going, of course."

She'd promised Bell.

That's what she told them.

A dirty magic-stone lamp cast faint light onto the stone walls.

Feeling a cold slab against her cheek, Lilly's eyes fluttered open.

She lay on her stomach, hands tied behind her back. Ignoring the aches and pains in her body, the prum girl lifted her head to look around. Nothing had changed in her dark prison cell since she was first brought here. Locked in a cage, she couldn't help but feel that she was a sorry sight to see.

She followed Zanis's orders to the letter and was brought to the *Familia*'s wine cellar. She'd been locked up in here ever since.

This floor was designed to hold the *Familia* members who had violated the rules or gotten a little bit too drunk off the divine wine. She was bound with a metallic wire strong enough to keep lower-class adventurers restrained indefinitely. Several of these compartments were used to store tools as well as serve as a makeshift jail inside the complex. Lilly was being treated as a prisoner as a punishment for the extended length of time she'd spent away from the *Familia*.

Having lost all sense of time, Lilly had no idea how many days had passed since the battle in the streets.

Lilly wiggled her body into the corner of her cell where a small dish of water had been mercifully left for her. Lifting her head off the floor, she put her lips into the liquid.

Part of her was embarrassed about her miserable condition, but she had been expecting something like this.

The days that she'd spent with Bell were special, but now she'd live her life by slurping the dirty water she was given.

Mr. Bell, Mr. Welf, Lady Hestia...

Were they okay?

That was all she thought about.

No one was guarding her outside of the prison, and stone bricks don't make the best conversation. She had no way of knowing what was going on outside. But not once did she consider trying to escape. The knowledge that she had fallen to the same level as a prisoner tore a fresh hole in her spirit.

The stone floor was cold and damp. Her body shivered as she drank.

The magic-stone lamp outside her iron cage flickered like a candle about to go out.

"..."

Ker-tap, ker-tap. Noises started coming from the end of the hallway outside her cell, the sound of someone coming down the stairwell.

Lilly willed her body off the floor and into a sitting position. Sure enough, a long shadow was growing on the other side of the bars. Zanis's shadow.

"How are you feeling, Erde?"

"...Horrible."

The man looked down at her through the bars as Lilly practically spat her answer at his feet.

He smiled ironically at her, his arms folded behind his back.

"Sorry about this. You see, the past three days have been very busy, collecting information and whatnot. I haven't had time to step away until now. Forgive me."

"...Mr. Bell is still okay? Mr. Zanis really hasn't done anything to him?"

"I'm a man of my word. I swear on the name of Lord Soma."

Lilly finally got an opportunity to ask the question that had been burning inside her for three days. While she didn't entirely trust him, she decided to believe his words for now. That settled, there was something else that she wanted to know.

"Why...does Mr. Zanis care about Lilly?"

She asked in the most serious, dry voice she could muster.

She knew he'd said that he needed her when the man took her away. She clearly remembered that moment.

Just like Kanu, the man who had left her for dead, Zanis often took money from her. Never once had he offered a helping hand. She believed him to be a man who saw her only as an insect that occasionally had vals worth taking.

"It's come to my attention that you are worth quite a lot." Zanis's smile deepened. "You can't imagine how happy I was to learn you were alive. I considered capturing you the other day when you appeared before Lord Soma by yourself...but we were already in negotiations with *Apollo Familia*. We still needed you for our justification after we had secured their payment. You played your part very well."

As a result, everything went according to plan, or so the man claimed. Lilly was vaguely aware of her gaze sharpening as she listened to more of his story.

"...Lilly is useless, not worth anything."

"No, no, I have a use for you. I realized that you were saving up a great deal of money in secret. I believe that anyone with fingers as sticky as yours deserves to be recognized for their talents.

"But above all..." He let his words hang as he pushed his glasses back up his face with one finger.

"You have a rather 'unusual' kind of Magic, do you not?"

Lilly's eyes shot open at the mention of her magic, Cinder Ella.

With the exception of Bell, Welf, and Hestia, she had never told the secret to anyone. "Lord Soma told me," said Zanis in response to the look of surprise on her face. Soma was the one who'd found that Magic in her excelia and enabled her to use it. Of course he would have known.

Lilly thought about the time frame and came to the conclusion that Zanis probably knew about her Magic before she'd feigned her death.

"Just to check...Erde, you can transform yourself into a monster, correct?"

"...What would it mean if Lilly could?"

A dark crackle of laughter escaped the man's lips.

Zanis's eyes narrowed in an evil grin as he looked down at Lilly like a wolf that just cornered its prey.

"There's a project in which I would love your participation. Nothing much, just a new business venture."

"And that is...?"

"Luring out monsters, capturing them, and selling them for profit...Isn't that simple?"

That's insane!—Lilly mocked him in her thoughts.

Even if a wild monster were tamed, said monster would only listen to the tamer. Should the tamed monster be locked inside a small

room and ordered to wait by its tamer, it would still mercilessly
attack anyone else who came near it. That's why tamed monsters
were never used for the carriages and other difficult tasks around
town.

Monsters considered humans to be their mortal enemy; there was
no way around it.

They were completely different from obedient slaves.

"Monsters have no value."

"Heh-heh...I'm not so sure."

An unmistakable twinge of greed passed through Zanis's smiling
eyes as he laughed off the girl's remark.

Anger began to take hold of Lilly. She glared daggers back up at
the man. Even her vain attempts to show respect disappeared.

"Is that the reason you brought Lilly back, back into *Soma
Familia*...The reason you got involved in the attack on Bell?"

"Yes, that was regrettable."

The tone of his voice turned up a notch, getting excited.

His mask of intelligence gone, Zanis's true character was beginning to emerge.

"I want Lord Soma's Divine Wine. I want money and women, too.
I want to taste the most exquisite dishes—I want every pleasure this
world has to offer!"

BAM! Zanis slammed his boot into one of the iron bars.

The cage had been designed to be strong enough to keep unruly
adventurers under control without breaking. But Zanis's Status was
too high for it to withstand that kind of blow, and it bent under the
impact. Lilly stared in silence, eyes trembling, at the boot-shaped
dent in the bar.

The avarice in his voice was far beyond anything Lilly had ever
heard before—much more hideous than those under the influence
of the Divine Wine, soma.

"I *love* this *Familia*. No matter how many questionable endeavors
I try my hand at, our god doesn't say a word. He's too busy with
that hobby of his to give a shit what any of us do. It's the ultimate
freedom!"

"...Lilly can see your true colors."

"Oops."

Zanis tried to cover half of his malicious smile with his hand. Taking his boot out of the bent iron bar, the man straightened his posture and continued on, business as usual.

The anger in Lilly's stomach burned brighter when she realized that this man cared nothing for Lord Soma. It went without saying that *Soma Familia*'s current condition was partly due to their god's neglect, but the man standing in front of her deserved a great deal of the blame.

Lilly's eyes flared as she looked up at the man, a thin smile on his face. That's when it happened.

"...?"

"The alarm bell...Are we under attack?"

Even the thick stone walls of this prison couldn't keep out the piercing resonance ringing out upstairs.

The hurried thuds of hundreds of footsteps sounded above their heads, mixed in with the high-pitched tone of the bell. Falling to her stomach, Lilly looked up, down, and all around for a clue as to what was going on.

"Chandra! Where are you?! Tell me what the hell is going on!"

Zanis yelled at the top of his lungs down the hall toward the staircase to the surface.

The hallway was still for a moment as the man's voice faded into nothingness. A few heartbeats later, a very annoyed-looking dwarf appeared at the base of the stairwell.

"You could go have a look fer yourself...or are those feet of yers fer decoration?"

"Enough sass. What's happening?"

"A few 'mice' got into the maze. From a few *Familias*...A young-lookin' goddess was with 'em."

A bearded dwarf with short hair and an inhospitable air about him, Chandra glanced at Lilly as he approached the prison cell.

The girl's heart jumped at the mention of a "young-looking

goddess." Zanis's eyes narrowed as he came to the same conclusion about the identity of the intruders.

"Where are they now?"

"Fightin' in the first-floor foyer."

"Is that so? In that case—we need to exterminate the pests. I'll take command."

Lilly's face turned a shade paler in fright. Frantically kicking her legs, she managed to get her body up against the bars with her hands still tied behind her back.

"You're breaking your promise?! You said that Lady Hestia wouldn't be harmed!"

"She came to attack us. It's not my fault if she gets burned by her own flame."

"Lilly will convince her to leave! Please, let Lilly talk to her…!"

"Absolutely not. I can't allow my *beloved ally* to be put in such danger. I bet they're here looking for you."

Zanis's claim that he needed to protect her was the final straw. Lilly's fury ignited.

"Lilly refuses to work with you if the promise is broken!"

"How unfortunate…"

Zanis closed his eyes and calmly walked up to the iron bars.

A sneer on his lips, he leaned down to look Lilly in the face.

"Then it can't be helped. I've got a bottle of soma with your name on it. I'll make sure you drink every last drop."

"—"

Lilly froze.

"Soma's influence should turn you into a very dependable servant…You'll be happy to comply with every order I give you."

The "absolute" that was created by Soma.

A merciless drink that turned the hearts of the people of Gekai into an endless spiral of drunken ecstasy and unbearable craving.

Not too long ago, one sip of the concoction was enough to make Lilly covet it more than life itself.

"!"

Not caring if her skull cracked, Lilly whipped her head forward in an attempt to inflict any amount of pain possible on Zanis.

Dunnnn. But the iron bars got in the way. The sound reverberated throughout the cell as her head bounced off. The man just smiled as he watched a trickle of blood work its way down the girl's face, thoroughly enjoying every second of the hatred emanating from the girl's eyes.

"Chandra, keep Erde in here for me."

"Humph…"

The dwarf didn't respond to his leader's order, only turned his back on the prison cell and sat down. Zanis only shrugged in response before disappearing from Lilly's line of sight.

She wanted to yell out, get him to come back, but no words would come out of her shaking throat. The man had been planning on breaking his promise and even intended to turn her into nothing more than his drunken pet from the start.

Dammit all! Lilly gritted her teeth and decided that now was the time to break out of her cell.

The only reason for her to stay was gone. She had to help Lady Hestia and the others escape.

"…!"

She worked her way into Chandra's blind spot and began to vigorously pull at her bindings.

But the dwarf just sat there, taking swigs of wine from the calabash strapped to his back. The wires dug deeper and deeper into her wrists as she fought. She called upon every trick she'd learned as a thief—including how to quietly trigger her magic. The claws of a werewolf grew on her fingers, allowing her to loosen the grip of the wires just enough to get her hands free.

However, she kept her hands behind her back to hide the fact that she was loose. Now all that was left was figuring out how to escape without the guard noticing.

Lilly's mind kicked into high gear as she tried to find a way to get out of the cell without drawing Chandra's attention.

But it was the dwarf who spoke up.

"Ya want out, get out."

Lilly was stunned.

Chandra didn't even bother to look at her, only wrapped his massive palm around the lock of the cell and yanked it clean off the door frame.

"Wh-why...did you go against Mr. Zanis's order?"

"I hate his guts."

The loathing in his voice was more intense than the sounds of battle raining down from upstairs.

"I came ta this city 'cause I heard I could drink the most fillin', most delicious wine around. That's how I found this *Familia*. But now it's nothin' more than that man's toy. No amount of our god's wine can satisfy me."

Lilly stared at the side of the dwarf's face as he took another swig from his calabash.

Chandra Ihit, an upper-class adventurer at Level 2, same as Zanis.

Never once had he extended a helping hand when Lilly was alone and tormented by other members of the *Familia*. At the same time, he had never joined in.

"Got a feelin' you hate him just as much as I do. So, I'm lookin' the other way."

He took another look over his shoulder. Chandra's deep brown eyes met Lilly's chestnut gaze.

Lilly decided to believe his rather simplistic desire for delicious wine and seized the opportunity.

"Thank you very much."

After a quick show of gratitude, Lilly ran out of the cell.

Being restrained and locked up for three days had taken its toll on her body. Tripping over her feet several times, Lilly ascended the stairwell to the surface as fast as she could.

"...?!"

She emerged at the end of another long stone hallway, but the sounds of battle were coming from the other side of the wall.

The clash of metal on metal, desperate yells and screams of

pain—every sound was like a knife through Lilly's heart. She couldn't stand it. Looking around to find a way through, her eyes managed to catch light coming through a window at the other end of the hallway. She wasted no time getting there.

The window was slightly higher than her head and barred off just like her cell was belowground. She jumped off the ground, grabbed the bars, and stuck her head between them.

"Mr. Welf, Miss Mikoto, too...?!"

Despite her very restricted view of the battle, Lilly saw many familiar faces engaging *Soma Familia* in combat.

The inner courtyard was wide and littered with piles of boxes, some of which stretched all the way up to the roof. However, the area was absolutely flooded with enemies. Welf and Ouka protected the front lines, Mikoto providing them with blind-side protection. Nahza and Chigusa supported them from a slight distance. Their whole group had been forced into the corner of the courtyard by the seemingly endless onslaught of *Soma Familia*.

Most of their enemies were lower-class adventurers, but their numbers were overwhelming.

"Please get out of here! Run, hurry!"

Lilly's face turned blue as she used every bit of air in her lungs, pleading with them.

There was only one reason why these kind people had come so deep into enemy territory: her. All the damage they took, every injury they sustained was her fault.

She yelled with all of her might in hopes that the battle would stop. It just so happened that Hestia was holding her head in both hands behind a storage box near the same window and heard Lilly's cries.

"Miss Supporter?!"

"Lady Hestia!"

Nahza was using one stack of boxes as cover; Hestia had been even farther behind her. Keeping her head low, Hestia went to Lilly's window.

The two were reunited, face-to-face through a hole in the thick stone wall.

"Don't worry about Lilly! Please escape now!"

"I can't do that! I'm not leaving this place until you come with us!"

"WHY?! Lilly won't cause any more trouble! Lady Hestia won't get dragged into any more bad situations without Lilly! So please...!"

The two young ladies argued back and forth, stay or go, through the iron bars of the window until Hestia screamed back:

"We're going to face Apollo in a War Game!"

"?!"

"It's a Castle Siege! Two *Familias* will collide head-to-head with their full strength!"

Lilly was lost for words as she heard Hestia's blitz of an explanation.

The thought of *Hestia Familia*, which only had one member, taking on the full force of *Apollo Familia* in a War Game was beyond belief. Bell was going to have to attack a castle by himself?

Hestia paused for a moment to catch her breath, not taking her eyes off of the flabbergasted Lilly.

"I'm doing everything I can to give Bell a chance to win!"

"Eh..."

"Right now, that boy is going through hell to prepare for the War Game! But it won't be enough! We need you! It's hopeless unless you're with us!"

—*What was that?*

They need Lilly in order to win the War Game?

She didn't believe her. Lilly always held other people back—how could she possibly be the key to victory?

Other people had used her as a doormat, taken advantage of her at every turn, and stolen many things from her. How could one prum girl trapped in this dark reality possibly be of any use?

Why was she worth saving?

Hestia was spouting nonsense.

"We can't win without you! It has to be you, no one else!"

The young girl objected.

She had never been needed before, and yet this goddess said she was.

That boy was the only one who ever helped her, who ever said that she was needed—now it was time to help him.

Hestia wanted Lilly to come to Bell's aid.

"Please, help us——help Bell!"

She ran.

She ran as if shot out of a cannon.

Hestia's pleas on replay in the back of her mind, she zipped through the dim stone corridor doors of *Soma Familia*'s storage facility with nary a sound.

It wasn't something that weak little Lilly should be able to do. How could she possibly be able to save Bell? Hestia overestimated her worth despite her divinity.

But…!

She said Lilly was needed.

She asked for Lilly's help.

She wanted Lilly, no one else.

No one had ever wanted her before, no one had needed her. But now, there was.

"Wah…!"

Her vision blurred, head feverish. Her chest felt so tight that her ribs might strangle her lungs.

There was no way to describe the onslaught of emotions that tore through her. Her only desire now was to help Hestia and those fighting for her in the courtyard. And to do that, she had to move.

With Zanis at the helm, there was only one way to stop this battle: appeal to the only person with more authority in the *Familia* than its leader, the god Soma. Lilly desperately searched through her memories of the day she was brought here and remembered seeing the deity in the building. He was also her only hope for being released from her contract with the *Familia*. She had to persuade Soma.

She used her memories to piece together a small map of the facility. There was an observation tower that overlooked the entrance to the underground holding cells. She was almost certain that the highest room of this tower belonged to Soma himself. That's where she'd find him.

Leaving clear tears in her wake, Lilly rushed to find the stairwell that would lead to her god.

"They don't know when to quit…"

Zanis watched the battle in the courtyard unfold from the roof of the storage facility.

Soma Familia's soma wine cellar was a central tower at the front with five more towers on each side encompassing an open court-yard below. His subordinates were engaging intruders who had been forced underneath one of the lookout towers in the corner of the courtyard.

Zanis chuckled to himself as the group of less than ten desperately tried to fight back. He silently applauded them for making it this far despite the overwhelming odds.

If he were able to capture the young goddess below, it would be easy to strike a profitable deal with Apollo. He was already working out the finer details in his mind as he ordered his subordinates to surround the enemy.

"…?"

Zanis watched the battle like a hawk until a flash of color caught his attention.

It was Lilly, on her way to the main tower.

What the hell is Chandra doing?! he silently snapped, his cheek twitching in agitation. But his smile returned a moment later.

"Interesting. What do you think you can do?"

Leaving one of his high-ranking subordinates in charge, Zanis took off to intercept Lilly.

Lilly ran through the vast complicated passages of the main tower. At long last, she found the stairwell leading to the second floor. Emerging from the narrow confines of the lower floors to this new open space felt extremely liberating. The lower hallways were narrow and there were many doors leading to small rooms and other passages. She could see blue sky outside the open windows and the candlestick-style magic-stone lamps were bright and clean.

Soma's room was on the third floor.

Every adventurer who should have been on guard had gone to join the fight. It was eerily quiet.

"Where do you think you're going, Erde?"

"?!"

A voice came from behind Lilly as she ran down the open corridor. *CRASH!* A window out of her line of sight was destroyed.

It was Zanis. The upper-class adventurer had broken the second-story window before jumping through. Casually stepping on shards of broken glass, the man taunted Lilly again.

—He found me!

Willing more speed out of her weak legs, Lilly zipped around the corner and out of sight.

"The stairwell in that direction only goes up?"

"?!"

Lilly suddenly felt a pressure from behind her before she was tapped on the shoulder.

The palm of Zanis's hand was all it took to send the girl crashing to the floor.

Nauseating pain overtook her as her body tumbled forward on the stone floor. Fighting through it, Lilly climbed to her feet and started running once again.

"Fu...ha-ha-ha-ha-hahahaha?! Now now, Erde, what's the rush?!"

The man's menacing laughter sounded from behind her. Lilly frowned and continued pressing onward.

A moment later, the man's boot plowed straight into her ribs.

"Agh!"

"Don't tell me, you're going to try to meet with Lord Soma? Pointless! Absolutely pointless!"

His kick sent her face-first toward the wall. Fighting to find her balance, Lilly kept moving forward.

Her thin legs reached their limit and Lilly had to thrust her hand out to the wall to catch herself.

"What makes you think that he'll listen to you? The only thing our god cares about is his wine!"

"Ighhh...!"

"Runts like you are nothing but background noise to him! No matter how much you revere him, asking for help will leave you with nothing but dismay!"

He let Lilly gain some distance before catching up and striking her again. Then he'd do some more taunting and repeat the process over and over. Be it his fists or his feet, one strike was enough to send Lilly's small body flying in any direction he wanted.

It'd become a game to him. His black shadow would overtake Lilly, then he'd decide how to hit, enjoy her squeal of pain, and then look down over her as she got up and kept going forward.

All the while he would jubilantly remark about how all her effort was for nothing.

"You're a strange one, Erde! I thought you were smarter than this! I liked that cold look in your eyes, like you hated the world and everything in it!"

In her darkest days, she had tried many times to escape the abyss only to have her connection to *Soma Familia* drag her right back in. The shell of a man who was Zanis sneered at Lilly.

However, the tears welling up in Lilly's eyes were not caused by her dark past but by the pain coursing through her body. She would never show tears of sadness again. She had already shed far too many.

Overcoming Zanis's physical and verbal attacks, Lilly pressed on. Forward, forward until she finally found the stairwell and climbed to the third floor.

There were only a few walls on this floor, making one large room with one area portioned off—Soma's private room. Lilly channeled all the strength she had left into her legs and made a break for it.

"Three, two...WHAM!"

"AGUHH!"

Zanis counted down and playfully announced his own kick, hitting Lilly right between the shoulder blades with all of his strength. The girl's body whipped through the air like a rag doll.

However, his kick sent her hurtling toward the door to the private chamber. Lilly folded her arms across her chest and used that momentum to break it open.

SLAM! Lilly tumbled into the chamber as the doors creaked on their hinges after slamming into the walls on both sides.

"..."

Soma was there.

He stood in front of the wide balcony, tending to many different kinds of plants growing in the sunlight.

He paid absolutely no attention to the sounds of battle outside the window or even to Lilly's loud entrance. The amount of water that each plant received, future ingredients for his wine, was the only thing on his mind at the moment.

"Lord Soma! Lord Soma! Please listen to what Lilly has to say!"

The deity kept his back to her as Lilly tried to peel her injury-ridden body off the stone floor.

At first, the god continued working in his slightly dirty robe despite Lilly's pleas until finally turning around with a slightly annoyed look on his face.

Zanis had entered the chamber—it was he who Soma was looking at through his long bangs.

"This is much too bothersome, Zanis. I left all trivial matters in your hands."

Ignored by her own god. Lilly was shocked.

Zanis enjoyed the look on her face to no end, gleefully chuckling under his breath. He kept his eyes on the girl and said:

"I apologize for the abruptness, Lord Soma. It appears that one Lilliluka Erde wishes to speak with you directly. Won't you lend her your ears?"

Zanis spoke with a calm and almost mocking tone, as if he knew what was about to happen.

Looking even more perturbed, Soma shifted his gaze down toward Lilly.

The girl managed to force her aching body into a kneeling position.

"I beg you, Lord Soma. Please bring an end to the battle taking place outside—please save Lady Hestia and those fighting alongside her! Please, please...!"

Soma's cheek twitched as if Lilly's voice had hurt his ears. He slowly squared his shoulders in front of her.

He opened his mouth to speak, but the expression on his face showed that he believed it to be a waste of time.

"What good are the words of a child who succumbs to wine so... easily?"

"—"

Lilly fell silent after hearing Soma's monotone words. A cold chill swept through her veins.

But it was the look in his eyes that did it, made Lilly realize the truth.

Soma was disappointed. Disappointed in his own followers, disappointed in the world of Gekai.

The Divine Wine, soma, had caused *Soma Familia* to collapse from within. Just as he said before, the children succumbed to the power of the drink he was giving them as a reward. They soon began fighting amongst themselves for more, became selfish beyond belief.

From the god Soma's point of view, all he did was reward them with delicious wine for their services. But rather than thank him, they turned on one another for more drunken pleasure. He had become disillusioned by their primitive reaction to his more refined methods.

—Soma harbored no ill will. He had no urge to inflict pain. At this point, he had no interest in any followers like Lilly at all. He was completely detached.

The divine being who'd had enough of the crude people of Gekai continued to produce soma and reward the children who made it possible for him to focus on his craft.

"The words of children who succumb are...irrelevant."

Soma's eyes, black as ink, were finally pointed in Lilly's direction. However, Lilly's face was not reflected in them, only empty disappointment.

Lilly remained still, unable to find any words in the face of her god's cold stare. It was Soma who moved first.

He took a bottle of white wine off one of the shelves built into the wall of his chamber.

Lilly watched in dumbfounded silence as Soma took a glass from a different shelf and said to her:

"If you can say the same thing after drinking this, I'll listen."

—She couldn't breathe.

The deity poured the wine into the glass, its cool yet sweet aroma filling the room. He held the glass out to her. Lilly looked at her own reflection on the surface of the white liquid.

Divine Wine.

Her throat clenched. Sweat poured down her face. The glass nearly slipped from her grasp as she tried to take it with both hands.

Memories of the dark days when she was under the influence of soma's power rampaged through her mind. She looked back up at Soma, shoulders shaking in fright. The god's face was void of emotion as he watched her from behind his bangs.

Zanis watched all of these events unfold, smiling as if he'd seen this coming.

"Ah, aah…!"

Lilly stood up on unstable legs.

Her breaths very shallow and staggered, she took another look at the glass in her hands.

She had no choice. In order to save Hestia, in order to finally break her ties with this *Familia*, she had no choice but to drink it.

Lilly brought the glass to her lips, hands shaking and palms clammy.

This wine had once turned Lilly into little more than a monster.

It had stolen her life from her, caused all of her problems.

Under the watchful eyes of Soma and Zanis, Lilly willed her mouth open and drank it down.

"—"

The world warped around her in the blink of an eye.

A boundless drunken euphoria enveloped her. The bliss was intense enough to bend her consciousness.

Tink! The glass fell out of her hands, hit the floor, and rolled away.

Her arms and legs quivered. She couldn't keep standing and fell to her knees like a puppet whose strings had just been cut.

Acute warmth filled her cheeks as her eyes went out of focus... Lilly giggled.

"—a...haa."

The flavor of the most delicious wine in existence made her heart melt.

Soma watched the girl's spirit disappear and turned his back to her without a second thought. Lilly's ears stopped picking up the sounds around her, with only one exception: Zanis's bloodcurdling laughter.

Overwhelming contentment spread throughout her body. Memories flashed before her eyes before disappearing again. Nothing inside this room mattered to her, was worth seeing. Even her purpose for being here, why she was so determined to drink the soma, felt like nothing more than a passing thought. Everything that made Lilly who she was evaporated in an instant.

She saw everything in the room with a white hue.

Her body, mind, and spirit were warm.

Down, down, down she went.

Then, just as the white was about to embrace her, she saw something.

A boy, a smiling boy.

"—"

Her craving intensified. The animal that demanded soma within her was on the brink of taking over.

But amid all the white around her, she saw how the boy smiled when he saved her that day.

It remained deep within her soul even after everything else had been erased. His smile stayed with her.

"..."

A single tear slowly rolled down her cheek.

Her slack, open mouth smiled for a moment before weakening again. Lilly's head started to rise.

The warmth of the boy's smile had awakened her heart, filled her with new emotion, and caused a tear to be shed.

Lilly had returned.

".......Please."

Not much sound escaped her lips, but it was enough to stop Soma in his tracks.

A moment later, he spun around with vigor.

His long bangs swung out of the way, revealing his black eyes. Lilly's trembling figure reflected within them.

"...Stop it, please."

Her words were getting clearer.

Soma and Zanis looked on in disbelief.

Lilly made eye contact with Soma.

"Lilly's begging you—stop the fight!"

Her words were unchanged as even more tears trickled down her face.

"Wha..."

She didn't know if that sound came from Soma or from Zanis.

She persevered. Lilly held off the effects of soma.

Countless people had fallen under its spell, becoming little more than savages in the process. And yet this little, fragile girl had not.

It didn't matter that her Status was low, that her body was weak. She defeated soma with sheer willpower.

"Lilly wants to save those people!"

She yelled her most earnest desire as loud as she could.

She sounded no different from a sobbing child.

Bonds with her allies had been forged in the fire, and she was a Phoenix emerging from the flame, guided by them.

"Lilly knows, even without any gods telling her, Lilly knows that she was born for this moment!"

It was highly unlikely that Lilly would ever forget.

Even if she died and was reborn many times, even in the deepest pits of hell...

Lilly would never forget the smile on that boy's face.

"Every mistake Lilly has made was in preparation for this day!"

The warmth of the hands that reached out for her, the kindness of his embrace.

She'd never forget the smile of the one who rescued her.

The image that had been seared into her very soul would never fade.

"This time, it's Lilly's turn to save him!"

Bell's smiling face and warmth filling every corner of her mind, Lilly yelled once again.

She had not forgotten all of the mistakes she made and the gray areas of her past. Those memories gave her the strength to keep shouting.

"Please, bring an end to this battle!"

Lilly's voice was loud enough to be heard outside the tower.

"......"

Soma stood, unblinking eyes locked on the girl.

Gods did not grow or feel distress of any kind. It was hard to comprehend what just unfolded.

Seeing a person of Gekai change right before his eyes for the first time left Soma speechless.

"No way...?!"

Zanis sensed danger in the expression on his god's face.

His feeling of invincibility gone, he pleaded with the deity.

"Lord Soma, you mustn't listen to her! Our *Familia* is under attack—!"

"Quiet, Zanis."

Soma turned away without so much as a glance in his direction.

Zanis fell silent, face twitching as he knew that there was no chance for a counterargument. Soma made eye contact with Lilly once again.

His ink-colored eyes clearly reflected the young girl's gaze. Then he walked toward the end of his chamber and opened the large window.

The empty wine bottle still in his hand, Soma stepped out onto the balcony. He could see the battle raging in the courtyard beneath him. Standing next to the railing, he raised the bottle high above his head and threw it into the courtyard.

Spinning end over end, the bottle sent flares of sunlight flashing all over the battle before crashing into the middle of it.

The shattering sound made all members of *Soma Familia* come to a halt.

Every head in the courtyard turned toward the balcony, waiting with bated breath.

"Stop fighting."

Soma looked down on the rest of his followers as he made his declaration.

Soma Familia's members were blindsided by a direct order from a god who had never shown any interest in anything other than his hobby before. No one even considered going against it.

Ignoring Zanis's commands, they listened to a higher power and put down their weapons.

"Soma moved on his own…?!"

An uneasy silence descended over the battlefield. Zanis couldn't believe what he was seeing, his eyes glued to Soma's back. He shook his head from side to side, refusing to accept what was happening. His mask of refined intelligence broken once again, muscles all over his body began twitching nervously.

He rocked on the balls of his feet—*BANG!* The main doors at the base of the tower had been kicked in. His shoulders flexed.

Knowing that the intruders would soon arrive, Zanis looked around the room in a panic. His eyes narrowed as soon as he saw Lilly on the floor.

"Damn you! At least give me the pleasure of slicing you open before—!"

Zanis jumped toward Lilly like a beast capturing its prey.

The man had only seen her as possible profit; he captured her out of greed. His avarice made him torment her and now she was too physically weak to run away or defend herself. She was the reason why his perfect world had come crumbling down. Withdrawing a rapier from the hilt on his belt, he smiled to himself, believing that she should be punished for what she had done to him. He reached out with his left hand.

However, just before his fingers reached her collar...

An arrow was fired at his chest.

"?!"

Zanis barely managed to avoid the attack that came from outside the window.

The arrow buried itself in the wall behind him, making a small web of cracks in the stone. Zanis looked back outside in shock.

There, standing on top of the nearest lookout tower, was a Chienthrope wielding a longbow.

"I'm ready! Fire away!"

"You don't have to tell me."

Zanis heard the voice of a young man and saw a flash of gold as the Chienthrope took a new arrow from him and promptly slid it over her bow. She pulled this new golden arrow back, took aim, and fired in one swift motion. But she wasn't targeting Zanis. The arrow plunged deep into the stone wall next to the balcony.

The man had only a moment to feel surprise—he saw a very thick wire attached to the end of the arrow. His surprise turned to disbelief.

As if to confirm his wildest fear, a young man with red hair and a greatsword over his shoulder ran across the wire toward him.

"?!"

The red-haired man kept his balance, pulling off some very acrobatic moves as he raced across the wire bridge connecting the two towers. The wire held firm under his weight. Sword balanced against his shoulder, Welf quickly reached the balcony, jumped over the silent Soma's head, and landed just in front of the window.

The smith's black jacket unfurled behind him as he stepped inside the chamber and came to a stop in front of Zanis and Lilly, both wearing looks of astonishment.

"It's time for you to come back, Li'l E."

"Mr. Welf..."

"We're gettin' outta here."

Welf set his jaw, smiling at Lilly before turning to Zanis.

"I've come to collect this one. I've got a partner who is waiting for her."

"Rrrgh—*Like hell you are!*" Zanis charged without hesitation, brandishing his weapon high in the air. Welf held his own weapon in his right hand and rushed to meet him.

A rapier against a greatsword in a duel.

The two blades collided in a shower of sparks, the opening bell.

"Come at me, smithy!"

With the ferocity of a madman, Zanis stepped into a forward slash before whipping his blade around and into an upward slice.

All he managed to do was take a small slice out of Welf's black jacket. It was an attack that would have skewered any lower-class adventurer, but the young man dodged it handily and used that momentum to slash his own sword diagonally upward at his opponent. Zanis was unable to step into his next attack.

Both Level 2 adventurers, they matched each other blow for blow, and their movements gradually picked up speed.

The shock waves generated on impact were strong enough to make Lilly lean backward as the echoes of their clashing blades filled the chamber. Welf deflected Zanis's spinning strikes and high kicks with the armor on his left arm, not allowing any attack to hit home.

Zanis used his rage to fuel an onslaught of slashes.

Welf held his ground, using his sword like a highly mobile shield despite its weight.

Considering the weapons the combatants were using, Zanis held several advantages. He knew speed was on his side and he could use it to overpower his red-haired adversary. Welf calmly read his movements and narrowed his eyes.

"Tough to bully an upper-class adventurer."

Welf's back, shoulders, and arms all flared to life at the same moment.

The massive blade whipped around the young man's body in a powerful arc. It met Zanis's downward slash head-on, overpowered it, and sent the rapier flying.

"—"

Time stood still for Zanis.

His techniques and maneuvers were useless in a contest of strength—a "warrior smith" like Welf wasn't about to fall for the same tricks that adventurers who relied on a high Status would overlook.

Lilly heard Welf's black jacket swish as the man closed the distance between him and his unnaturally rigid opponent.

Seeing everything in slow motion, Zanis tried to jump out of the way but watched helplessly as Welf's left foot collided with his chest.

Then he saw the blade flash as it spun around.

Welf had flipped his hold on the weapon so that the blunt edge was facing his enemy.

"Sloppy. That weapon of yours is crying."

With that said, Welf drove the entire blade forward in a rising arc aimed right for his opponent's head.

"GHEEEEE—!"

The blow struck Zanis with such precision that it split his glasses right down the middle before launching him backward.

Momentum carried his body straight into the wall, the man's scream of pain cut short by the impact.

Zanis fell to the stone floor like a bag of potatoes. The blunt edge of Welf's greatsword left a thick red line down the center of the motionless man's face. What was left of his glasses lay on the floor beside him.

"That should do it," said Welf as he returned the blade into its sheath at his shoulder and looked down at the white eyes of his unconscious foe.

"Ya really got it done...Won't have ta drink as much tonight."

"...Mr. Chandra?"

Soma Familia's Chandra had appeared in the chamber and stood behind Lilly, commenting on Welf's victory in the duel against Zanis.

The usual unfriendly expression on his face, Chandra turned the man's body over and fitted him with sturdy handcuffs that even upper-class adventurers would have difficulty breaking.

"He was stealin' soma, usin' it for his own profit. Deserves some time in the slammer."

"What happens now...?"

"I'll make sure ya get no trouble. It's all up to our god after that... Maybe now our voices will reach 'im."

Apparently, Zanis had hijacked the *Familia* using Soma's name and punished anyone who dared say anything against him. Now that his treachery had been exposed right in front of Soma's eyes, Chandra felt that the new era was about to begin.

The god himself was still out on the balcony, assessing the damage to his chamber—but his gaze always came back to Lilly.

"Are you all right, Supporter?"

"Lady Hestia..."

It wasn't long before Hestia and the other adventurers led by Mikoto and Ouka made it to the third floor of the main tower.

Truly grateful to Lilly for all of her hard work, the two made eye contact for a moment before Hestia walked over to talk with Soma.

"I would like to make a deal for the supporter, Lilliluka Erde, to join my *Familia*."

"..."

Soma stood silently on the balcony as Hestia stopped just before the open window, neither of them blinking.

"Please accept this knife as collateral for payment."

"L-Lady Hestia, that's—?!"

"It's all right. I've talked with Bell."

Lilly gasped when she saw the goddess hold out the Hestia Knife and hand it to Soma.

"This knife is a very expensive weapon. If we should lose the War Game, you can get a lot of money for it."

" "
...

"But if we win, I'll buy it back from you with our reward money...
I'll make Apollo pay for it in full. Once you have the money, I'll take
my knife back."

She explained that should *Hestia Familia* win the War Game, she
was planning to take a large sum of money from Apollo. Soma held
the weapon in his hands, running his thumb down the Ἥφαιστος
logo engraved into its sheath. He looked up at her.

"Indeed, this is more than satisfactory. She may leave my *Familia*."
His lips barely moved as he spoke to Hestia.

Welf, Mikoto's group, and Chandra stood quietly in the doorway
as Soma once again cast his gaze upon Lilly.

Badly injured and still bleeding, she managed to make eye contact. The two stayed still until finally an answer was heard.

Soma shifted his posture to face Hestia head-on and nodded, saying, "I accept."

Hestia, Soma, and Lilly went to the second floor of the main tower,
leaving everyone else behind.

All three of them entered a small room that had no windows.
There was no need to worry about any information being exposed to
prying eyes or ears. The three set to work in the dim light.

Lilly sat on a chair, pulled off her shirt, and exposed the Status on
her back. Soma made a small cut on his finger and ran it across the
hieroglyphs, the ichor in his blood making the markings glow.

His finger made quick movements across her skin, as if unscram-
bling a puzzle. The hieroglyphs glowed brighter with each passing
moment until every mark started to blink.

Now it was Hestia's turn. Pricking her finger, she added her own
ichor to the mix, gradually erasing several hieroglyphs as their color
faded. The markings indicating Soma's contract disappeared from
sight as Hestia's name and symbols engraved themselves above Lilly's name at the top of her Status.

Conversion.

A ceremony that allowed a child of Gekai to be transferred from one *Familia* to another.

A ring of light worked its way around the girl's Status, making it look like an epitaph in the dimly lit room. The markings for *Hestia Familia* shined brightly at the top.

From this moment onward, Lilly was now one of Hestia's followers.

"Lady Hestia...is this really okay? Using Mr. Bell's precious weapon in a trade for Lilly...?"

"Perfectly fine. Everything will be back to normal if we win the War Game. And we need you for a chance at winning. No problem at all."

Lilly's nerves had settled down considerably now that the ceremony was complete and she was fully dressed. However, the collateral made her uneasy. Despite that, Hestia puffed out her chest and said everything would take care of itself.

"Trust me, no problem. Now let's go."

"Y-yes..."

Lilly's eyes kept jumping from one deity to the other. Hestia placed both hands on the girl's shoulders and guided her out the door.

"...Hest...ia?"

"That's me. What is it?"

Hestia closed the door behind Lilly and turned to face the god she was meeting for the first time. Soma wasn't even sure how to pronounce her name.

Only the two of them remained inside the small room.

"...Did that girl actually receive my Blessing?"

Even now, he remembered the strong look in her eyes. And yet Soma had no memory of her. Hestia was the only one he could ask.

"Without a doubt, she is one of the children who suffered due to your selfish discontent. She's a little girl who grew strong as a result of your neglect."

Hestia took it a step further, telling him to imagine how much Lilly had suffered after being abandoned by her own god.

The blue in her eyes became intense orbs in the dark as Soma was unable to respond to her accusations.

"You should think long and hard about why she changed, the meaning behind it."

Hestia had her hand on the door handle as she wrapped up her lecture with that and left the room.

Soma was left alone with his thoughts.

He stood there quietly, Hestia's words running through his mind.

Hestia and Lilly rejoined the others at the base of the main tower and exited *Soma Familia*'s wine storage facility.

Miach had been waiting one block away in case of an emergency. Joining the group of more than ten, they all ran together through the backstreets.

"Lilly's very sorry for the trouble she's caused...Thank you."

"It's all right..."

"Think nothing of it, Miss Lilly."

"That's right...It's nice to see you again."

Nahza, Mikoto, and Chigusa—her eyes hidden behind her bangs as usual—responded to Lilly's apology.

Welf and the massive Ouka, holding a greatsword and a battle-ax over their respective shoulders, were having their own conversation next to the girls.

"That wire, did you bring it with you?"

"Nah, found it in that tower. Thought it might be useful so I picked it up."

The sun seemed to be smiling down at them as everyone celebrated the success of their mission.

Lilly moved closer to Hestia.

"But, Lady Hestia, Lilly doesn't understand how she can make a difference in the War Game by herself..."

Hestia smiled at her confusion and then looked back at the path ahead.

"Not quite."

Hestia shook her head as Miach spoke up.

"You won't be alone."

All they had done was increase Lilly's confusion. She tilted her head in their direction and Miach smiled back at her. Feeling another gaze on her, Lilly looked the other way to see Mikoto with a very determined look in her eyes.

Even Welf was smiling at her.

The group reached a four-way intersection.

"See ya later, Li'l E."

"...Lady Hestia, we'll take our leave here."

Welf peeled away from the group and went down the right path. Ouka, Mikoto, and Chigusa led their group down the road to the left.

Miach, Nahza, and Lilly watched them leave from the center of the intersection when a sudden breeze swept through the backstreet.

Hestia held her black hair out of her eyes with her right hand.

She looked up at the blue sky, where the wind was blowing in a new direction.

"Hmmm—gahhh..."

Takemikazuchi groaned.

He was pacing back and forth inside his own room in an old building designed to house multiple families, built on the side of a narrow street. The god lived alongside his six-member *Familia*; this building was their home. Arms folded in front of his chest, he wore a troubled expression.

"The War Game...I want to assist Hestia, but..."

The Guild had already announced the details of the War Game. Takemikazuchi knew full well that it was a castle-assault style and everything that entailed.

His good friend needed military might and he wanted to help her. But he was in a quandary.

Should he transfer one of his own followers to *Hestia Familia* with a conversion ceremony, or not?

"It's impossible for Miach. He only has one and his *Familia* will collapse should she leave..."

Without any members, *Miach Familia* would be disbanded by default and revoked by the Guild. Miach would lose the reputation and recognition he'd worked so hard to gain. There was also the possibility that he could be forced to sell his home in order to pay off current debts.

Takemikazuchi completed yet another lap around his room, mumbling to himself as he considered every possibility.

"Even among my own children, the only two who could compete with Apollo's children are Ouka and Mikoto. Chigusa and the others would only weigh them down..."

Chigusa and the other three were still Level 1 adventurers. Only Ouka and Mikoto made sense.

"Ouka is the captain. I can't send him..."

Which would mean the only option was Mikoto—

"Would she be willing to go to a different *Familia*...?"

Mikoto loved *Takemikazuchi Familia* too much.

She'd always had a strong sense of justice and an urge to do what was right. Was she capable of betraying Ouka and her allies? There was also the mission given to them by their hometown in the Far East to consider—Mikoto would never abandon it.

"I'll just have to find some way to convince her...After all, I'm the one who wants to help Hestia...But wait, if I did that...Ghaaaaaa...!" Takemikazuchi stopped in the middle of the room and scratched his head with both hands as he groaned at the ceiling.

Caught up in a fit of very ungodlike indecision, he almost didn't hear the knock outside his door.

"Lord Takemikazuchi, it is Mikoto...May I speak with you?"

"Ohh!" The deity jumped on the spot in surprise at the girl's visit.

Mikoto must've interpreted his surprise as an affirmative and opened the door with a slight bow.

"...? Has something happened, my lord?"

"N-no. Everything's fine. Nothing to worry about."

The girl tilted her head as Takemikazuchi hastily straightened his hair.

Forcing an air of calm, the deity closed his mouth and looked upon his follower. She, too, wore a distressed expression similar to his own.

Her silky black hair was tied back in its usual style. However, she carried herself without her normal level of confidence, shoulders uncharacteristically drooping. Even her violet-colored eyes were trembling as she met his gaze.

The two stood face-to-face in silence.

The tension building, Takemikazuchi gave in and opened his mouth.

"—Mi-Mikoto."

"—Lord Takemikazuchi!"

The two spoke at exactly the same moment.

Both paused, saying, "My apologies, go ahead," and, "Speak first, I insist," back and forth.

Mikoto was the first to accept the offer.

She took a deep breath and made eye contact with her god.

A moment later, she threw herself to the floor at his feet. *Takemikazuchi Familia*'s special technique, the prostrate bow.

"Please forgive me!"

"Wh-what?"

Takemikazuchi was taken aback by Mikoto's sudden plea, her hands, knees, and forehead on the floorboards.

She didn't look up, only raised her voice to be heard clearly despite speaking directly into the floor.

"Please allow me to go assist Sir Bell!"

Takemikazuchi's eyes shot open.

"Despite nearly causing his death, I haven't done anything to atone for my actions! I also made a promise; we made a promise to help each other!"

Mikoto's body shook as her voice took on a more serious tone.

"This is my chance. I can't abandon him in his time of need…"

The look of surprise gradually left Takemikazuchi's face as he watched his follower bare her soul to him.

His shoulders relaxed, arms hung loosely at his sides.

So we both came to the same conclusion...

He had been with her for so long and yet he had failed to anticipate how she would react to the situation. It was shameful.

Takemikazuchi grimaced before a genuine smile grew on his lips.

"Ahhh..." He let out a long sigh. Mikoto's shoulders shook once again.

The deity looked back up at the ceiling and mumbled under his breath.

"One year...Such a long time."

Mikoto looked up with a start.

It was a rule among *Familias*: A child who had been transferred to a different group with Conversion could not be transferred again for at least one year.

Mikoto immediately understood what his words meant. Her face grew brighter and brighter by the second.

"But it will pass. Learn as much as you can from Hestia's children and come back stronger than ever."

"—Yes, sir!"

Mikoto brought her fist and palm together as Takemikazuchi smiled upon her.

Lastly, she gave him her *Familia* emblem for him to hold on to until she returned.

Mikoto Yamato had joined *Hestia Familia*.

"..."

Hephaistos sat at her desk, examining a dagger in her hands.

She was visiting one of her *Familia*'s shops located on Northwest Main. Rather than working in her private office, she was focusing on this particular weapon.

There was a story behind its maker. A rather difficult child, his skills had been rather unpolished at the time he forged this dagger, but passion for his craft alone gave him incredible potential—that "passion" could be felt by anyone who used the blade.

Hephaistos herself could feel it coursing through her when there came a knock at her door.

"Enter."

She opened one of the desk drawers at her side, returned the blade to its sheath, and placed it inside.

Closing the drawer, Hephaistos looked up to see the silhouette of a young man in a black jacket standing in the doorway: Welf.

"What is it?"

Rather than answering, Welf walked up to the other side of her desk.

Showing no hesitation, he came as close as the desk would allow and met her gaze.

"I've come to say good-bye."

He closed his eyes and continued.

"I'm joining *Hestia Familia*. Please allow it."

This was not a request for permission, but a demonstration of strong will and determination.

Leaving *Hephaistos Familia* would mean that he would be forbidden to use her logo as a smith. Despite attaining his dream of becoming a High Smith at long last, he was willing to forfeit the right to engrave ""Ηφαιστος" into any of his work and leave Hephaistos behind.

"And what makes you think I would allow such a selfish decision?"

"Because the goddess I know and love would scold me if I didn't."

Welf responded without missing a beat.

Hephaistos displayed no emotion, her face stoic as she asked another question.

"Didn't you want to overcome the blood in your veins, create a weapon that exceeds magic swords?"

"As long as I have a hammer, metal, and a good flame, I can forge weapons anywhere. The one who taught me that was you."

Even apart from her, he would work to spread his name and reach a higher plateau.

He answered her without any hesitation.

"And what was it that inspired this intense enthusiasm?"

Welf raised his chin and grinned.

"Friendship."

At long last, a smile appeared on Hephaistos's lips.

"Then I accept."

Hephaistos stood up from her desk and walked toward a long line of hammers on a shelf behind her.

She selected one that was the same crimson color as her hair and eyes, and picked it up.

She approached Welf, still standing in front of her desk, and handed the hammer to him.

"A parting gift. Use it well."

Hephaistos said her good-bye by bestowing him with the soul of a smith. Welf grinned from ear to ear and graciously accepted it with a bow.

"Thank you for everything."

The fabric in his black jacket ruffled as he turned to leave.

Leaving the goddess he revered behind, Welf confidently strode out of the office.

Welf Crozzo had joined *Hestia Familia*.

"...So that's how it is. Would you mind helping out again?"

Hermes kept a close eye on her face as he asked.

They were a little ways away from The Benevolent Mistress, inside of the wooden building where the employees lived. The elf Lyu sighed at Hermes's forced smile.

"God Hermes, are you mistaking me for some handmaiden?"

"Sorry! But do this for Syr. Bell needs your help!"

"I would like you to refrain from using Syr as a bargaining chip..."

"S-sorry, Lyu..."

"Syr, your apology is unnecessary."

Three figures huddled together inside Lyu's private quarters: Hermes, Syr, and Lyu herself.

There were only a few days left before the War Game. Hermes had lobbied to allow outside involvement for just this reason, to request her help.

The condition: said outsider must belong to a *Familia* outside Orario—must have the blessing of a deity from outside its walls. Since Lyu's goddess, Astria, had not been in the city for some time, there would be no objection to her participation.

Hermes felt slightly guilty for being directly responsible for forcing Bell and Hestia into the extremely disadvantageous Castle Siege and this was his way to, kindly, offer his assistance.

"Should I fight, there is a high probability that my identity will be revealed during the War Game."

"Don't worry about that. I'll convince everyone that you came from someplace on the other side of the mountains before the fight begins. No one will believe you're a waitress at a bar once I'm through with them."

Several events in the recent past had landed a hooded adventurer on the Guild's blacklist—there were still many who resented the "Gale Wind." Hermes already had a plan to help keep her and those living with her anonymous and safe.

Lyu sighed. "Mother Mia will scold me again."

Either way, the ex-adventurer couldn't abandon Bell to his fate. The elf agreed to Hermes's request.

The room itself had very little decoration. Lyu walked a few paces to the corner and grabbed a knapsack along with a wooden sword.

"I'll handle the paperwork with the Guild. It'd make it a lot easier to jump through the hoops if I had your *Familia*'s emblem. Do you still have it?"

"I do. Be sure not to misplace it."

"It'll never leave my sight," he said with a nod as he took the badge engraved with the sword of justice and wings from her.

Lastly, Lyu approached Syr, who was holding out her cape.

"Do your best, Lyu. I'll come up with something to say to Mama."

"You have my gratitude, Syr."

Lifting the string of her knapsack over her shoulder, Lyu flashed a soft smile.

Hermes and Syr saw her out of the building and watched as she disappeared into the night.

Lyu Lyon had joined the War Game.

Blades clashed in vicious flurries.

A silver flash, lashing forward at tremendous speed, was blocked head-on by the downward swing of a crimson blade. Knife and saber collided under the reddish glow of dusk, their wielders' blond and white hair flowing in the breeze.

The boy's long shadow passed over the stone surface, slamming into the girl's shadow over and over. Each time he was thrown backward and each time he charged again.

Their brutal training was taking place on top of the city wall around Orario.

"You learned how to...react without seeing..."

"D-do you really think so...?"

It was already the fifth day.

Aiz lowered her saber, signaling a brief pause in the action. Bell took a deep breath and took a look at his own body. What was left of the evening sunlight illuminated all the cuts, scrapes, bruises, and dried blood that littered his skin. Completely covered in sweat, the boy's condition showed just how intense these training sessions had been.

After gathering supplies and setting up a small camp, Bell had committed himself fully to sparring with Aiz. They started just before the sun rose each morning and continued until the stars lit up the night, dramatically increasing the length and intensity of their sessions from the last time they were here. They ate meals together and slept at the same time; neither of them had gone into the city even once. A dirty pot and the remains of a fire sat on top of the path just inside the chest-high stone wall, a guardrail on the city side of the wall. Three water bottles and three sleeping bags also sat at the base of the guardrail.

Bell had his eyes focused on the cuts crisscrossing his arm when suddenly—*whoosh!* A saber came at them from his blind spot without warning. His instantaneous reflexes brought his weapon into the path of the oncoming blade, deflecting it before he jumped backward.

Looking very rabbitlike, standing with his left shoulder higher than his right, he stood at the ready for the next attack. Aiz seemed very satisfied as she nodded over and over.

"Guess who's back!"

Bell and Aiz turned to face the owner of the cheerful voice.

Emerging from the doorway of the tower that housed a stairwell connecting to the city street was Tiona with a very large backpack over her shoulder. She skipped her way up to them and plopped the backpack at their feet on top of the stone path with a light "Hup!"

"Picked up a ton of meat and fish! Bread and water, too!"

"Thanks, Tiona..."

"Sure thing! Ah, Argonaut, these blades work okay for you? I bought about five of them."

"Y-yes, thank you very much...s-sorry for the trouble."

Bell stood next to Aiz, scared stiff, as Tiona withdrew the weapons from her backpack one after another.

Tiona had been supplying the two of them with food and items for the past five days. It was thanks to her that Bell and Aiz could focus solely on training.

Bell couldn't shake the feeling that he was building up quite a large debt to the always smiling, happy-go-lucky Amazonian girl Tiona. With the exception of Ushiwakamaru, he couldn't count how many blades had snapped in half or been damaged beyond repair during their combat sessions.

"Well, I heard quite a bit around town. First off, the War Game is four days from now."

"Four days..."

"Yep. It's gonna happen outside of Orario, so we have to think about travel time...I'd say you've got maybe two more days left."

Tiona continued to relay the information she had collected that day.

Her update complete, Bell looked out over the guardrail and across the beautiful cityscape.

"Exactly one week...Goddess."

The five days of training plus two more would make one week. Bell said a quick thank-you to his goddess, who had managed to deliver on her promise.

Bell's ruby-red eyes smiled; he knew that somewhere in this gorgeous city, Hestia was smiling back.

"Also, you'll never guess what was posted on the Guild's bulletin board. *Hestia Familia* has some new members."

"Eh?!"

"Soma, Takemikazuchi, Hephaistos...Looks like all three of them transferred someone."

Bell fought to contain his surprise and delight until Tiona was finished talking. The two girls watched as his face lit up and tears of happiness rolled down his face.

Hestia had saved Lilly, plus Welf and Mikoto were coming to help him. He didn't need to know the details because he already understood. The black void that had been eating away at him finally lifted, a new warmth flooding his soul.

Bell stretched out his arms. He looked at Aiz and Tiona with renewed strength and willpower, feeling stronger than ever.

"Another round, please!"

The look in his eyes made Aiz and Tiona smile.

"Yes..."

"Try to keep up!"

The two girls went on the offensive beneath the red sky.

Three sets of legs dashed about with blinding speed.

Aiz, Tiona, and Bell mixed attack with counterattack in the very limited space on top of the city wall. Two daggers, one silver saber, and two insanely wide swords struck with jolting impacts, sparks lighting up the twilight sky.

"Ehsaa!"

Bell did everything he could to keep the attacks of two top-class adventurers at bay. All the while he couldn't take his eyes off the massive blades in the Amazonian girl's grasp. Despite learning how to defend against attacks from the side, knowing that another blade exactly like that edge of death was following right behind it sent shivers up his spine.

He knew immediately that the weapons were order made. Seeing her wield the thick, heavy blades as if they were nothing more than shortswords was the stuff of nightmares. The Amazonian girl smiled, practically laughing as she danced her way into every strike.

Rather than trying to defend against such an attack head-on, Bell chose to get out of the way.

Jumping back to avoid the first and to his right to dodge the second, the boy managed to get clear. However, Tiona charged forward even though her weapons weren't poised to strike.

"Hup!" Spinning in midair, Tiona unleashed a kick right into Bell's face.

"Geh?!"

The wheat-colored skin of her bare foot buried itself in his cheek, sending the boy flying backward. Hitting the stone floor and bouncing several times, Bell rolled to a merciful stop.

"Try not to use potions. If you take one after every hit, you'll run out really quick. Better to kick the habit."

"I-I'll try..."

Tiona approached him with her swords over her shoulders, looking like wings from hell. Aiz wasn't too far behind. Tiona gave him some advice as soon as she saw the boy's hand reach for his leg holster.

"That's the thing about being an adventurer. We still have to be able to move even after the crap's been beaten out of us!"

Although she was holding back, the kick of a top-class adventurer to the face can inflict immense damage. Bell slowly nodded as feeling returned to his head. Just as she'd suggested, it would be a good idea to learn how to fight well when not at full strength. The lesson had literally been beaten into him.

Gritting his teeth, Bell climbed to his feet as Tiona looked on with a satisfied smile.

"My turn."

"?!"

The session started back up. Bell was forced to use both knives in order to repel Aiz's direct attack.

Not only that, Tiona circled around to his blind side and continued her assault. Two of the greatest sword wielders in Orario weren't holding back any techniques on top of the city wall. Bell desperately intercepted each strike, deflecting the blades out of his ever-changing path. However, he hadn't come here to learn how to defend. He had to find a window for counterattack.

Fighting off his own cowardice, Bell surprised both of them by charging forward.

"!"

Aiz's posture slipped ever so slightly.

Her feet and shoulders weren't on the same page, moving in different directions as Bell came in for his attack. Bell couldn't believe his luck. The girl's feminine frame was trying to retreat, leaving her side wide open. This was his chance and he didn't hesitate.

A golden opportunity—score a hit on the Kenki.

Taking aim for her ribs, Bell took a quick step forward and thrust the dagger in his left hand toward his opponent.

"Hm."

"—"

But Aiz spun her body around like a top, armor a blur.

Taking advantage of his outstretched position, Aiz easily dodged the weapon and traded places with Bell. Now directly behind him, she whipped her saber forward with less than her full strength and nailed the light armor protecting the boy's back.

"BuuHA?!"

"You dove for the opening..." said Aiz as Bell landed flat on his chest on top of the stone floor.

Only then did Bell realize it was a trap. She had baited and set it for the rabbit as though to demonstrate the prowess of a skilled hunter. Bell's head hit the stone surface in disappointment.

The boy pushed off the stone floor into a sitting position. Aiz crouched down in front of him and continued her lesson.

"Monsters and people fight differently..."

"Y-yes."

"Monsters always attack head-on, aiming to kill...but people read each other, change their strategy."

Unlike monsters that used their full power all the time, people used techniques and experience to gain the upper hand in a fight. This was especially true of the combatants of similar strength and skill.

"People become easier to read when they see a window. Just like now."

"...!"

"Guard is lowest when the final blow is near...That's what I was taught."

People became overconfident when they saw victory within their grasp, which meant they neglected to cover their blind side.

That was especially true during a duel.

Bell looked up, making eye contact with Aiz as she finished her impassioned explanation.

"Your best opportunity lies in the moment you've been cornered. Don't forget."

Bell carved her words into his very soul.

Aiz held out her hand. Bell nodded and took it.

She pulled him to his feet.

"How about some more?"

"Yeah..."

"Yes!"

Both combatants nodded at Tiona's invitation and their battle heated up once more.

Lessons of the top-class adventurers fresh in his mind, Bell continued his training long into the night.

In order to grasp victory or to rescue a friend.

Each of the people caught in the whirlpool was taking their own actions for their own reasons and coming together.

The city of Orario might appear calm on the surface, but excitement was building underneath its placid exterior.

The War Game was fast approaching. With each passing day, the average citizens of the city discussed it on the streets, at their workplaces, and over a jug of ale at their favorite bar. The number of adventurers going into the Dungeon fell dramatically, forcing disappointed shops to close early. No one seemed to want to do anything else. Even the children seemed to sense that something was different. Many of them gathered in city parks wielding toy swords and staging their own games.

Orario was quietly, but undoubtedly, boiling over with excitement. It grew more intense as the War Game drew nearer.

Most of all, the ones closest to the people caught in the whirlpool had their own reactions as they watched the preparations unfold.

The curtain of night fell over the city, revealing a star-filled sky.

The white tower in the middle of it all looked over the city as magic-stone lamps gradually lit up its surroundings.

"Lady Freya, it has been completed as ordered...Lady Freya?"

In the highest room of Babel Tower.

While Freya heard the words of her follower, Ottar, she didn't respond in the slightest.

The man looked upon her in concerned confusion as she ran her fingers through her long, gorgeous silver hair. The goddess sat in her usual chair facing the window, watching something outside with so much intensity that Ottar was afraid the glass would melt.

"...Fu-fu."

Her silver eyes were being drawn to a fierce battle taking place atop the city wall.

The blond-haired, golden-eyed knight along with the warrior wielding massive twin blades fought two-on-one against a white-haired boy. Two female, one male, three different spirits "glowed" as they clashed. Freya was enjoying every second of it.

She felt no pity for the boy whenever he was launched into the air by the Amazonian girl or cut down by the long-haired human.

This was because every time the boy got up, his soul shone brighter. It was as if this training ground was a forge and the girls were eliminating all impurities, like a smith prepping metal. They were drawing out his soul's clear glow.

It was that glow that originally drew Freya to him and would hold her interest until the end of time. Every hit the boy took added a new sparkle. The goddess sat there, completely transfixed.

"...Are you certain that we can allow Apollo's followers to go through with this?"

Ottar tried once again to draw her attention away from the city wall.

Her eyes stayed put, but she used one thin finger to pull a lock of her silver hair behind her ear and grinned.

"I thought about crushing them for trying something so stupid but...No."

Her silver eyes narrowed as they followed the boy charging back into battle against the human girl and the Amazon.

"No goddess worthy of her divinity wouldn't want to see how this turns out."

Her cheeks pulled back into a full smile as she looked down from her spot among the stars.

Unable to rest, the stars twinkled brightly through the night.

Even at this late hour, the Guild headquarters was alive with activity. Clerks holding stacks of papers, receptionists carrying boxes upon boxes, and employees with no time to sit down were busily working in every corner of the Pantheon decorated with white pillars.

With the War Game only four days away, there was enough work to be done to make their eyes spin.

"No more! I'm gonna *die* right here!"

"Misha, you're too heavy..."

The human receptionist Misha set yet another stack of papers down on her desk before drifting over to Eina and collapsing onto her back amid the commotion. The half-elf looked at her old friend with tired eyes as she spoke again.

"Eina, wha'cha doing...?"

"Making a plan to keep people away from the war zone...Advising, I guess."

A small mountain range of paperwork encircled her desk, each pile bearing Eina's handwriting.

"Do not enter" was written in big, bold letters—all referring to the Shreme Castle ruins located southeast of Orario.

"Shreme Castle...Didn't that group of robbers decide to move in a while back?"

"Yes. *Ganesha Familia* accepted our request to remove them ahead of time. A few quests have also been issued to help them out...It's a good opportunity to catch them while we can."

Eina continued writing while she responded to Misha's question.

Misha could hear the constrained energy in Eina's voice despite her weak tone. The girl looked at the side of Eina's face before standing up and bringing her chair next to her.

"Eina...are you worried about Bell?"

"...Worried? How could I not be worried..."

Her expression became cloudy as her emerald eyes trembled.

Her head drooped as she brought her hand to her chest. One of the adventurers assigned to her, practically a little brother at this point, was caught up in a battle between *Familias*. And now he'd been forced into a War Game in which it wasn't uncommon for participants to die. Needles pierced her heart just by visualizing the boy's innocent smile—would she never see it again?

If she could convince him to run away or maybe assist him, maybe she wouldn't be in this much pain.

"But I'm an employee of the Guild…I can't interfere in any way."

However, the situation had progressed so far that one half-elf couldn't have any influence at all. Eina knew that she was powerless in the face of the forces at work.

That fact had soaked in completely. The tone in Eina's voice bordered on despair. She felt utterly useless.

"We——ll, you know…You could root for him?"

Misha could tell that her friend was upset and tried to cheer her up.

Eina looked up at her.

"Root…?"

"Yep. 'Go for it!' and stuff like that? I'm sure that if he had your support, he'd do the best he could to win, right?"

Eina looked at Misha's childish smile for a few moments.

Finally, she stood up and walked over to the window at the end of the office.

The moon shone brightly down on her as she looked up at the night sky.

"…Go for it."

Eina whispered to the moonlight.

"Ahh, how patient must I be…"

The deity's eyes slowly closed in a dark room illuminated by moonlight.

Sitting on an ornate throne made of gold, Apollo brought a glass of wine to his lips.

The manor that he called home was tranquil, a good distance away from the noisy areas of the city. Tonight, it was much quieter than usual. The bulk of his *Familia* had already left to prepare the castle ruins that would become their battlefield. As it was their role in this battle to defend it, *Apollo Familia* had a lot of work to do.

If his only goal was to steal Bell away from Hestia, it would've been easy enough to continue their assault and capture him even without the cooperation of *Soma Familia*. If he had done so, the boy would already be his.

However, Apollo was partial to the idea of a War Game.

There was a very clear difference between a conflict fought on the streets and the War Game. Crushing a foe in battle to obtain an objective left everyone involved with a sour taste in their mouths. On the other hand, should he obtain his prize by following a set of rules, then he would be able to bask in the glory of victory and enjoy the spoils. It was, after all, a game. He would not allow the Guild or any other group to profit from this situation. With victory, he would gain the authority to take the follower of the enemy god—if Hestia refused to perform a Conversion, it was impossible to make Bell *his own* both in name and reality.

Above all, the other gods would not be satisfied by such a quick turn of events. Apollo had gathered the support of many gods who were starving for some "entertainment" in order to capture Bell. He owed them the show they were dying to see.

He also wanted some amusement.

A war of gods fought by mortals. By far the most delicious flavor of Gekai, it was enjoyed by all gods.

There was no greater excitement than to be able to move their followers like pieces on a board game without any kind of interference.

Those were Apollo's true feelings—the influence of his own divinity.

His wants and desires swirling within him, the god wearing a crown of laurels looked toward the sky.

"Oh, my beloved Bell Cranell...will there ever come a day I can embrace you in my own arms?"

He wasn't sure when he first knew of the boy—most likely when the rumors of a new record holder came to light. Apollo had a habit of indulging in everything new and fresh. Picturing the events that would soon unfold brought him great joy. His very body shook with anticipation.

—Ahh, Bell!

—No, my Belly-boy!

—You won't get away!

He could see the boy now, a tear in his eye. But something else was swelling up within him. This heat surging through his chest was proof of his love. Apollo's craving for the boy was on the verge of driving him insane. His thin, compact build and rabbitlike features with white hair and young, red eyes that were untainted by the truths of this world—everything.

Apollo's cheeks flushed like those of a drunken man.

"…If our love is to grow, Hestia, you will only get in the way. Once he is mine, I will drive you out of this city—no, out of Gekai entirely."

Coming back to reality, Apollo opened his eyes and looked up at the stars.

The moonlight reflected off his suddenly serious eyes as his lips curled upward.

"I'm counting on you, my cute little children…"

A low laugh resonated from his room beneath the calming moonbeams.

Click. A few moments later, both hands of his clock joined him in looking skyward.

The time drew near.

The city was filled with a morning chill just before sunrise.

The streets were lined with silent and motionless shops. Shutters were closed over windows and doors; it was unbelievable how lifeless the city seemed. The city wall cast a tall shadow over the buildings, the streets covered in shade.

Two figures ran quickly through East Main Street toward the brightening horizon through the unnaturally quiet morning air.

"You have to hurry, Bell! The caravan's about to leave!"

"Right behind you!"

Hestia and Bell ran through what was left of the morning fog. Their destination was the East Gate. They kept talking as they ran.

"They already know you're coming. There's a spot for you on one of their horse-drawn carts. Get off at a town called Agris, it's pretty close to the old castle! Guild employees will give you instructions from there, so pay attention!"

"Will do!"

The War Game would start the day after tomorrow.

Bell had finished training with Aiz and Tiona and had received a Status update from Hestia. Now all that was left was to travel to the battlefield. It would take a day to get there, so arrangements had been made for Bell to travel with the caravan of merchants for most of the trip.

He was dressed in light but strong traveler's clothes with a cloak around his shoulders. Everything else he needed was in a bag over his shoulder, the drawstring held tight in his grasp.

"Everyone else is already there, so meet up with them in town! Also, here's your travel permit issued by the Guild—show it to the gatekeepers and the leader of the caravan!"

Orario was set up so that it was relatively easy to enter the city but extraordinarily difficult to exit. An individual needed several documents approved by the Guild before they were allowed to pass. Bell took the signed sheets of paper identifying him as a War Game participant from Hestia and said a quick "Thank you."

At last, they arrived at the heavily fortified East Gate. Somehow, it looked a lot smaller to Bell now than it did when he'd passed through a few months ago. Members of the caravan were already here, talking excitedly amongst themselves. Bell and Hestia worked their way through lines of horse-drawn carts and large storage containers on wheels toward the head of the caravan before stopping in front of the first gate.

"...I'll be waiting right here for your glorious return."

"...See you then, Goddess!"

Hestia smiled at him. Bell smiled back.

That's when Hestia jumped onto his chest, wrapped her arms around him, and squeezed with all her might. Bell's body tensed out of embarrassment, but he didn't try to escape. He couldn't. Hestia ignored all the commotion around them and enjoyed the warmth emanating from his chest as long as she could. Bell's face turned beet red as her arms worked higher, going above his shoulders and around his neck as she started to pull back. Meeting his gaze, she opened her mouth into a bright, gentle smile as she said, "Now go."

Bell took a step back, a shy smile on his face. Wiping his hot cheeks with his free hand, the boy turned and ran to the front of the caravan. "Wait for me!" he yelled to the front and took off into the maze of carts. The caravan leader was talking with one of the gatekeepers. Both looked up as the boy approached, holding out his paperwork for them to see.

The gatekeeper was an adventurer—probably someone who had accepted an assignment from the Guild. Two Guild employees emerged from the gate office from behind him and took Bell's paperwork. Reading it over, they nodded to each other. The caravan leader pointed to a cart in the line and told Bell to take a seat.

The horse-drawn cart that Bell climbed into was more spacious than he thought. It had a roof as well as windows on each side. A few people—some travelers, merchants, and a hired guard—were already on board. Each of them had a very distinct look about him or her, a few in light armor and others in comfortable clothes.

"...Hey, you there. Aren't you the Little Rookie from *Hestia Familia*?"

"Ah, yeah, that's me."

"Thought so! On your way to the War Game, huh? Give 'em hell!"

Bell took a seat at the back corner of the cart next to a rather friendly animal person who immediately recognized him and started a conversation. The smiling young man had the aura of a drifter and a bushy tail wagging cheerfully behind him. The tension in the cart dissipated as the other passengers came over to break the ice.

"Those guys are rough, but give it your best shot!" "This is our tradition, we have some snacks before every trip!" "How 'bout this?!"

Each of them came over with handfuls of nougat, dried fruit, and tarts. Surrounded by kind and welcoming people, Bell couldn't help but smile, nod his head, and manage to say, "Th-thank you..." He didn't really like sweet foods but he didn't want to reject their goodwill and decided to eat everything he was offered.

The cart lurched beneath him as it started to move forward.

The cries of many horses cut through the morning air. The East Gate was open; the caravan started to move.

Bell felt every bump in the road through his wooden seat when suddenly—

"—Bell!"

He heard someone call his name.

He leaned over to look out the window and saw Syr running right beside the cart.

"Syr?! What are you doing? It's dangerous!"

Bell lifted the window open and called out to her.

She was out of uniform, wearing a cape over her usual clothes and running as hard as she could to keep up with the cart. She thrust her right hand toward the window.

"Take this...!"

"Huh?"

Something golden glinted from within her outstretched hand. Bell reached outside out of reflex.

She gave him an amulet. It was in the shape of a golden teardrop, a jewel in its center. It had to be an accessory that granted the wearer some kind of power. Bell raised his eyes from the item in his hand to look at Syr.

"It was a thank-you gift to the bar from an adventurer a while ago...A good-luck charm!"

Bell's eyes shot open as he listened to her explanation.

"Do your best! And please come back to our bar!"

The cart picked up speed and Syr couldn't stay beside it, almost tripping a few times.

"I-I'll have a lunch ready for you! I'll be waiting!"

The girl's cheeks blushed a light pink. Bell couldn't help but smile.

He leaned out the window and waved good-bye as she fell farther and farther behind. She came to a stop, put her hands together in front of her chest, and watched the cart disappear through the East Gate.

"..."

Bell returned to his seat and looked again at the shining amulet in his hand.

Sliding the thin chain around his neck, he tucked the amulet under his shirt.

—Win.

—Win and come back.

The faces of everyone he'd met in Orario flooded his mind as he swore to see them again. Squeezing the amulet with his right hand through his shirt, the boy suddenly realized he was smiling.

He looked outside the window as he felt every bump in the road shake his seat.

The sun was just peeking over the mountains in the distance.

Bell shielded his eyes from the bright morning light.

The ruins of Shreme Castle.

Standing in a field void of trees or hills, the castle had been built in ancient times as the first line of defense. Completed before Babel Tower served as a "lid" over the Dungeon, it was used to stop the advance of monsters that emerged from the hole to attack nearby towns and villages. Many castles just like this one were built relatively close to Orario for just this reason. Most of them had been destroyed or collapsed after centuries of neglect, but Shreme was used as a staging point by the kingdom of Rakia in the war almost one thousand years ago. Several of its main towers were damaged, but the castle's main wall and other defenses were very much intact. Now it had been selected to host the War Game.

The outer wall stood an impressive ten meders high, even higher in the areas where the towers once stood. The wall itself was more than thick enough to withstand the strongest of attacks—perhaps with the exception of a powerful blast of magical energy. Even top-class adventurers would have difficulty cracking it. The castle was located in an open area and very easy to attack. This wall was the main reason it had lasted so long.

"Get some clay over here. Reinforce everything that's fixable."

Night had already fallen, the moon shining brightly overhead. *Apollo Familia* was hard at work making their final preparations for the War Game that would begin in a few short hours.

One hundred ten of them had arrived three days ago and had been working around the clock to make sure the castle was ready. That was almost all of their *Familia*. Working in groups, they had made repairs to the castle itself as well as set up hidden stores of spare weapons and items in various places inside the structure.

"Humph, pointless...Why bother?"

The fortress's main tower stood above the wreckage of the other towers in the very middle of the castle. Hyacinthus watched the other members of his *Familia* work from the top floor.

The time limit for the Castle Siege War Game had been set at three days. *Apollo Familia* would win if either he was alive after that time or if the enemy general—without a doubt, Bell Cranell—was defeated in combat.

It was their role as the defender to make sure the castle was ready, but it was obvious that they could win without all this fuss. Hyacinthus had heard that the enemy ranks had increased as of late, but they would face no more than five combatants. What point was there in having more than one hundred warriors repair a castle when they could crush their enemy outright in a head-to-head battle?

"Lord Apollo, why? Why a castle siege...?"

Hyacinthus was very confident that he could win without all of these favorable conditions. Did his god not trust him and the rest of the *Familia*? The man was feeling underappreciated, as though Apollo had forgotten what he was capable of.

The disgruntled man walked away from the window and took a seat on the throne at the back of the room. The throne itself had been there when *Apollo Familia* first arrived, but they had made a few modifications. Very comfortable, the back of the ornate chair was an enlarged version of the *Familia* emblem, a burning sun with a bow and arrow. The rest of the room was decorated with artwork and had been cleaned spotless because Hyacinthus had ordered everyone under his command to make the space pleasing to the eye.

Leaning back on his throne, Hyacinthus begrudgingly laughed through his nose.

"What a boring game…"

"—Yeah, Hyacinthus would say something like that…"

The short-haired woman, Daphne, grumbled to herself as she looked up at the throne room from her post on top of the solid castle wall.

Rakia had made a few strange modifications when they occupied the castle. Their god must have really enjoyed showing off because the main tower had many complex designs built onto its surface. It had a luxurious feel to it despite being the castle's last line of defense. Seeing her own *Familia*'s emblem attached to the top of the main tower made her want to laugh out of sheer absurdity. That hunk of metal was so big it could probably be seen from Orario.

Daphne sighed to herself and continued with her own assignment. It was her job to motivate the other members to hurry up with the wall repairs. The hard part was that most of them shared Hyacinthus's opinion of the upcoming battle and couldn't wait to watch it unfold. Despite having more than one hundred workers under her command, making sure that there were no weak points in any of the walls of the castle had been frustrating beyond belief.

Also, *Ganesha Familia* had arrived at Shreme a few days before Daphne and the rest of *Apollo Familia* in order to clear out the group of thieves and marauders that had been living in the castle. Since they'd been ordered not to damage the castle in any way before the War Game, the eviction had been carried out by digging holes under the wall and catching the squatters by surprise. They'd captured every single one of the criminals in less than a day. Daphne made sure that they filled in the holes before returning to Orario.

"Daph…"

"Cassandra?"

Magic-stone lamps lit up the top of the wall in place of the torches of old. Cassandra approached Daphne, nervously calling out to her.

She came to a stop in front of one of the lamps, only half of her face illuminated in the light. She embraced her own trembling body with both arms as if she were afraid it would fall apart.

"It's no good…We need to get far away from here."

"Huh?"

"The castle, the castle will fall…"

Daphne's expression turned to annoyance as she listened to the nonsense coming out of Cassandra's mouth.

"Another dream? You know it's too late to do that now. Get it together."

"Please, please, Daph, believe me…!"

Cassandra desperately begged her friend to take her prophetic dream seriously even though there was no way it could come to pass.

Daphne ignored her and continued inspecting the wall, but Cassandra was much more persistent than usual. The long-haired girl's shoulders slumped as if she were debating whether or not to keep trying, before freezing on the spot.

Surprised by the sudden silence, Daphne turned around to face her. Cassandra's face was pale and gaunt as if she were moments away from death, eyes transfixed on a spot below them.

"No, we can't let it in. There's still time; it mustn't come inside…"

A small line of horse-drawn carts carrying the last of their supplies was approaching the wall just outside the gate. The girl watched, horrified, as the gate opened.

"Heey! Wait up, will you?!"

Luan yelled at the top of his lungs, chasing the last cart as he watched the castle gate start to close.

The driver of the last cart ordered his horse to gallop to cover the distance, forcing the prum into an all-out sprint just to make it inside the gate before it shut completely. A dull thud sounded a moment after he slid between the massive iron blocks.

"Why, why would you shut it when I'm *still out there?*" the small prum man asked in a pathetic, panting voice to the exceptionally large animal person standing at the gate controls.

The large man just laughed. "Hee-hee, so you were there, Luan. You're so tiny! Couldn't see you at all."

The lower-class adventurer known as Luan Espel looked much younger than his age, almost like a child. Other members of *Apollo Familia* treated him like the bottom of the barrel because of the combination of his rank and his appearance. That was why he'd been assigned to bring supplies to the castle at this late hour.

Prums were often discriminated against because of their short size and unintimidating presence. "Come on," he retorted as other members of the *Familia* joined in the laughter.

"...Quite a large shipment you brought in."

"Three days' worth of weapons and rations. Best to be ready, you know?"

The animal person laughed again, saying that he was being a little too careful considering their opponent. The large man didn't even look at Luan as he started to inspect the shipment.

In moments, other members of the *Familia* were unloading box after box from the carts and taking them to the castle's already well-stocked storage rooms.

"Aaah..."

Cassandra watched it all unfold from her spot on top of the wall.

Daphne had never seen her friend like this. Although she felt something was wrong with the girl, Daphne turned to leave.

"Wake up, we have work to do!"

Cassandra watched Daphne's back pass in and out of the light of the magic-stone lamps. She took a deep breath and let out a long, heavy sigh.

Then she whispered in a shaking voice like a prophet who'd seen the end of the world.

"It's too late…The Trojan horse is inside the wall."

"What took you?"

"Sorry."

"Are your preparations in order?"

"Yes. My goddess upgraded my Status already."

"Great. Now, here's the knife I promised you. The cutting edge is way better than the first one, I guarantee it."

"Thanks."

"Sir Welf…What about *those*?"

"Ready and waiting. Didn't have much time, so I could only finish two."

"…Um, Welf, are you sure this is all right?"

"Yeah…I've stopped compromising allies for pride."

"?"

"Never mind…Yo, you can take these now. But I warn you, they were very rushed so I'm not sure about their full power or how long they'll last. Don't waste them."

"Understood."

"Well, then…Everything is going according to Lady Hestia's plan."

"Yep. And tomorrow—we take down the castle."

"Yes…Let's win this."

Several voices went unheard under the cover of night.

War Game versus *Apollo Familia*. Classification—Castle Siege.

Victory condition: defeat the enemy general.

The long night was almost over.

CHAPTER 5 OUR WAR GAME

© Suzuhito Yasuda

The city was bustling.

The War Game everyone had been waiting for was finally here. There was an atmosphere of energy and passion not normally seen within the city wall.

Every bar opened early; workers at restaurants and food stands stood ready for the incoming onslaught. The reason this game had received so much attention was due to a few gods demanding that posters be hung all around the city as advertisement. These deities wanted as big of an audience as possible to build tension. The posters themselves were dominated by *Apollo Familia*'s burning sun and bow emblem. Since *Hestia Familia* didn't have any kind of symbol, a white rabbit had been painted into the corner.

Almost no adventurers even considered prowling the Dungeon on a day like today. Instead, they were jam-packed into their favorite bars with even more adventurers coming in every moment. As for the workers and citizens who managed to get the day off, they made their way to Central Park. Not a single one could contain their anticipation as they waited with bated breath for the opening bell.

"Test—test, one...two...Ahem. Gooood morning and good day! I'll be providing blow-by-blow analysis of today's events, the chattering fireball himself, *Ganesha Familia*'s Ibly Archer! Some of you may already know me as the Fire Inferno Flame. Remember that name!"

A temporary stage had been built in the front garden of the Guild headquarters. A dark-skinned man claiming to be a commentator for the War Game stood at the front of it with a magic-stone voice magnifier clutched in his hand. A large crowd had already gathered in front of him.

"Joining me today to add his own insights into the festivities is none other than Lord Ganesha himself. Lord Ganesha, a word, please!"

"—I am Ganesha!"

"Yes, thank you very much for that!"

A god wearing a large elephant mask climbed up to the stage at Ibly's prompt and struck a pose as he yelled at the top of his lungs. The god received a round of applause.

The Guild had worked with the merchants to turn this match into a holiday of sorts. Many people from other cities around the world would come to Orario to watch the battle, meaning more customers for the merchants. At the same time, the Guild used this opportunity to advertise Orario's image and draw more adventurers into the city.

But, of course, no one was looking forward to the War Game more than the gods.

"Woah, they're livin' it up out there!" said Loki with her face plastered to the window, looking down at the crowds.

Many deities had gathered on the thirtieth floor of Babel Tower. All of them were on the edge of their seats, overflowing with excitement. Hestia and Apollo, the two gods at "war" in this battle, were among them.

The ones not present in Babel Tower had chosen to watch the game in the bars among the people or with their followers from the comfort of their own homes.

"Lord Hermes…are you certain I am allowed here?"

"Yeah, don't worry about it. The only ones who would care aren't here anyway."

One very uncomfortable mortal woman was among the gods and goddesses inside the wide confines of the thirtieth floor. But Hermes laughed off Asfi's concern. She tried her best to make herself as small as possible as Hermes reached inside the front of his shirt.

"…Should be about time."

The damaged pocket watch he withdrew showed three minutes until noon.

Hermes lifted his chin toward the ceiling and took a deep breath.

"Well then, Uranus, we need your permission to use our 'power.'"

Hermes's powerful words echoed around the chamber. They were answered a moment later.

"—Granted."

The response spread throughout the city, the heavy syllables heard everywhere from the Guild headquarters to the bars to the crowd gathered in Central Park.

Deities all around Orario cracked their knuckles and set to work.

"_____!"

Mortals far and wide gasped in amazement as hundreds of "windows" appeared all over the city.

The gods were only allowed to use one specific type of Arcanum—the "Divine Mirror." Any god or goddess could use their power of clairvoyance to show what was happening at a different location at any time. It went without saying that it was to increase their enjoyment of life on Gekai.

This way, every deity in Orario could watch the War Game alongside their children, even though the battle would take place far from the city.

"Now that the mirrors are in place, I'll set the stage once again! Today's War Game is a Castle Siege battle between *Hestia Familia* and *Apollo Familia*! Both factions' combatants are already in place and waiting for the signal to begin!"

Magic "windows" of various sizes filled the bars, the Guild's front garden, and Central Park. Each of the circles hovered in midair, showing different angles of the castle, *Apollo Familia's* oversize emblem, and the surrounding prairie. A roar of excitement erupted from the crowd as Ibly raised the voice enhancer back to his lips and started giving background information.

"All bets in—?! Won't accept any once things get under way!"

Ibly's voice echoed through all the bars in the city. The owner of one such establishment raised his voice to cut through the din of his patrons as well as the commentary. Merchants and adventurers alike were laying odds and making bets on the outcome of the War Game between *Hestia Familia* and *Apollo Familia*. Their favorite ale in one hand and large amounts of money in the other, the patrons made their bets and took their seats in front of one of the many "windows."

"Team Apollo and Team Hestia, outnumbered almost twenty-five-to-one..."

"But the odds are twenty-to-one in *Apollo Familia's* favor...Lower than I thought it'd be. What idiot bet on the little guys?"

Two adventurers sitting side by side at the table looked over the information they were given at the betting counter. Team Apollo was the overwhelming favorite and betting on them should be the smart thing to do, and yet there were some who had put money on Team Hestia.

"Gotta be those deities over there..."

Gods and goddesses were known for going after the jackpot rather than making safe bets. The two adventurers looked at three in particular with blank stares as the deities became more and more enthralled with the mirror in front of them. "Uahh!" "It's time, it's time!" "Come on, lucky rabbit!" Tickets in hand, all three were shaking with anticipation and praying with all their might.

Meanwhile, at another bar...

"What's this? Borin' as hell if everyone bets on Apollo..."

Another bookie looked around the bar, a bit disappointed. At that moment, a human adventurer walked up to the grumbling dwarf and set down a large bag of coins on the counter.

"—one hundred thousand on the rabbit!"

"Whoa, whoa, whoa!"

"Are you serious? Hit your head or something, Mord?!"

"Anyone else willin' to ride *Hestia Familia*'s luck? Aha-ha-ha!"

The excitement level in the bar doubled as the tough-looking human placed his bet. The man smirked at his companions' looks of disbelief—for he had once attacked Bell with seething hatred on the eighteenth floor of the Dungeon. Mord sat down on the nearest chair, folded his arms, and thrust his chin forward with unwavering confidence.

Every corner of the city had been whipped into a frenzy. Their furor would boil over at this rate.

"I hope you've said your last good-byes to Bell Cranell?"

"..."

High above the whirlwind of tension and street level, Apollo approached Hestia inside Babel Tower.

The god's hair had been perfectly set for the occasion. He approached Hestia's seat with a smug grin plastered on his lips.

Hestia didn't respond, only turned her back to him with her eyes glued on her own personal mirror.

"My, my," said Apollo with a shrug. He started back to his own chair, calm and extremely self-assured.

"We are just seconds from noon!"

The commentator's voice filled the thirtieth floor.

Waves of cheers ran through the garden in front of the Guild headquarters.

"Here we go..."

"Yes..."

Eina and Misha talked quietly as both girls watched the large Divine Mirror floating behind the stage.

The eyes of adventurers, bar owners and staff, merchants, and gods all focused on the images inside of those "windows."

And then...

"The War Game—has begun!"

Loud, deep bells rang out to signal the start of the battle.

At that moment, inside the castle ruins...

The ringing of the bells that signaled the start of the War Game wafted through the windows from afar.

Compared to the thrilling atmosphere in Orario, the battlefield itself was underwhelming.

Since this was a castle siege, the time limit had been set at three days. The vast majority of *Apollo Familia* believed that their opponent's strategy would be to wait until the last day when their concentration would be lowest because they didn't have the numbers to attack the castle head-on. As long as they kept their eye out for any probing attacks, they should be fine right where they were.

The mood inside the castle walls was relaxed.

"Hey, Luan. Go take a lookout post."

"Wha......Why do I have to?!"

Luan the prum's superior ordered him to leave the meticulously cleaned and decorated inner sanctum. "You've got good eyesight, right? Since you can't fight, go do some laps around the wall like you did yesterday. Might as well be useful while you can."

The castle itself was deceptively wide, big enough that one hundred people would have difficulty maintaining a constant visual around its entire circumference. They would always be shorthanded somewhere. Luan didn't want to leave the comfort of the inner castle, but he begrudgingly obeyed the order.

He could hear the others laughing at him as he closed the door to the chamber and climbed the stairwell leading to the top of the wall.

"Hey, Luan. What are you doing here?"

"...Looking out."

Two archers on patrol spotted him immediately when the prum emerged on the north edge of the wall. The two chuckled to themselves as soon as they heard those two words, knowing exactly what had happened. Luan turned his back on the two of them and looked out at the northern plains.

There was almost nothing out there. Sure, there was a random tree or boulder here and there, but no place for anyone to hide. The grasslands spread out from the north and out to the east. A river ran past the castle to the south and the edge of a forest was visible to the west. A gust of wind passed through the prum's hair as he narrowed his eyes toward the north, when he heard voices coming from behind.

"Magic is really the only threat."

"What're you worried about? This big guy's got a few presents for anyone who shows up."

An animal person stroked his longbow and bared his fangs in a long grin, completely brushing off the other archer's warning.

The power and range of all Magic was determined by the length of its trigger spell. The defensive wall was so thick and sturdy that only a really powerful type of Magic would have any hope of doing damage, let alone cracking it. Magic with a long trigger spell would be the enemy's only option.

Any mage who wandered within range of their bows would be

greeted by a rain of arrows long before they could finish reciting their trigger spell. The animal person wasn't worried in the slightest.

"Keh," coughed Luan in disgust, knowing that the two of them had everything covered. He had been given a pointless errand.

It was then—

The prum's eyes caught something moving in the distance.

Someone walking through the grassland to the north straight toward the wall…A vaguely human figure completely covered by a cloak.

"H-hey!"

"What's that…?"

It was very strange attire for anyone to be wearing. Most likely, the person had a hooded cape on underneath a long cloak that hid everything above the ankle. The archers took notice of the hooded figure as well.

There was no doubt it was an enemy. However, the enemy warrior was alone and not casting a spell. The hooded figure was walking slowly but surely in their direction. Luan's eyes opened in fright at the mysterious warrior's aura of calm, which smoldered like hot coals buried under ash. The breeze made the figure's cloak sway, the flapping sounds reaching the sentry's ears.

All three of them stood, watching the figure come within one hundred meders of the castle wall.

The hooded figure chose that moment to make its move.

Whoosh! It spread its arms out wide, outer cloak flying open, exposing what was hidden underneath.

Two thin, feminine hands held on to scarlet and violet blades—twin magic swords.

"Huh?"

Luan's eyes became as round as the full moon as he watched the two long blades swing forward at the same time.

An overwhelming mass of magical energy was reflected in the eyes of everyone present on the north edge of the wall.

"Wh-what—wassat?!"

Utter chaos broke out within the castle the second that the magical energy hit the wall.

Screams echoed through the stone hallways as more impacts rocked the structure. Those who emerged from the main tower were immediately lost for words when they saw what had happened to their precious wall.

The breeze took enough of the clouds of smoke away for them to see that a piece of the wall *was missing*.

"U-unbelievable! It's them—they're attacking!"

Luan, who had been knocked off the top of the wall by the first blast, climbed back up. The same people who ordered him to "look out" a few moments ago brushed up to him in a panic.

"How many?!"

"J-just one!"

The prum's superiors squinted at him, as if trying to make sure they'd heard him right. Luan, himself, was visibly shaken by fear. Still, he forced trembling words out of his mouth.

"C-could that be...N-no, it has to be! Crozzo's Magic Swords! They're going to break down the wall with legendary weapons?!"

A collective gasp emerged from the small group of people who had gathered around him. They knew he spoke the truth.

There was no other magic sword in this wide world that could possibly break through a wall of that size in one hit. Since this wasn't cast Magic, Luan's suggestion was the only explanation that made sense. Any doubts they had instantly disappeared.

Almost on cue, the voices of lookouts on top of the main tower rang out. "One enemy?!" "Attacking with magic swords!" Words that started as a call to arms ended in screams laced with fear and surprise.

"The castle'll be blown sky high at this rate!"

Luan yelled in sheer terror, his comrades frozen on the spot. Suddenly, *KA-BOOM!* The remains of the lookout tower only a few meders away took a direct hit. Large chunks of stone flew in every direction, showering the archers and onlookers with debris.

"UWWAAAAAHHHHHHHHH!" Luan shrieked at the top of

his lungs. Leaving his allies behind, he rushed back into the relative safety of the inner sanctum.

"To think, there would come a day when I would use *this* magic sword…"

The hooded figure, Lyu, whispered to herself as she swung both blades toward the castle.

One flick of the scarlet blade sent a giant, crackling fireball hurtling toward the target. Bringing down the violet blade brought forth a thick column of electricity that snaked its way to the castle in less than a heartbeat. Both were powerful enough to pierce the outer layer of rock, sending bits and pieces high into the air.

The weapons had been prepared by Welf in less than a week. Crozzo Magic Swords.

The blades created by men with cursed blood were so powerful that they overpowered opponents to the point a counterattack was impossible. The kingdom of Rakia had demonstrated their power during the war, and the world had not forgotten the devastation they wrought.

There were even stories about how they'd used Crozzo Magic Swords to turn a previously impenetrable fortress into a pile of rubble in one night. The ultimate siege weapon.

"You cannot hit me from there."

Archers hastily brought down a rain of arrows from the still-intact parts of the wall. However, Lyu had no trouble dodging them. Every time she spun, she swung one of the magic swords forward, engulfing the archers and magic users with flaming explosions and electrical eruptions. The sound was deafening even from this distance as even more of the castle wall came crumbling to the ground.

Its structural integrity gone, the heavily damaged northern wall started to tilt inward. Hurling a series of magical attacks stronger than regular Magic, Lyu worked her way east as she continued the assault. It wasn't long before the castle's eastern wall began to crumble under their power.

"If you insist on doing nothing, I'll bring the castle down on top of you."

Her sky-blue eyes narrowed from beneath her hood.

Another beam of electricity shot straight through the opening in the castle wall, lighting up the inside like a storm cloud. It didn't take long for screams of pain to reach her ears.

"Now, come out."

One more spin, and yet another explosion rocked the castle.

"S-status report! What the hell is going on?!"

Screams of panic and terror replaced the relaxed atmosphere inside the castle as Lyu continued her bombardment. Everyone was at a loss as to how to handle such an unpredictable and dangerous opponent.

Their arrows weren't connecting, spells couldn't be finished—Luan emerged from the middle chamber, running as if his life depended on it.

"Orders from Hyacinthus! Take fifty fighters and take that guy out!"

"Fifty?!"

Everyone present inside the sanctum was taken aback by that number. That would slice the forces defending the castle in half to take care of one enemy. Luan was quick to cut them off.

"Those magic swords will mow down any small groups we send! They don't even have ten fighters—just get rid of that one and get back here!"

Everyone fell silent in the face of reason. Yet another explosion rocked the wall, sending shock waves through the stone and cracking the surface beneath their feet. "UwaHH!" Luan jumped back as small stones fell from the ceiling, and he ran away.

"C-come on, let's get going!"

"Tsk...No choice. Move out!"

Luan's message being the final push, fifty adventurers gathered around the elf, Lissos, and rushed toward the east gate. The iron doors swung open, an early afternoon breeze hitting their faces as another round of explosions made their ears ring.

"Spread out!" Obeying Lissos's command, the adventurers split into ten groups of five as they converged on the hooded attacker from different angles.

"Guh, guahh…?!"

As predicted, the group that had taken point position was blown backward by a sparkling electrical explosion. One group after another was mercilessly knocked out of commission every time their enemy swung one of those two magic swords. Lissos jumped over the burning grass and weaved his way through the electrical strikes as he closed the distance.

Then he heard a cracking sound immediately after dodging a fireball. A moment later, the crimson blade shattered into thousands of pieces.

"Now! Attack as one!"

The magic sword had exceeded its limit. The violet blade began to crack the moment that Lissos ordered a full-out assault to seize the opportunity.

The hooded adventurer threw the remains of the weapons into the dirt and withdrew a wooden sword from beneath her cloak to engage the thirty remaining adventurers in close-quarters combat.

"S-so fast?!"

"Stay in formation; do not break ranks!"

It didn't take long for the group under Lissos's command to fall into chaos as the hooded adventurer sprang into action. Most of them were third-tier, Level 2 adventurers facing down an enemy who was on her own—yet she unleashed a massacre, wielding her wooden weapon with the force of gale winds. Cape flapping vigorously behind her, she deflected three oncoming swords with one upward sweep before sending a human who got too close twenty meders into the air, using the momentum of her backswing to propel her blade forward.

Thirty adventurers couldn't even land one blow against a single enemy.

"Haa!"

"!"

Lissos timed his sneak attack to land the moment the hooded adventurer was repelling another weapon. The tip of his dagger cut across the enemy's cheek.

The side of her hood had been sliced open enough to reveal, for just a moment, a long ear in the shape of a leaf. Time froze for Lissos as he realized the hooded adventurer was another elf. Fury spread through his veins like wildfire.

"Bastard! An elf dirtying her hands with foul weapons such as magic swords—have you no shame?!"

Rage filled Lissos's body to the point that his ears were burning red as he dove toward the hooded adventurer.

Crozzo's Magic Swords had turned an elvish forest into ash. "Those weapons destroyed the home of your people! How could you not know?!" He roared with the anger and grudge of an entire race. In response, the hooded adventurer—Lyu—remained expressionless and calm as she sideswiped the dagger, breaking it in half.

"—"

"Regrettably, there is something more important to me than the animosity of one people."

Time stood still as Lissos watched his opponent step in, her words overpowering him as her weapon came forward.

"If it is shameful to rescue a friend, I shall gladly accept that."

Lissos saw her feet leave the ground in a spin before losing consciousness on impact.

"This is incredible! Could *Hestia Familia* be looking to end this sooner rather than later?!"

Cheers of surprise and excitement erupted all over Orario.

The mirrors floating in the air showed images of the smoking north and east walls as well as the damage already taken by the inner tower of the old castle. Still others focused solely on the relentless attacks of the mysterious hooded adventurer who eliminated upper-class adventurers one by one in the blink of an eye. She was gaining fans by the moment. Onlookers filling the streets shouted cries of encouragement to the beautiful elf.

"Please tell us, Lord Ganesha, just what are those ferocious magic swords?"

"Those are—Ganesha?!"

"If you don't feel like adding anything to the commentary, please go home, Lord Ganesha!"

The atmosphere in the Guild's front lawn was absolutely electric as the announcers' voices rang out throughout the city.

Meanwhile, inside the confines of Babel Tower in Central Park, many gods and goddesses voiced admiration for her exploits.

"That hooded adventurer—damn good, am I right?"

"According to Hermes, that's a 'helper' from outside the city."

"Hooded adventurer...Leon something or other..."

"*Apollo Familia*'s response time is very quick."

Three gods had gathered in the corner, all watching the same mirror and exchanging opinions. Back at the main table, "Cheh!" Apollo snapped his tongue in disgust. He bared his white teeth menacingly at Hestia, but the young-looking goddess didn't look up from her own mirror.

"Look at that—here comes another one!"

Movement could be seen in a mirror showing the northern grasslands. This time, it was a human girl racing across the landscape like a predator on the hunt.

Wearing camouflage to conceal herself in the grasslands, Mikoto took advantage of the chaos of battle to approach the castle unseen.

Thanks to Lyu's distraction, she was able to climb over the rubble on the north side of the castle and get inside. Holding a rustic longsword in one hand, she ran into the damaged remains of the base of a lookout tower. Small piles of debris had accumulated inside, but she simply jumped over them.

"*Fear, strong and winding—*"

Then she began *casting while running*.

"A sneak attack—! Another enemy coming in from the north!"

The prum Luan was the first to recognize the danger and alerted his allies to Mikoto's presence.

She used the stairwells inside the tower to emerge on the roof of the inner sanctum, all the while keeping her eyes locked on the strange tower where the enemy general was waiting on his throne. Her enemies moved to surround her and cut off her advance.

"I call upon the god, the destroyer of any and all, for guidance from the heavens. Grant this trivial body divine power beyond power."

"That one's got a magic sword, too! She's going for Hyacinthus!"

Luan's keen eyes had caught sight of the unorthodox weapon in her grip. Members of *Apollo Familia* swarmed in, flooding the roof from both sides.

"Saving, purifying light. Bring forth the evil-crushing blade!"

Arrows and spells shot from higher towers peppered the stone roof at her feet. Mikoto pushed on, the song of her spell dancing on the breeze.

Heat welled up as magic energy swirled within her body, splashing with every step and hit taken. Her skin was slick with sweat, droplets flying in her wake.

"—?"

"Hey! That's no magic sword!"

An archer fired an arrow from below and managed to hit the longsword dead on. The blade snapped on impact.

Her ruse was over. The next wave of arrows ripped the camouflage clean off her back and exposed her lithe limbs. The attacks of her pursuers intensified; arrows buried themselves in her battle cloth and spells burned her tender skin. Fragments of stones flying through the air left cuts and bruises on her face and neck.

She almost fell countless times, but never did she stop conjuring her spell. Mikoto pressed forward at full speed.

"Bow to the blade of suppression, the mythical sword of subjugation."

Every nerve on fire, Mikoto conducted a very unpolished Concurrent Casting. There was a very real danger of Ignis Fatuus— unstable magic energy exploding before release. Every attack that connected, every step she took made even more energy churn within her. She was already on the brink.

Keeping the magic energy under control through sheer willpower, a memory flashed within Mikoto's eyes: the song of the "Gale Wind."

The exquisite melody produced by that amazing warrior while engaged in fierce combat with a strong enemy was still ringing in her ears. Mikoto had seen the next level; she had sworn to do whatever it took to reach that plateau.

No matter how many arrows hit her, how many spells barred her path, she would grit her teeth and press on.

Conjure and run—that was all. That fairy warrior managed to attack, move, dodge, and cast her spell at the same time. But that was still a distant dream, one that she would never realize if she failed to complete her mission. What's more, she would be unable to face her new allies should she come up short.

More and more enemies emerged from the castle. Mikoto forced her legs to move even faster.

"I summon you here now, by name."

Mikoto raced across the stone roof. Knowing full well that she would be unable to finish her spell if drawn into combat, she made a hard turn and rushed toward the central tower, arriving at the castle's inner courtyard.

Doing her best to evade incoming arrows and keeping her eyes focused on the looming tower, she jumped off the roof and into the air.

"Descend from the heavens, seize the earth—"

Enemy warriors appeared in the courtyard, emerged from the castle, jumped down from the roof in hot pursuit.

The threat of a magic sword had drawn them in. The adventurers in the courtyard looked up at the girl in the air as she focused her gaze toward the clouds.

Countless sets of eyes on her, Mikoto finished her incantation.

"—Shinbu Tousei!"

A wave of magic energy was released the moment Mikoto landed in the courtyard. Her enemies only gawked for an instant and threw their swords, spears, axes, or anything else on hand in a desperate attempt to silence her before she could flip the trigger, but it was too late.

The wave spread out fifty meders in every direction, maximum range.

A glimmering pillar of light in the shape of a sword appeared above Mikoto's head—her Magic had been activated.

"*Futsu no Tama!*"

Many rings of light shot out from beneath her as the sword of violet light came crashing down to her feet.

An immense gravity field forced all of the airborne weapons straight to the ground before they could find their target. All adventurers within the outer ring, including Mikoto herself, fell to the ground under the tremendous weight.

"Gh-gahhhhhhh…?!"

The adventurers trapped underneath the violet dome generated from the top of the sword cried out in pain.

Apollo Familia members who had been lucky enough to be outside the ring launched arrows and threw even more blades at Mikoto, but all of them crashed to the ground the moment they hit the light purple barrier. "*Ka-ting!*" The sound of metal on stone echoed throughout the courtyard. Humans, elves, and animal people inside the outer ring fell to their knees, some on all fours as they fought to keep their heads upright under the insane pressure of Mikoto's gravity magic.

The girl had her fists clenched, feet planted firmly on the ground as she endured the full brunt of her own spell.

"Are you freakin' serious…?!"

Self-sacrifice.

By getting caught up in her own Magic, she had managed to capture every adventurer inside the courtyard and keep them there for as long as she could hold out.

Mikoto watched as more and more of the adventurers collapsed. However, she didn't budge at all. Her eyes met the closest human's gaze as he howled at her.

In the middle of this test of endurance, Mikoto responded in a resolute voice.

"You shall remain here with me for the time being…!"

"Stay strong, Mikoto…"

Takemikazuchi watched the battle from a mirror he'd summoned into his *Familia*'s home.

"Hang in there…"

"She plans to keep the enemies in the courtyard?"

Chigusa and Ouka were by his side, grimacing as they watched the sweat pouring down Mikoto's face.

Twenty-two enemy combatants had been trapped inside Mikoto's gravity cage. Anything that touched the outer layer of Futsu no Tama, be it physical or magical, instantly came crashing to the ground. Nothing was coming close to the magic user at its center, which meant that the spell would not be broken until she collapsed from exhaustion.

Including the group that had gone to engage Lyu during the magic-sword attack, *Apollo Familia*'s forces had been cut by almost 80 percent.

—At the same time on the thirtieth floor of Babel Tower…

Hermes spoke as he followed the tides of battle on the mirror in front of him. "Much too fast."

"What is?"

"Team Apollo's movements. They're reacting too quickly."

His eyes jumped from person to person reflected in the mirror as he responded to Asfi's question.

"How they responded as a group to the power of Crozzo's Magic Swords, how they all ganged up to stop little Mikoto's sneak attack—don't you find it a little odd? It's almost like…they're being guided somehow."

Asfi's eyes went wide in recognition as Hermes looked away from the battle to enjoy the look on her face.

"Information is a weapon in war."

"The better the quality, and the faster word comes in, it can be the ultimate trump card."

"However, should a little bit of *poison* be mixed in with said information...it spreads much faster."

Asfi exchanged words with her god before looking back at the mirror. Only one person was reflected inside: a prum with his head on a swivel as he ran through a hallway. Luan encountered no guards as he ran quietly to the fully intact west gate of the castle.

"Just one drop of poison can lead to unthinkable tragedy."

Then the man opened the west gate by turning a wheel with his own hands—granting Bell and Welf entrance to the castle.

"A traitor—?!"

Townspeople all over Orario stood up, heads between their hands and jaws slack in surprise.

In the main streets, in front of the Guild, in Central Park, no one could believe what they were watching and yelled at the top of their lungs.

"That guy just betrayed *Apollo Familia*?!"

The many "windows" floating in midair showed two humans running side by side with the prum man. Everyone seemed to be drawn closer to the mirrors in shock.

An unthinkable betrayal—Bell and Welf entered the castle without any resistance whatsoever thanks to Luan. What was left of the fifty adventurers dispatched to take care of Lyu were still fighting in the east. Almost half of the castle's remaining troops were currently trapped by Mikoto's magic in the courtyard. The passages in the western part of the castle felt deserted. The guards who were originally stationed there must have gone to protect the heavily damaged north and east walls, creating this blind spot. One unlucky adventurer who happened to be passing through the hallway stared at the three for a moment before taking off and yelling at the top of his lungs. But he wasn't fast enough to get away from the white rabbit and was knocked unconscious with one quick strike.

Absolutely floored by the turn of events, waves of excitement and anxiety passed through the spectators.

"Wha...Eh...Hah...?!"

A speechless Apollo was one of them.

He stood up from the table with such force that his chair flew backward, slamming to the floor behind him. Anger had boiled up inside him to the point that his face started to contort and change color as he opened and closed his mouth.

Yes...!

Hestia made sure to keep her celebration out of sight of the visibly shaking god as she silently pumped her fist beneath the table.

She gazed at all the members of *her family* with trusting eyes in the mirror in front of her.

"You get them goin'?"

The castle ruins, inside *Apollo Familia*'s castle. Welf ran up to Luan's side.

"This is the only way Lilly can be useful."

It was most definitely a man's voice, but Luan's tone was surprisingly feminine. His face was male, too, but the way he smiled at Welf was the spitting image of their young ally. Bell ran up along the other side and grinned at their unsung hero, their supporter.

Luan the traitor was actually Lilly in disguise using her magic.

The real Luan had been captured almost four days ago on the night that *Apollo Familia* first set out to the castle ruins. He was currently in a random shed outside the city wall—no doubt viewing the War Game under Miach's watchful eyes. Lilly had taken his place, copying his voice and mannerisms to the point that no one noticed a difference. She'd been collecting information from inside the castle ever since.

She had an opportunity to reunite with Welf and the others the night before the War Game after being assigned to bring the last of the supplies into the castle. That's when this plan all came together.

Being Level 4, Lyu would draw out half of the enemy's forces and keep them busy while Mikoto cut the remaining forces in half yet again by restraining them inside the castle grounds.

Lilly would manipulate the commanders as well as anyone else from the inside to ensnare as many as possible in their trap. With their numbers reduced, she would then let Welf and Bell into the castle.

Lastly, Welf would escort Bell all the way to the throne room.

Everything was going exactly the way that Lilly and Hestia had drawn it up.

A traitor in their midst—Lilly in disguise had been the Trojan horse all along.

"I told you yesterday, but the enemy general is at the top of a strange-looking tower. In order to get there, you have to go through a long hallway connecting to the third floor."

Returning to Luan's speaking style, Lilly explained everything to Bell. Rakia had made some serious design changes, the largest of which was an enclosed bridge that connected the whitish main tower to the rest of the castle. She pointed to it through the window as they ran.

"We can't break in from the outside?"

"No, there's no entrance. The thing may look pretty but it's sturdy as a rock. It'll take time to get there and enemies will swarm in. But, once you get inside..."

"Straight shot to the throne room?"

The small man nodded and grinned at Bell's words.

"There'll be a ton of magic users in that hallway. Counting on you?"

"Yeah, I got this."

The prum "man" asked Welf to watch Bell's back and grinned.

Then he split off from the two humans. The only people who knew "Luan's" true allegiance were the people watching the mirrors in Orario. Lilly could still stir up enough chaos inside the castle to keep the remaining enemies away from her allies.

"Let's do this."

"Yeah!"

Bell, wearing brand-new, refurbished light armor, and Welf, greatsword balanced on his shoulder, raced up the nearest staircase toward the sky bridge.

"Tell me, what's going on?! Out with it!"

Daphne yelled as she watched the tide of battle turn against them from her post at the base of the main tower.

"You don't need to tell me the wall's been destroyed, I can see that from here! Why is the castle so empty?!"

Eyes widened, a tinge of fear in her loud voice, Daphne shook her hair as she yelled.

Smoke was still rising from the north and east walls; she had a direct view from one of the many windows around her. She was trying to get a straight answer out of the messenger who had brought news from the front lines.

Daphne, along with only eight other adventurers, stood at the end of the sky bridge as the last line of defense.

"L-Luan said Hyacinthus ordered a direct attack..."

"HHAH?! That man ordered no such thing! I've been right here the whole time! I'd have been the first to know!"

Indeed, she had been ordered to stand guard in front of the only entrance to the main tower. No messenger carrying word from Hyacinthus would have reached the troops at the front line without her noticing.

The elf messenger shrank backward in the face of Daphne's intimidating aura.

"Luan...betrayed us...?"

It was believable, especially considering that Daphne doubted most of her comrade's allegiance to Apollo in the first place. She bit her lip before pressing the messenger for more information.

"What about Lissos and his troops?"

"E-eliminated, by the looks of it. The enemy used some kind of magic in the courtyard and trapped many of our warriors inside it. I don't know how many are left who can still fight."

She quickly reasoned that all of this had to be Luan's handiwork; he had to be the reason that things fell out of hand so quickly. Not even an hour had passed since the start of the War Game, and the enemy had already made this much progress with almost no resistance.

Daphne cursed through her teeth. Not only was she angry at Hyacinthus's way of looking down on their enemy since before the War Game, but also at herself for hesitating to act the moment the north wall collapsed.

"Daphne, they're here! Two humans...The Little Rookie!"

"...This ends now. Alto, deliver a message to Hyacinthus for me: Bring reinforcements down from the throne room and we'll crush Bell Cranell."

One of the adventurers had spotted the two advancing up the outer tower and alerted Daphne to the danger. She issued her orders to the elf, who immediately bowed and disappeared into the main tower.

Daphne's plan was to flood the sky bridge with so many warriors that it would be impossible for Bell and Welf to pass. The hallway in the sky was surprisingly wide—it would take more than ten large men in full body armor, standing shoulder to shoulder, to seal it off completely. She knew it would take several seconds for them to approach from the other side. Windows dotted the walls, a very solid ceiling above and a red carpet running down the full length of the floor. There were no obstacles in the way, no cover. Daphne ordered the mages to start casting.

Finally, the two humans appeared at the other end of the hallway.

"Archers to the front! They have nowhere to run—shoot everything you've got! Mages, fire on my command!"

Each archer and magic user had a straight shot to their target, a literal firing range. Magic with a decent blast radius would wipe out anything in this confined space. There would be no escape.

Daphne's eyebrows sank, visions of these would-be attackers' demise in her head. Withdrawing her shortsword from the hilt at her waist, she pointed it directly at their oncoming enemies.

Archers nocked their arrows; magic users reached the final phrases of their trigger spells.

"—GO!"

At the same time, the man with the massive sword over his shoulder—Welf—yelled.

The white-haired boy beside him leaned forward for an instant before taking off in a mad dash.

"FIRE!"

Bow strings cracked as arrows hurtled forward. Magic users moved their lips to bring their magic to life. At that moment—

Welf thrust his right hand forward.

"Blasphemous Burn!"

A short-trigger spell.

Silver, murky mist silently flowed like mercury from the palm of his hand.

The mist overtook Bell and inundated the enemy ranks around Daphne.

"____"

She watched in horror as the bodies of each of the magic users started to glow, flickering like flames inside a furnace as the mist washed over them.

A heartbeat later, each of them flinched awkwardly as their bodies flashed from within.

KA-BOOM!

"Huh?!"

Sparks erupted like flower petals all around her.

Every single magic user in front of her had failed to cast—victims of Ignis Fatuus.

—He turned the mages into bombs?!

Welf's anti-magic Magic. Archers caught up in the blasts were tossed like rag dolls left and right. The mages lay where they fell, black smoke steadily rising from their limp mouths. They would not be casting again anytime soon.

The series of explosions shook pieces of rock loose from the ceiling and walls of the hallway, the singed red carpet in shambles. Daphne managed to brace herself just before the explosion and kept her feet despite the raging winds howling inside the stone bridge.

A swirling cloud of black smoke in front of her, Daphne steadied herself as the white-haired boy burst through it.

"?!"

Bell bounded right by her like a rabbit on the loose, making a break for the staircase at the base of the main tower.

Dammit! Daphne turned to give chase when suddenly, "Ekkkk—!" A scream stopped her in her tracks.

Spinning on her heel, Daphne saw an archer bounce face-first off the floor and a red-haired man walk toward her over the remains of the carpet.

Black jacket rustling in the wind, Welf came to a stop a stone's throw away from Daphne —*THUD*.

The tip of his sword on the floor, Welf looked Daphne in the eyes just over the hilt of his weapon.

"Real adventurers settle things with blades, don'cha think?"

The young woman's eyes trembled as she looked at the smith's fearless grin.

Welf's and Daphne's blades flashed in what little sunlight came through the sky-bridge windows.

Loki watched the two battle on her own mirror, a playful grin growing on her lips as she watched the red-haired man force Daphne away from the main tower.

"Fei-fei, that kiddo's somethin' else!"

"Why, thank you."

The main table inside Babel Tower. Loki sat next to Hephaistos, who had just allowed Welf to join *Hestia Familia*. This was the trickster's chance to have a little fun.

"Those flashy magic swords—forged by him, right? Regrettin' lettin' him go?"

"Who knows."

Loki's pearly white teeth glistened as her grin grew even deeper. Hephaistos looked at her with a warm smile, as if happy about something.

Elsewhere, the conversations taking place just outside Babel Tower were nowhere near as high-spirited as the two goddesses'.

"I'm screwed at this rate..."

"There's still a chance, there's still a chance..."

The atmosphere inside the bars had become thick with tension, adventurers restless.

Many eyes twitched as they watched Bell run on one of the many mirrors floating in the air. "Give up already!" one shouted as he stood up, shaking his fist at the boy. "Like hell you can lose!" yelled another, cheering on *Apollo Familia* with all of his might. Every adventurer who had bet money on Apollo's victory was suddenly extremely vocal. Their shouts could be heard all around the city.

"Go, Whitey! Make 'em cry, meow!"

"Did she place a bet behind our backs...?"

"Be glad she didn't bet on *Apollo Familia*, meow..."

West Main Street, The Benevolent Mistress.

There wasn't a single empty seat at the bar. Chloe screamed at the mirrors along with the adventurers while carrying jugs of ale in her arms. Runoa and Ahnya watched her in disbelief.

"..."

Syr stood next to the two girls, unable to focus on her job in the slightest as she watched Bell on the mirror.

Her silver-gray eyes traced the boy's every step, as if pleading for him to make it out alive.

"—Wow, just wow, Aiz! Look at him go!"

"Yes."

On the northern edge of the city...

Loki Familia's home was also brimming with excitement despite being far away from the bars.

Tiona's eyes sparkled as she watched *Hestia Familia*'s carefully crafted attack unfold on another mirror.

Aiz stood next to her, golden gaze nailed to the boy reflected inside.

"Yes, they're doing very well...But even without all the tricks, couldn't they have just sent that hooded adventurer with the magic swords straight in and let the cards fall as they may? That would've been so much easier."

Tione stood behind the two girls, watching the action over their heads as she asked her own question.

"Amazonian to the bone, thinkin' like that..."

"Hmm, simply put, would a Goliath stand a chance charging into a battle party of one hundred?"

"...Impossible."

"Additionally, those two magic swords alone would have been unable to destroy the entire structure. There is no doubt that Apollo's forces are much better organized. Hestia's group couldn't afford to have a wide-scale battle, chaotically mixing friend and foe."

Gareth, Finn, and Reveria rolled their eyes at Tione's proposition and each explained their reasoning in turn.

A battle party composed of only *Apollo Familia* members led by the Level 3 Hyacinthus was already powerful enough to take down a Goliath on their own.

The three started calmly breaking down the group's tactics for her when—

"Doesn't mean shit."

Bete entered the conversation.

"Rabbit Boy wants to settle the score with the perv himself."

Many members of *Loki Familia* had gathered in the common room of their home. Loki had set up many Divine Mirrors before leaving earlier that morning. The young werewolf was watching a different one from the girls, one that showed the side of Bell's face as he ran.

"He's a man, that one."

Talking loud enough to be heard by everyone, his amber-colored eyes didn't leave the mirror.

"Do you know something?"

"...Nope."

Bete spat out a response to Reveria's question.

"This'll work, this'll work! They've already come this far!"

Completely ignoring what was going on behind her, Tiona started running around Aiz and pumping her fist in the air. Tione, Bete, and the others watched in annoyance as the young Amazonian girl started jumping up and down as well. Tiona didn't care as her cheering became even more acrobatic.

Her face beet-red, the girl came to a stop and punched toward the mirror with each word.

"Fight! Win—! Argonaut!"

Bell made it through the sky bridge and into the main tower by following the instructions that Lilly had given him.

The tower containing the throne room was expansive. Old rugs covered the stone floor and the walls were decorated with dust-covered artwork. Bell felt like he'd walked into a mansion that had been abandoned by its owner.

"SHAA!"

"!"

An animal person jumped out at him from the shadows. Bell calmly moved to engage.

Handily dodging two swings of the attacker's white blade, Bell knocked the sword out of the way on the third swipe and swung his left leg out and high. "Gah!" His left foot buried itself in the attacker's cheek, sending him crashing to the floor. The animal person's body rolled two or three times before lying still.

—Mr. Cranell. I am only lending you my strength.

As more enemies appeared from the shadows, Bell's mind flashed back to the conversation he had last night.

They'd spent the night before the War Game in the forest to the west of the old castle. The experienced elvish warrior had pulled him aside under the moonlight.

—This conflict must be resolved by your *Familia*—no, by *your* hand.

Thanks to the hastily forged magic swords, Bell and the others wouldn't have to worry about directly assaulting the castle. Considering the defensive advantage given to an already powerful enemy, a plan to have the "Gale Wind" spearhead an attack was also scrapped.

But that was all just a premise.

Without a doubt, everyone was hoping for a defining moment.

Hestia, Lilly, Welf, Mikoto, the audience, and most likely every god—but most of all, Bell himself.

Everyone wanted to see the boy bring an end to this War Game.

—*I want to beat him.*

Determination burned within him.

He wanted to roar out with the pain of not being good enough, the tears he'd shed.

The bar, in the middle of the city, and today. Bell swore that he would surpass that man on their third encounter.

To regain his honor, to claim victory for his goddess, and to reach that next plateau.

Today, Bell would settle everything with his own hands.

I think that's the last one…

Leaving the bodies of his assailants on the floor, Bell advanced to a circular hallway where he couldn't sense anyone else.

The last of his enemies were in the throne room. The general, Hyacinthus, and his personal guards were waiting for him there.

Returning all weapons to their sheaths, Bell looked at the palm of his right hand.

Clenching his fist, the boy looked up—*ring, ring, ring*. A chiming sound echoed around him.

"We're under attack! The Little Rookie is here!"

The messenger elf flew through the main doors and instantly sent a wave of panic through the throne room.

The fact that Bell had penetrated this far into the inner defenses of the castle left all of them in shock. Word that reinforcements were needed below made all of them draw their weapons and dash toward the door. That is, all but one.

"Denied. What is running through your heads?!"

Hyacinthus was seated on the throne at the back of the room. He slammed his fist down on the armrest.

Cape swishing behind him as he stood up, veins in his head pulsing with anger, he looked around the room. Everyone present recoiled in fear.

"Displaying this much cowardice is beyond shameful. How can we face our Lord Apollo in such dishonor…?"

His normally charming and beautiful face wrinkled into a horrifying expression.

Hyacinthus couldn't hide his annoyance at the fact that his own forces had allowed the enemy to come this far, as well as the anger he felt toward himself.

"General? General, sir! I beg you, please leave this place at once!"

"Cassandra, enough already!"

The girl shouting from beside his throne had provided Hyacinthus with an outlet for his anger.

The girl, wearing a dress-style battle cloth, her long hair tied back, had been pleading with Hyacinthus to vacate to the throne room since early that morning. Everything about the desperation in her cowardly message made his skin crawl.

"Please, please believe what I'm telling you...!"

"Silence! Keep your nonsense believable!"

Hyacinthus waved her off in anger.

Apollo had appointed him as general of his forces. A leader could never abandon his post without reason. A loss was still unthinkable, even with the current conditions.

"Can you not see?! I'm here along with several other warriors. Bell Cranell coming in here alone would spell his own demise!"

The man gestured to the other adventurers in the room. They had been hand selected by Hyacinthus for their skills in battle. Ten in all, they would be more than enough to handle a Level 2 rookie. Victory was all but guaranteed with their Level 3 general leading the charge.

Every person in the room stared at Cassandra as her eyes started to well up with tears. She looked down at her feet in terror.

She held her quivering body, her line of vision jumping from stone to stone on the throne room floor.

"Ah...ahhh."

The long-haired girl started to moan, her face losing color every second.

Hyacinthus's cheeks twitched out of annoyance as he turned to face her. That's when the girl looked up and whispered:

"Lightning..."

Ring, ring.

Bell kept moving, chimes echoing around him until he found a staircase leading higher up the tower.

There wasn't a soul in his way. His ruby-red eyes traced the path of the spiral stairwell before focusing on the specks of light circling around his right arm.

The Grand Bell had not been heard since the battle on the eighteenth floor of the Dungeon.

There must be some kind of trigger because Bell was sure this was exactly the way he charged his attack before. Scouring his memory, he got the feeling that the voice of a divine being came to him at that time.

It revived him, provided vision, filled him with a burning desire—that was all Bell could remember. Something had just suddenly come to him during that battle. At the same time, Bell realized that the power he wielded that day was not something he could conjure up each time.

But he didn't need it right now.

"…!"

Argonaut's trigger, a clear vision of a hero. This time, he saw the warrior Argis.

The seemingly immortal hero had fought to his dying breath, slaying monster after monster in order to take back a stronghold that had been overrun by a horde. His courageous deeds were legendary.

Every nerve in Bell's body came to life as he visualized the hero storming the castle on his own. Light started to flicker in the palm of his right hand.

"Lightning—really?"

Hyacinthus slowly exhaled through his nose, his voice laced with sarcasm as he responded to Cassandra.

The man looked outside each of the windows that surrounded the throne room. Still facing away, he looked at the girl out of the corner of his eye.

"The sky is an azure blue, white puffy clouds here and there. And you're telling me lightning will fall?!"

With no hint of a storm on the horizon, Hyacinthus laughed at the prospect.

However…

"Not fall..."

Cassandra's rebuttal barely squeaked out of her lips.

Grasping her pale face between her hands, Cassandra made eye contact with the man and whispered:

"Lightning...*will rise.*"

Once again, her gaze fell to the stone floor.

"What?"

The base of the stairwell directly beneath the throne room.

The massive spiral spread out to his left and right. Bell stood directly in the middle, looking straight up like an archer sighting a target.

The footsteps of an adventurer trying to descend echoed down the wide tube and reached his ears.

Bell reached skyward as if he were trying to grab hold of the sun.

—One minute.

A sixty-second charge. Pulsing white light had come together around him.

Next, one voice.

"Firebolt."

A white inferno of electricity burst forth.

"___"

Cracks ran through the bulging stone floor, light leaking through.

All words left Hyacinthus the moment he saw the first blast break through and continue into the ceiling.

A deafening explosion.

"What was that, did you see that———?!"

Babel was full of screaming deities.

"No trigger spell?!"

"That kind of power without casting—?!"

"I want that human soooooooooooooooo bad!"

Not a single deity in the chamber kept their seat as they roared with excitement.

Most of the gods and goddesses were filled with a mix of shock and admiration for Bell's trigger-less spell.

"…,…?!"

Separated from the gods enjoying the moment, Apollo stood frozen in place with his mouth wide open.

"…!"

Hestia didn't move, either, eyes not budging from her mirror.

She watched as the enemy general emerged from a pile of rubble on its surface.

"Haa—, ghaa—…?!"

Bits and pieces of stone fell off of Hyacinthus as he sat up, writhing in pain.

The upper half of the main tower was gone. The throne room itself had been completely destroyed by a blast that came from directly beneath it. Even now, the last of the electrical blasts were carving their way through clouds high in the sky, on their way toward the shining sun.

"What…what just happened?!"

Hyacinthus climbed to his feet. The once perfectly set and clean cape around his shoulders was torn and badly damaged. His normally stylish hair was ragged and filled with dirt.

—Cassandra had tackled him just as the first electrical burst came through the floor, knocking him out the window.

He could vaguely remember hearing the glass break as everything went white and his body was pelted with thousands of stone fragments. He must have lost consciousness during the fall, because he couldn't remember how he'd ended up on the ground outside the castle. Looking around, all he could see were small mountains of debris and thick clouds of smoke obscuring his vision.

"Cassandra?! Ron?!"

He called out to his allies in confusion, anger, and an emotion he couldn't recognize that was welling up inside of him. There was no response.

The smoke lifted enough for him to get a better view of the pile of stones a few meders away from him. A chill ran up Hyacinthus's spine when he realized there was a human body buried in the rubble.

—Wiped out.

He was the only one left. His normally calm and refined demeanor crumbled.

Eyes flashing in fury, Hyacinthus drew his sword as the sky bridge fell apart, collapsing onto the castle below.

"Where are you?!"

Flamberge firmly in his grasp, Hyacinthus roared into the smoke.

His enemy was still alive—he knew it. The urge to tear that boy into pieces consumed him.

His heart was racing; sweat continually poured down his face. The enemy was hiding in the smoke, blade trained on his throat.

Hyacinthus spun to the left, looked back to the right, and then turned all the way around. The coolheaded warrior was gone. He couldn't stand still, watching every single twist of the rising smoke in all directions.

At last, the sun's rays started to pierce the smoky clouds. He could see deeper and deeper—until…

"___"

The air seemed to shiver.

Two dots of ruby-red light flickered deep in the smoke behind him.

Hyacinthus could sense it: the beast covered in blood. It made his skin crawl.

A heartbeat later, Bell burst through the smoke cover. Hyacinthus spun to meet him.

Two red knives and one long, rouge blade collided in an explosion of sparks.

"UWHHAAAAAAAAAAAAAAAAAAAAAAAAAAAAAAA AAAAAAAAAAAAAAA!"

Orario shook.

Adventurers, commentators, and gods alike.

A duel between enemy generals. This highly unexpected turn of events sent the city into a frenzy.

Thousands of sweaty palms were clenched into fists as unblinking eyes watched the mirrors with the utmost intensity.

None of the onlookers could form actual words, only make as much noise as possible as the duel of the century unfolded before them.

"...?!"

A forward thrust. Two whirling crimson blades.

Their attacks were too fast to follow. As soon as the mirror reflected one successfully blocked attack, the echoes of the next three came through loud and clear. The moment that Hyacinthus squared his shoulders, the white-haired boy darted away, rolling to his side, then to a blind spot, always staying out of the flamberge's path.

Forced to go on the defensive, there was no window to counterattack.

The man could feel every impact of the two knives against his weapon in the bones of his fingers. Pain shot through them every time.

Hyacinthus's eyes shook as he watched Bell's double-bladed onslaught, desperately trying to keep up.

—Who?

The boy's strikes increased in ferocity. What was worse, he couldn't predict them.

Hyacinthus had the Strength advantage. But strangely, and obviously, the boy was faster.

—Who is this?

Techniques, footwork, nothing mattered if his blade couldn't connect. What's more, the boy got behind him.

His Agility had increased so much that memories of their previous battles became cloudy.

—Just who is this?

The word "growth" didn't do him justice.

Barely managing to block the boy's attack, Hyacinthus looked at him in disbelief and screamed at the top of his lungs:

"—JUST WHO THE HELL ARE YOU?!"

Abilities, strategy, techniques—everything was on his own level.

The boy who had been easily overpowered by simple, straightforward strikes in an instant only ten days ago was nowhere to be seen.

The man put all of his strength into one overarching swing at the head of this strange adventurer and yelled:

"I'm Level Three!"

Hyacinthus swung again and again, attacking wildly, when suddenly Bell's body became a blur.

Catching the oncoming flamberge between both knives on a down stroke, the crimson blades flashed as they broke the rouge sword in half.

"What's wrong with you, Hyacinthus?!" shrieked Apollo as he watched his prized follower lose the sword that symbolized his *Familia*. The deity's face couldn't hide the amount of stress he was under.

Angry jeers could be heard from the city below as every god inside Babel watched Hyacinthus draw a shortsword from his belt and continue the fight. Hestia bit her lip as she watched the two engage in a highly mobile, hit-and-run style of combat on her own mirror. Hermes cocked an eyebrow and made his way to her side.

"Well, well, it seems Bell had some extra excelia stocked up when he became Level Two."

Hermes flashed his usual charming smile as he looked at the side of Hestia's face.

There had been no announcement that Bell had reached Level 3. So the only way that it was possible for him to keep up would be for his Level 1 abilities to have combined with his current Level 2 stats. It made Hermes tingle inside just thinking about how high his basic abilities must've been to produce such a result, and he just had to know.

"What was his Status before ranking up? Come on, I promise I won't tell anyone else. The secret's safe with me, so please?"

Hestia's eyes didn't leave the mirror. She didn't even move as she responded in a quiet voice:

"You won't believe me anyway, so no."

"Of course I'll believe you, so please, tell me."

Hermes kept pressing, so Hestia told him Bell's basic ability levels after his battle with the Minotaur.

"Everything but Agility was SS."

"Ha-ha! You must be joking."

"See?"

Hestia continued watching the mirror, her serious face in stark contrast to Hermes's laugh.

Hermes came to realize that Hestia wasn't smiling and the reality of what she had said began to sink in.

"Really?"

"Really."

Hermes took a step forward, the tingly feeling flooded his body as yet another smile grew on his lips.

"...So, what was his Agility?"

"Quiet, Hermes."

Bringing an abrupt end to the deity's questioning, Hestia returned her focus completely to the mirror.

She was determined to watch this fight to the very end.

"Hu...!"

"_____?!"

Crimson arcs sliced through the air as Hyacinthus absorbed each hit with his shortsword.

His main weapon, the Solar Flamberge, lay in pieces on top of the rubble. One direct hit from the weapons in Bell's hands was powerful enough to break it in one strike. Covered in sweat, the man was suddenly being driven backward.

Ushiwakamaru-Shiki.

Welf, now a High Smith, had put his heart and soul into forging this new weapon from the remaining half of Bell's Minotaur Horn. With far more destructive power than the original Ushiwakamaru, the menacing spirit of the Minotaur seemed to reside within the blade itself. In fact, Bell had to concentrate with all his might to prevent the Minotaur's bloodlust from overtaking him as he advanced on Hyacinthus.

However, just because he'd disarmed his enemy and had him against the ropes didn't mean Bell was confident of victory.

Using Argonaut had taken a heavy toll on his body despite

drinking one of Nahza's dual potions. Bell knew that he would lose this battle should his opponent draw it out. His arms and legs were getting heavier by the second.

Bell needed to end this in less than a minute. Every ounce of his strength, every drop of energy was going into each strike.

Body and mind working as one, the boy's movements picked up even more speed.

"Guhh...?!"

Hyacinthus's handsome face, one that his god adored, twitched violently as anger mixed with desperation.

One week of combat training under Aiz and Tiona had come to a head. Bell was on par with his opponent in terms of technique and footwork; everything was coming together. Every lesson that had been pounded into his body by fist, foot, and blade by the top-class adventurers was pushing Hyacinthus farther and farther back across the field of debris.

The boy's focus and greatly improved Status were overwhelming the second-tier adventurer.

"U-OOHHHHHHHHHH?!"

"?!"

All of the accessories attached to his body flailed in the air as Hyacinthus spun and twisted to dodge the crimson blades. Yelling at the top of his lungs, *Apollo Familia's* general slammed his shortsword into the debris under his feet.

The resulting impact sent a fresh cloud of blinding dust into the air. The strike was powerful enough to reach the soil, adding a plume of dirt to the explosion. Bell was quick to react, his reflexes sending him backward before the cloud could overtake him. At the same time, Hyacinthus kicked off the ground, launching himself away from the boy like an arrow shot from a bow.

Then—

"*—My name is love, child of light. Glorious son, I offer you my body!*"

Hyacinthus played his trump card.

A good deal of distance between them, he started casting Magic.

"My name is sin, jealously of the wind. This body calls forth your gust!"

Magic—the power to come back from the bleakest situation in the blink of an eye.

Unable to hold his own in hand-to-hand combat, Hyacinthus decided to try a different strategy to turn the tide of battle to his favor.

"Come forth, ring of fire—!"

Bell could sense a large amount of magical energy gathering on the other side of the swirling dust cloud.

Returning Ushiwakamaru into its sheath, Bell thrust his left arm forward in an attempt to stop the magic in its tracks.

"Firebolt!"

It took less than a second for Bell's Swift-Strike Magic to cut through the cloud and tear into Hyacinthus.

"_____?!"

The thundering inferno enveloped him, dispersing the dust.

The man's long body bent backward. His battle cloth was now nothing more than rags covering charred skin. However, Hyacinthus endured.

Not only that, the magic power gathering in his hands was unaffected. The man gritted his teeth, stood up straight, and continued casting.

"—on westerly winds!"

Bell's eyes opened wide. He watched the man in disbelief.

He took in a deep breath, preparing to hit his enemy with another round of the Swift-Strike Magic, when out of the blue…

"YAA–?!"

"?!"

A long-haired girl had emerged from the rubble and attacked Bell from the side.

Cassandra's tackle made contact with his arm at the same instant the boy's magic was released, protecting Hyacinthus from the blast.

"Well done, Cassandra!"

Apollo yelled into his mirror inside Babel Tower. Another shadow appeared in the field of rubble, this one making a beeline for Cassandra.

"Mr. Bell!"

"Kyaahhh?!"

Lilly, undisguised, had arrived to provide support.

The girl was the first one to arrive from the castle. Tackling Cassandra from behind, the two of them rolled down the pile of stones and onto the grass below.

"—Nuuuahhhhh!"

Bell immediately stuck out his left hand to fire again, but Hyacinthus had finished casting. The man pulled his shoulders back as his torso twisted at the waist.

Bending his knees to lower his center of gravity, Hyacinthus reached his right hand high into the air and dropped his left to just above the rubble beneath his feet—a discus throw.

The boy watched in horror as Hyacinthus's eyes locked onto him, right hand pulsing with magic energy. A heartbeat later, the man triggered his Magic.

"Aro Zephyros!"

A ring the size of his body appeared between his hands, shining bright as the sun.

Hyacinthus flung the ring forward in one swift motion, his right hand aiming the disk at Bell. It spun with blinding speed as it rushed forward.

"Firebolt!"

Bell launched his own Swift-Strike Magic a second later.

A burning disk the size of a human torso; a snaking pillar of violet, flaming electricity.

The two Magics collided, but the disk had no trouble cutting through the electric flames.

"?!"

Sparks flew in every direction as the violet light was swallowed up by the burning rays of the "sun."

Firebolt had been overpowered. That was the weakness of Bell's Magic—it might be quick, but it lacked destructive force.

In the face of Hyacinthus's Aro Zephyros, it didn't stand a chance.

"Guh!"

Bell managed to dodge the oncoming disk by the slimmest of margins.

"Pointless!"

However, the disk suddenly turned skyward as if guided by Hyacinthus's voice. Flipping around, it set a new course for Bell. The oncoming flames reflected off Bell's ruby-red eyes.

Homing Magic. The magical energy would not disburse until the disk hit its target.

A westerly wind pushing his body to the east, Bell made a desperate jump to get out of the disk's path.

"Rubele!"

A blinding flash and then a sudden explosion.

"—GAH!"

Bell's body had been extended, arms reaching out, when Hyacinthus triggered the explosion of the disk.

The explosion threw the boy's helpless body several meders, careening into another pile of debris.

"Mr. Bell?!" screamed Lilly as she clung to Cassandra's body, watching the battle from the corner of her eye.

Hestia forgot to breathe as she stared, eyes transfixed on her mirror. Everyone cheering for the boy around the city suddenly fell silent.

Body shrouded in smoke, Bell bounced off the debris two, three times, droplets of his blood flinging through the air around him. *Clang!* The knife fell from Bell's right hand on the next impact.

Finally coming to a stop, the boy managed to climb to his feet. However, the armor protecting his right shoulder was gone, his arm hanging limp and useless at his side.

"Now I have you!"

Drawing the shortsword from the sheath at his waist, Hyacinthus charged.

Bell watched his enemy pick up speed, but he couldn't react.

The sun reflected off Hyacinthus's blade as it homed in on its motionless target.

(——)

Bell saw his opponent charging in slow motion. Meanwhile, far away in Orario...

Hestia's eyes shook.

Apollo smiled with glee.

Eina's face turned pale, Syr prayed, Bete snapped his tongue.

Tiona held her breath—but in the golden eyes of the girl sitting next to her...

Was the same memory that was flashing before the boy's ruby-red eyes.

(——)

Two shadows colliding above the city wall, the sky orange before sunset.

I told you. I listened to you.

—People become easier to read when they see a window.

The boy had paid attention to every word.

—Guard is lowest when the final blow is near.

Their hearts were connected by this one memory, accidentally, inevitably.

—Your greatest opportunity lies when you are most vulnerable.

She'd taught him. The boy took it to heart.

—Don't forget.

So, not yet.

((—Now))

Hyacinthus's arm pulled back, the blade of his shortsword even with his shoulder.

All of the emotions stewing inside him were focused into the point of his sword for one deadly thrust. He was going to end this by running Bell clean through.

The man's face morphed into that of a wolf salivating over a kill. Bell started to lean backward.

The corners of Hyacinthus's mouth curled upward, interpreting Bell's movements as cowardly. He sliced the air with his sword once, taunting his foe before resetting for the final approach.

Bell bent his knees and rolled onto his back a moment later.

Forcing his center of gravity as far back as possible, he rolled backward over his shoulder.

Seeing his enemy less than three meders away, Bell vigorously rolled backward once again in time to dodge the incoming blade.

He used that momentum to swing his legs upward.

The shortsword was held in his opponent's outstretched right hand. Bell felt the tip of his right boot brush against the hilt.

From there, he kicked with all his might.

"___"

CLING! The shortsword flashed in the sunlight as it spiraled upward and out of sight. Disarmed, Hyacinthus froze on the spot.

His enemy's confidence and carelessness had opened the path to victory.

Bell rolled over his shoulder once again and felt his feet connect with soil—he sprang forward.

"—Haa!"

Point-blank range.

"—W-waaaaaaiit!"

Limp right arm at the mercy of centrifugal force, Bell made a fist with his left hand.

Hyacinthus saw the boy coming but was unable to evade his attack because his body was still stuck in the same thrusting position, right arm forward, left arm back.

The Vorpal rabbit was a fearsome, murderous white rabbit that lurked in the deeper floors of the Dungeon. And yet, here was one aboveground. That's what Hyacinthus saw as fear overtook him.

Every muscle in the boy's body tensed before filling the "fang" of his fist with every ounce of energy he had left.

"UWAAAAAAHHHHHHHHHHHHHH!"

Impact.

"GeHAA?!"

Bell's fist buried itself in Hyacinthus's cheek; shock waves rolled all the way around the man's head. A heartbeat later, his feet left the ground.

A sharp thud rang out before a loud crash. The man's body hit the ground with such force that he flew high into the air on the first bounce; what was left of his cape was torn to shreds as he spun like a top. He fell to the ground again only to have his momentum launch him skyward once more.

His body came to a merciful halt after a thirty-meder trip through the debris field. Hyacinthus lay on his back, arms and legs spread out like a fallen angel in the middle of the grassland.

Eyes rolled back in his head and the giant crater on his cheek, the man did not try to stand.

The wind stopped blowing as silence descended on the battlefield.

Cassandra was about to throw Lilly off her body when she saw the final blow. The long-haired girl fell to her knees.

"!"

The sky above Orario erupted in a tremendous outcry.

Church bells rang out throughout the city to mark the end of the War Game just as the final blow had been delivered at the castle ruins.

Demi-humans of every race looked at the young boy reflected in the mirrors and yelled at the top of their lungs.

"Eina, look at that!"

"Bell…!"

Misha wrapped her arms around Eina's shoulders in front of the Guild headquarters.

Emerald eyes tearing up, Eina forgot her position as a Guild employee and joined in the celebration taking place around her. The anxiety masked by refinement was gone, pure joy taking its place.

"There's the final bell! That was amazing, ranking right up there with the deeds of the 'Giant Killers,' *Loki Familia*! The victor of this War Game is *Hestia Familia*——!"

For some reason, Ganesha struck manly poses in the middle of the stage, completely ignoring the fact that Ibly was shouting through the voice magnifier with so much intensity that his face might explode.

His voice echoed throughout the city, enveloping every building and reaching the ears of every onlooker.

*   *   *

" " "Yahh HAAAA!" " "

Three deities, who'd bet on *Hestia Familia* at a certain bar in the city, jumped up from their table, celebrating their improbable winnings.

" " "SON OF A BITCH!" " "

At the same time, all of the adventurers who'd bet on Apollo swore at the top of their lungs and threw their tickets to the floor in disgust.
"Oh, oh? Lady?! You win, too?"
Judging from all the shrieks of agony, Mord had thought he was the only one who came out on top. That was when he saw a rather happy young woman sitting in the corner of the bar.
The man walked up to her, happy as could be. The Chienthrope woman—Nahza—smiled back at him, wagging her bushy tail and making a *V* with her fingers.

" " "YESSS–SAA!" " "

The cries of anguish were just as strong on West Main at The Benevolent Mistress. However, Ahnya, Chloe, and Runoa were jumping for joy, slapping their hands together over and over. Other employees of the bar came over to the three girls, exchanging hugs and smiling right along with them.
"…Bell."
Tears of happiness were flooding Syr's silver eyes. Her lips quivered as her face tried to express the intensity of her feelings all at once.
Her cheeks blushed as she finally looked away from the mirror floating in front of the wall and turned her attention toward the customers. "Dammit, I've lost everything!" "Hey, Syr, I'm gonna need a crap-ton of ale over here!" She managed to put her "work smile" on as the patrons began to drown their sorrow in as much alcohol as they could afford.
"Com–ming!" she responded in a bright voice, pep in her step as she went to take their orders.

*   *   *

"...Punk pulled it off."

Bete practically spat those words out of his mouth as he listened to the celebrations coming from outside his *Familia*'s home.

He turned his back on the common room and walked toward the exit.

"Bete, where are you off to?"

"Wherever the hell I feel like."

The werewolf responded to Finn's question before disappearing out the door.

Everyone left behind in the common room exchanged glances. They came to a consensus surprisingly quickly.

"Dungeon, huh." "Tha'd be da Dungeon." "The Dungeon, no doubt." "For sure..."

Finn and Gareth forced a smile as Reveria closed her eyes in frustration. Tione looked more bored than annoyed.

With Bete gone, everyone in the room returned their attention to the mirrors. Thinking back to the desperate boy who'd come to their doorstep almost ten days ago, it was hard to believe that pitiful rabbit had seized victory. No one said a word.

That is, until...

"...Good for him."

"Yes..."

Tiona had been literally dancing around the room just moments earlier, but now the Amazon stood next to Aiz as they watched a mirror. Slowly but surely the wheat-skinned girl turned to her friend with a radiant smile on her lips.

The blonde nodded in response and watched Bell's friends gather around him in the mirror's reflection. Her lips opened before she realized what was happening.

"Congrats..."

The largest mirror in the street showed the boy's allies gathering around him, ruffling his hair and congratulating him like family. Others showed scenes of other cities overtaken by the thrill of the good fight.

The same was true of the gods in Babel Tower. Several of them had gathered together, comparing notes and admiring the children or offering criticism in their own reviews of the War Game.

"Wha...ha..., eh...?"

One of them however, Apollo, looked like a ghost as he stood frozen next to the table.

His mirror showed nothing but reflections of his children, powerless and kneeling all over the castle ruins. The fact that he couldn't escape this reality just hit him like a brick wall.

He took two steps back, then another as his crown of laurels fell from his head.

"A-PO-LL-O."

Then, *schreee.*

The feet of Hestia's chair squeaked as they slowly slid across the floor. The goddess who had kept quiet all this time had broken her silence.

A dark aura emerged as she stood up from the table. Head angled down, no one could see her eyes behind her black bangs. Her chin suddenly jerked up, blue eyes flashing as they locked on her target: Apollo. *Tap, tap.* She walked toward him.

"Hy-hyeee!"

"You've made peace with yourself, I hope?"

Hestia's low voice sounded as though it were summoned from the deepest pits of hell. Apollo fell backward in fright.

Bell had nearly been stolen from her, her home was destroyed, and she'd been chased at arrow point around the city, among other hardships.

All of the pent-up anger that hadn't been allowed to vent until this moment was on the verge of exploding within her. The god on the floor could see it in her eyes. He shook as Hestia stood over him, glaring down with the utmost intensity. The god's eyes began to water.

"H-hear me out, Hestia! This was all just an impulse! That child of yours was just so cute, I couldn't help but pinch his cheeks a little... P-please, have mercy on me, O Goddess of Affection! We were once destined to share marital bliss!"

"Shut—your—mouth."

The young goddess cut off his pleading with the ferocity of Hades himself.

Apollo's face took on a shade of blue and fell silent. Even in Ten-kai, he had never seen Hestia be so terrifying.

Whoosh, whoosh, whoosh. Hestia's twin ponytails whipped about behind her head, riding the waves of her aura. It was proof of just how deep her rage ran.

"You promised to do *whatever my little heart desires,* yes?"

Apollo, who never even considered the possibility of defeat, had indeed said that.

All the other gods present had made a large circle around the two deities, enjoying every second of the climax. They couldn't wait to see the young goddess's Divine Judgment on the offender for his sins.

Apollo started to panic, gasping for breath as he looked to the faces of his former allies. They were now just faces in the dark, white teeth sparkling in the dim light from the mirrors. The deities were thoroughly enjoying watching him squirm.

Apollo's robes dragged across the floor as he squirmed away from them and backed into Hestia. Looking up, he saw blue orbs flash in anger the moment he made eye contact.

"Everything you own, including your home, is now mine. Disband your *Familia*—and you will go into exile! Never set foot in Orario AGAIN——!"

"HyGAHHHHHHHHHHHHHHHHHHHHHHHHHHHHHHHHHH-HHHHH!"

His scream sent a shiver through the city.

Hestia gave no quarter to the dangerous god who had very nearly taken everything away from her.

Far away from the battlefield, amid a swirling storm of emotions…

Another final blow had been struck.

At the now peaceful castle ruins…

Bell reunited with his allies inside the castle that was now missing its throne room and a good deal of its outer wall. Of course, all of them were elated by their victory.

"We actually defeated a *Familia* possessing that much power...by ourselves."

"Had to rely on a ruse or two but...Yeah, we can brag about this one."

Mikoto and Welf exchanged words, adrenaline still pumping through their veins. She had taken the brunt of her own Magic and he had crossed blades with one of the enemy captains, so the two of them were in rough shape physically. However, their faces were so full of life and a feeling of accomplishment that no one could tell if they were in pain at all.

Bell walked away from their conversation and approached Lilly.

"Lilly...Thank you for saving me."

"Mr. Bell..."

"Really, thank you..."

The sincerity in Bell's eyes, despite the fact he was covered in blood and beaten to a pulp, overwhelmed Lilly so much that she couldn't speak clearly. The muscles in her small body tensed up as she hid her face and worked up the courage to ask.

"Was Lilly...useful?"

"Yes. It's all thanks to Lilly that...I can go home to Orario."

Bell's words made Lilly's childlike face smile.

She hadn't felt like this since the day that their relationship had been reset. The prum girl blushed as she looked up at him with a smile as radiant as a blooming sunflower.

"Mr. Cranell, we should move out of this location. The Guild employees will be here soon; it is necessary to find a place to rest and recover."

"Ah, sure."

Lyu suggested from beneath her hood, eyes locked on Bell's injured right shoulder.

The taste of victory in their mouths, the group made their way through the debris inside the castle walls.

"...?"

Without thinking, Bell placed his left hand on his chest.

Taking a deep breath, he grabbed the string around his neck and pulled the amulet out from under his shirt.

However, it was broken.

The jewel had a series of spiderweb-like cracks running through it and the golden casing was falling apart. The radiance it had the moment that Syr gave it to him was gone.

...Did it protect me?

Hyacinthus's Magic packed a very powerful punch. Taking a direct hit, like he did, should've knocked him out of commission for good.

Bell couldn't help but feel that this amulet had sacrificed itself to save him.

Bell took a closer look at the broken jewel and saw something that looked like an emblem engraved in the casing behind it.

Due to the thousands of cracks in its surface, however, he could only see that it was someone's face in profile.

"Something wrong, Bell? We're leaving."

"Ah...yeah. Right behind you."

The boy stopped moving to look at the jewel. Welf had noticed and called out to him.

The white-haired boy nodded, keeping his gaze on the jewel in his left hand before slowly looking up to the sky.

"..."

Just who was the adventurer who gave Syr this amulet?

It was given to her for a reason, so that she would give it to him.

These thoughts ran through Bell's mind as he looked up at the azure sky.

He couldn't help but feel that someone watching him through a mirror in the city was smiling at him at that very moment.

And so the curtain fell on the War Game, with *Hestia Familia* standing victorious.

The exploits of combatants on both sides became the talk of the town. Bell and his allies became hometown heroes overnight. They were the center of attention wherever they went after returning to the city.

Obeying Hestia's demands, *Apollo Familia* was disbanded

immediately. Apollo said his good-byes and released every one of his followers from their contracts before being escorted out of the city for the last time.

As for the now *Familia*–less adventurers, they went their separate ways. Some went on journeys of self-discovery, others were scouted and joined other *Familias*, and a few fell into despair. A small group, including Hyacinthus, went against the laws of Orario by leaving the city to follow their god.

The effects of the War Game were felt in many places.

The fervor had yet to die down, but there was still something that needed to be taken care of.

"...This is the money owed for Lilly's release, as promised."

The small girl held out a bag stuffed full of gold coins.

Soma, clad in his dirty robe, took the bag from her without a word.

Two days had passed since the War Game ended. Lilly had journeyed to *Soma Familia*'s home by herself.

Every val that had been held in Apollo's name now belonged to *Hestia Familia*. Lilly took a large part of it and returned to her former home to exchange the money for the Hestia Knife, which had been used as collateral.

Her new family offered to go with her, but Lilly declined. She told them that she had to see this through to the end on her own.

"..."

She had a reputation to uphold as a member of their *Familia*. Soma accepted the money without a fuss.

He didn't even check the contents of the bag before pulling the knife out from inside his robe and handing it to Lilly.

Lilly was taken aback by how quickly this exchange transpired. In a room full of different types of plants and a wide array of wine bottles, she blinked a few times before straightening her posture.

Clearing her throat, she prepared to say her final good-bye.

"Thank you for everything, Lord Soma..."

There was no hint of irony or resentment in her voice. She wanted to end things well.

The Status on her back clearly identified her as a member of *Hestia Familia*. She no longer had any connection to *Soma Familia*.

Her loose robe bent around her small body as Lilly bowed. Her face down, she never had a chance to make eye contact with Soma. One step back, turn, a few more steps, and she paused for a moment in front of the door.

"..."

Soma was standing in the corner of his room, the muscles in his face shifting as if he were deep in thought. He stared at the back of his former child...and spoke to her.

"Lilliluka Erde...I have done you wrong."

Halfway out the door, Lilly froze on the spot.

She looked over her shoulder in surprise. The deity's expression was hidden behind his long hair as he continued.

"...Make sure to take care of your health."

The first words he had ever spoken to her.

Slowly but surely, Lilly's chestnut eyes began to moisten.

She had wanted to hear his words for the longest time, but at least now, at the end, she was grateful to hear them. Lilly nodded, her chin hitting her shoulder.

"Lilly will..." she said in a quivering voice to the deity who had remembered her name.

One last step, and she left the room behind.

"..."

Soma stood in silence for a while after Lilly disappeared from sight. Finally, he turned to face the shelves on his wall.

Removing all the wine bottles, he carried them to a wooden box in the corner of the room, slipped them inside, and closed the lid.

Filling the empty spots with the now useless wineglasses, Soma's eyes narrowed from behind his long bangs.

The conditions within *Soma Familia* gradually improved from that day.

EPILOGUE **HESTIA FAMILIA**

A large manor stood in the middle of a wide garden.

Hestia took a deep breath.

"Ta-da! This is our new home!"

""Ooohhhh—""

Bell, Lilly, Welf, and Mikoto stood in awe of the building Hestia pointed at.

It was three stories tall; they had to crane their necks to get a good look at the top floor. Hestia went on to say that there were covered passages along with more gardens inside. The property was surrounded by a tall iron fence. Flowers and trees hid most of the bars from view.

"But was it really okay to take *Apollo Familia*'s home...?"

"Oh yes, he blew mine into a million pieces. I don't want to hear any complaints!"

Lilly muttered as she looked up at the manor, but Hestia cut her off right away.

It was a prize from the War Game—the building that *Apollo Familia* had once called home was now theirs. Bell was just as surprised as Welf and Mikoto at this sudden upgrade in living conditions.

None of the mortals could believe their luck as they looked over their new home from the outside gardens.

"The ones who lived here before had...strange tastes. So, since we've got a lot of money, I say we do some remodeling! If you have any requests, let me know!"

"L-Lady Hestia, I humbly request a bathhouse!"

"Lady Hestia! Would you build me a forge?!"

Mikoto and Welf didn't waste any time in suggesting what to build to replace any remnants of *Apollo Familia*. Hestia turned to them, holding her arms out, saying, "Wait, wait," and smiling.

"Now that we can finally puff out our chests and say we're a proper *Familia*, don't you think we should decide on an emblem first?"

" "Good point!" "

All of Hestia's followers nodded in unison. Bell was the most excited among them. He'd been wanting to have his own *Familia* emblem for quite a while.

Hestia took a seat on the front steps of the manor. Pulling out a small piece of paper and a pen, she set to work on sketching a picture. Bell and the others formed a half circle around her, watching her pen move while standing shoulder to shoulder.

"Hee-heee, I put a lot of thought into this—"

Hestia's pen didn't stop for an instant until she turned the paper around to show her new family, grinning from ear to ear. Welf, Mikoto, and Lilly each held the paper in their hands and gave the design a once-over.

"This is fire and..."

"I see. This is the Lady Hestia's idea of protective flames."

"That's not it at all. This emblem, it's all about the relationship between Lady Hestia and Mr. Bell!"

Welf and Mikoto whispered to each other, but Lilly's eyes twitched in annoyance.

The three of them had different reactions, but Hestia used her authority as a goddess to ignore them and said in a very satisfied voice:

"What's the problem? This *Familia* started with me and Bell, after all."

At last, the paper made its way into Bell's hands.

His ruby-red eyes opened wide as he studied the emblem design.

"Goddess, isn't this...?"

Hestia giggled as she looked at the surprise on the boy's face.

Smiling once again, she made eye contact with Bell and said:

"Now, Bell. Today is the real debut of our *Familia*."

Bell looked back down at the paper as he listened to her words. A few moments later, he smiled back at her with an expression as radiant as the sun.

The boy held out the paper once again for everyone to see.

The design on the paper in his hands consisted of a bell surrounded by flames.

【BELL・CRANELL】

BELONGS TO: *HESTIA FAMILIA*
RACE: HUMAN
JOB: ADVENTURER
DUNGEON RANGE: EIGHTEENTH FLOOR
WEAPON: HESTIA KNIFE
CURRENT WORTH: 123,000 VALS

《 PYONKICHI MK-IV 》

- WELF'S DESIGN, FOURTH IN THE SERIES.
- SHINY SILVER LIGHT ARMOR CONSISTING OF
  A BREASTPLATE, SHOULDER GUARDS, WRIST
  GUARDS, A BACK PLATE, AND KNEE GUARDS.
- FORGED AT A FEVER PITCH BEFORE THE WAR GAME.
  IT HAS NO GREAVES. BELL WEARS BOOTS INSTEAD.
- IT IS THE STRONGEST AND LIGHTEST OF THE SERIES.

STATUS

Lv. **2**

STRENGTH: SS 1088   DEFENSE: SS 1029   UTILITY: SS 1094
AGILITY: SSS 1302   MAGIC: A 883   LUCK: 1

《MAGIC》

【FIREBOLT】   • SWIFT-STRIKE MAGIC

《SKILL》

     • RAPID GROWTH
     • CONTINUED DESIRE
【REALIS PHRASE】   RESULTS IN CONTINUED
     GROWTH
     • STRONGER DESIRE
     RESULTS IN STRONGER
     GROWTH

【HEROIC DESIRE, ARGONAUT】   • CHARGES AUTOMATICALLY
     WITH ACTIVE ACTION

《USHIWAKAMARU-SHIKI》

- WELF'S DESIGN, THE SECOND IN THE SERIES.
- THE BLADE IS LONGER AND A DEEPER CRIMSON
  THAN THE ORIGINAL USHIWAKAMARU.
- THE REMAINDER OF THE "MINOTAUR HORN" WAS
  USED TO FORGE IT.
- THANKS TO WELF'S ADVANCED ABILITY "FORGE,"
  ITS ATTACKING POWER FAR EXCEEDS USHIWAKAMARU.
- RECOGNIZED AS A THIRD-TIER WEAPON BY THE GODDESS
  OF THE FORGE, HEPHAISTOS.

Afterword

A dungeon fantasy story that never once ventures into a dungeon: that's book six. I suspect this pattern will continue for the next few volumes…However, you can visit the Dungeon many times in the spin-off! Please excuse the self-promotion. If you're interested, have a look.

I'm particularly fond of stories where the characters increase one by one.

The main character's journey is a solitary one until he or she meets a healer, then a beautiful and mysterious fortune-teller, then adds a young mage as the fourth member…I get excited when a new ally joins the fight in manga, novels, and of course video games. Nothing beats the feeling of accomplishment after assembling a well-balanced party.

At the same time, the early stages where very few characters must face difficult odds to build their relationships is one of the most important, and in my opinion the most entertaining, parts of the story. I took my time in developing this part of my own work in books one through five, sacrificing larger story arcs in the process. Back when I first started writing the stories, I don't know how many times I heard the phrase "Wouldn't it be a good idea to increase the party size?" I would like to thank everyone who worked with me for listening to my selfish desires and allowed me to take my time in developing each character in turn. You have my gratitude.

Gods, family, and *Familia* all came together to form the backbone of the story. As soon as the idea for a "War Game between the Gods" came to me, the story for this book fell into place with support from loyal readers. I can't thank you enough.

I would also like to recognize my adviser Mr. Kotaki for providing me with inspiration and guidance throughout this project; Mr. Suzuhito Yasuda, for producing beautiful artwork equal to or exceeding the magnificent designs from earlier installments; as well as every other person involved in this project. Thank you from the bottom of my heart.

Also, I would like to thank all of the guest artists who came together to produce the limited-edition art book that was released along with this volume. NOCO, Ms. Haruko Iizuka, Mr. Eiji Usatsuka, Mr. Noboru Kannadu, Mr. Ki Takaya, Mikeo, YASU: thank you for lending your talents and individual vision to this project. Each of you deserves great praise for your marvelous drawings.

I cannot wait to pick up my pen and start in on the next volume. Now then, I will take my leave.

Fujino Omori